BOOKS BY JANET RISING

The Pony Whisperer series:
The Word on the Yard
Team Challenge
Runaway Rescue
Prize Problems
Pony Rebellion
Stables SOS

The Blueberry stories, with Carl Hester MBE, FBHS:
Valegro, the Little Horse with the Big Dream
Valegro The Early Years
Valegro A Rising Star
Valegro Goes International
Valegro Going for Gold
Velegro The Legend

The Amazing Adventures of Superpony!
Jorja and the High Stakes Horse
Ponytalk – 50 ways to make friends with your pony
The Bumper Book of Horses and Ponies

For Grown-Ups

My Horsy Life – an Unconventional Equine Memoir

THE PECULIAR MADE-UP WORLD OF HENRIETTA MARSHALL

(It's out of control!)

JANET RISING

Copyright © 2022 Janet Rising

The moral right of the author has been asserted.

Apart from any fair dealing for the purposes of research or private study, or criticism or review, as permitted under the Copyright, Designs and Patents Act 1988, this publication may only be reproduced, stored or transmitted, in any form or by any means, with the prior permission in writing of the publishers, or in the case of reprographic reproduction in accordance with the terms of licences issued by the Copyright Licensing Agency. Enquiries concerning reproduction outside those terms should be sent to the publishers.

This is a work of fiction. Names, characters, businesses, places, events and incidents are either the products of the author's imagination or used in a fictitious manner. Any resemblance to actual persons, except where permission was granted to use real names, living or dead, or actual events is purely coincidental.

Matador
Unit E2 Airfield Business Park,
Harrison Road, Market Harborough,
Leicestershire. LE16 7UL
Tel: 0116 279 2299
Email: books@troubador.co.uk
Web: www.troubador.co.uk/matador
Twitter: @matadorbooks

ISBN 978 1803132 785

British Library Cataloguing in Publication Data.
A catalogue record for this book is available from the British Library.

Printed and bound in Great Britain by 4edge Limited
Typeset in 11pt Minion Pro by Troubador Publishing Ltd, Leicester, UK

Matador is an imprint of Troubador Publishing Ltd

To dreamers everywhere

CHAPTER ONE

Reaching the mountain summit the girl reined in her fiery, snow-white stallion. The horse's front hooves lifted from the rock in a half-rear before he stood, motionless like a statue. Billowing in the wind, the stallion's silver mane and tail provided a vivid contrast against his rider's long, black hair, dark tendrils of which entwined her slender neck. Beside the horse, the bewitching amber eyes of a grey wolf searched for an escape from the dead-end they had unwittingly entered – but he searched in vain. It was a sheer drop to the sea below, with no way down through the jagged rocks that glistened like jewels under the onslaught of the waves.

The trio – stallion, wolf and girl – all turned to face the foe that had forced them along this path, the rider tall and proud astride the elaborate high-backed saddle, the horse's bejewelled caparison swirling around his legs.

'Steady now, my Silverado,' whispered the girl, patting her stallion and glancing down. 'Easy now Wolf, for what shall be shall be, and we shall face the outcome together.'

'So, who can name any of King Arthur's knights?' asks Mr Taritt, my English teacher, interrupting my (much more interesting) thoughts. Blocking out all the annoying school noise, I return to Azbathria...

Drawing her sword, the wolf at her side curling his lip in a snarl, the girl locked eyes with those of the ugly figure facing them. His panting and gleeful companions followed in his wake, closing on their prey.

'Now, my pretty,' the poor excuse for a human form began, allowing himself a satisfied smile, 'now we will see who is to be ruler of Azbathria.'

'You may kill me, Tarituss, but you will never rule Azbathria,' the girl declared calmly and with quiet courage that hid her fears. 'Only those born to royal blood have the right to govern this land. Slay me and you slay yourself. The gods will see you fall as your sword reaches its target and I can promise you one thing: I shall fight you with all the determination of my people, and you would do well not to underestimate my strength and resolve.'

'Can I be of assistance, my fair Lady Estra?'

The girl looked up to see a handsome knight astride a majestic jet-black stallion approaching along the treacherous cliff-top path above her. A further army of knights stood behind him, all mounted and armed.

'Sir Nathan, the Black Knight!' gasped the girl.

'At your service, My Lady,' replied the knight, bowing his head and laying a comforting hand on the neck of his ebony stallion, who snorted and pawed the ground.

Tarituss drew back. The odds had shifted against him, and he knew that to engage in warfare with so fearful a foe now facing his army would result in a different outcome, an outcome that would not be in his favour.

'Your knight has saved you – this time,' spat the snarling Tarituss, and he turned to flee back down the mountain, his cowardly army following behind.

'I am indebted to you, good knight,' said the girl, inclining her head in a beguiling manner, her bouncing locks framing her perfect features. 'You have saved us from a battle with the Heratos, and blood surely spilt.'

'I sense victory would have been yours,' said the knight, 'for your reputation as a warrior is second only to your beauty, and I and my army are but...'

'Henrietta Marshall, are you with us?'

It is Mr Taritt's voice again, interrupting my Azbathria scenario, oblivious to the fact that his starring role, that of the ugly Tarituss, is over and done with, and droning on again about the legend of King Arthur. And where's the Black Knight going? He is fading away.

Oh don't go...

He's gone.

I'm back in double English. *Not* Azbathria.

Pity. I mean I know there is no such place as Azbathria, and that it only exists in my head where my name is more glamorous and my hair is the stuff of Hollywood sirens, but it's certainly more exciting there than here in double English – but then again, where isn't? Besides, it was all Mr Taritt's talk of King Arthur and his Knights of the Round Table that set me off in the first place.

'So do you have an answer for me?' asks Mr Taritt, raising his eyebrows. I can't understand how his eyebrows can make themselves look sarcastic, but they definitely have the knack. I wonder whether I can make my eyebrows do the same – I'll have a go at that in front of the mirror because it might be useful later if my first choice of career pans out.

Maybe I won't. Who wants sarcastic eyebrows?

I can't remember Mr Taritt's question because I've been in Azbathria with the Black Knight, with Mr Taritt in the role of the evil Tarituss far, far away from classroom seven with the time coming up to midday, my stomach rumbling and my packed lunch in my bag just waiting to be eaten.

My friend Hebe nudges her exercise book across her desk towards me. Pretending to screw up my eyes in concentration I glance down at the name written on it, underlined twice in pencil.

'Um, Sir Galahad?' I say, with just a hint of a question in my voice.

'Hmmm, yes,' agrees my teacher, grudgingly, his eyebrows drooping from sarcastic in order to register disappointment. Neat trick. I throw Hebe a grateful glance. She rolls her eyes at me just as the bell for the end of the lesson rings out and saves me from any more questioning.

'Phew, thanks Heeb,' I say, as we make our way along the corridor towards the lunch hall.

'Why can't you pay attention?' asks Hebe, throwing her bag onto one of the tables by the window and herself on a chair, sweeping her long, red hair out of her eyes and curling it up like a skein of wool behind her neck. I wish I had Hebe's hair. I wish I had my alter ego Estra's hair. I wish I had *anybody's* hair but my own tangle of wiry curls.

I just shrug as I take a bite from my goat cheese and watercress sandwich. It's a bit warm and squashy what with it being a hot day, and I'm sure I've just swallowed one of our dog's hairs along with the cheese. He's a small, grey, hairy mutt that we got from the rescue centre where he'd been for months because nobody else wanted him, probably due to him being a bit manic. All I can say is that they all MISSED OUT because Wolfie is the best dog EVER – if you don't count his hobby of digging up the garden, and his habit of redistributing loose hairs when he shakes himself. It isn't the first time I've found his hairs in my sarnies. I wouldn't be surprised if I'm developing a fur ball in my throat, like one of Hebe's cats. Whenever I go round to her place one of them is always honking all over the carpet trying to bring up a chunk of its own fur it had previously licked off itself in a self-washing frenzy.

'Wherever was your head?' Hebe asks, digging her fork into a pasta salad. 'You were staring into space again.'

She's a bit of a swot, is Hebe, soaks up lessons like a sponge – as well as being good at sports. With Hebe, what the teachers tell us all goes in somehow, almost like she doesn't need to try at all whereas I...

'Oh, um, I just drifted off,' I reply vaguely, having a good look through my remaining sandwich for rogue hairs.

'Besides,' I add, frowning, 'I don't know why we're learning about King Arthur in English, nobody's even sure he existed.'

'Well, you have a point there, babe,' agrees Hebe, 'I think Mr Taritt just likes Arthurian legends.'

My friend knows nothing about Azbathria and the Black Knight. Nobody does. It and he exist only in my head. Azbathria is where I go when I'm *not* soaking up lessons like a sponge.

'You'll never pass your exams.'

'You sound like Mr Taritt.'

'I'm just telling it like it is.'

'Well stop it. I really don't see how passing exams is going to help me at all when I'm a famous actress,' I say, unwilling to tell Hebe exactly what I think about when my body is in lessons and my mind is elsewhere. I fail to see how maths, English and history can be of any use when I'm up on the stage, or acting my way through a Jane Austin period drama. I suppose history might just be a bit useful, like research or something, but other than that what's the point?

My mum gave me the idea for my (current) career choice. She says I'm a born actress, and I reckon it's good to have a parent on board. 'She's a born actress, your daughter,' she tells my dad whenever I protest about having to tidy my room or do my homework. 'Has to make a drama out of everything.' Then she adds something about me needing to get good results in my exams whether I like it or not. She just doesn't seem to get it.

'You'll need a back-up, young lady,' Dad then chimes in. 'If you come out of school with low grades I'll have something to say about it.'

I wonder exactly what he'll have to say about it. I mean, what can he say other than I've come out of school with low grades? He doesn't get it either. Anyway, I do have a back-up. It is always good to have a Plan B in case Plan A doesn't work out. I know this because I have been caught out on more than one occasion by not having a Plan B, and it isn't a good look. So you see some things – important things – do go in.

Miffed with each other, Hebe and I both spend the next ten minutes scrolling through our phones. Judging by Hebe's giggles she's looking at cute cat videos again. I get onto Chesterton Riding School's website to see what's going on, hoping to see a new picture of Silver.

There are two things in my life I am totally in love with. I mean, I love my family and Wolfie of course, but these two things are different. I am totally MAD for these, like if they didn't exist I'd probably die, or at least whither away like lettuce does when it's been left in the fridge too long (but without all that horrid brown goo you get).

The first one is Silver.

Silver is the VERY BEST pony at Chesterton Riding School, which is where I have a lesson every Saturday at ten o'clock come rain, come shine (shine is better because the stables doesn't have an indoor school so when it rains we all get wet riding in the outdoor school which, in case you don't know, is called a *manège*).

I wish I could buy Silver and have him all to myself. I could keep him at Chesterton because they have lots of horses and ponies there which are privately owned. But whenever I ask for Silver for my birthday or Christmas I always get told (usually with a long, drawn-out sigh, like I've asked to go to the moon or something) that we can't afford it. This statement is always followed by my being reminded that riding lessons are expensive enough, and I ought to consider myself lucky to have those. I fancy I can detect a slight threat in this last remark, like if I don't stop asking to have my own pony the riding lessons could grind to a halt.

My parents have me over a barrel in this respect, as they pay for my lessons.

If I owned Silver I could ride him whenever I want, go to shows and win rosettes. This would happen because I would be a much better rider than I am now because I would be able to ride every day, instead of just once a week.

Silver is grey – well, he's almost white but Becky (who is my riding instructor) says white ponies are always called grey (I'm not sure why, they just are. This is handy to know because it means if you hear somebody talking about *white* horses, you can tell they really don't know anything about horses AT ALL).

Silver has a lovely dark grey mane which gets tangled up in his reins whenever I ride him. Becky has tried to train it so it all falls on one side of Silver's neck, but half still falls one side, half on the other. Having a half-and-half mane is Silver's USP, Becky says.

I didn't know what USP stood for but I didn't like to ask Becky at the time for fear of looking stupid, so I asked Hebe. She hummed and harred a bit, before saying she thought it was either something to do with alien spaceships, or how some people know what other people are thinking without them saying anything – only she admitted that she could have been getting confused with different letters. I couldn't see how either of those things could have anything to do with Silver's mane…

Etta felt a weird sensation in her head. It was as though someone was… was reading her mind! Turning to her favourite pony, Silver, Etta suddenly knew he was trying to communicate with her, due to their special bond. He was telling her that she was the only rider at Chesterton who understood and appreciated him, the only rider he really liked and with whom he had bonded. Somehow, Silver was doing this despite not being able to speak English, and Etta not knowing a word of pony. It was some kind of supernatural mind-meld.

'If only you could buy me and be my only rider!' Etta heard Silver say in her head. 'But now I have to go – my spaceship is waiting for me, and I mustn't keep the other ponies in the galaxy Ponio waiting.'

As Etta watched, the grey pony was suddenly bathed in a beam of light from the sky, and Silver was magically transported up to the waiting spaceship which hovered above the stables…

So anyway I Googled it and discovered USP stands for *unique selling point*. So there you are – nothing to do with spaceships or being able to read minds. I panicked a bit then, thinking Silver might be up for sale but apparently it can just mean something someone has that is unique to them – like my daydreaming, or Hebe's fascination for cat videos, or Mr Taritt's obsession with King Arthur – which was a relief.

Silver rubs his tail on his stable door so the top of it always looks like a loo brush (his tail, not his stable door). That's another of his USPs. I only know he rubs his tail on his stable door because Becky tells me – the riders at Chesterton are NOT ALLOWED in the yard where the stables are, we have to wait in the office or in the corner of the outdoor school until the ponies are led in by the students and grooms for our lesson.

I'm quite tempted to be a riding instructor instead of an actress when I leave school – it's currently my Plan B. I mean, I know I totally *could* be an actress, but I'm not one-hundred-percent positive I *want* to be. I'm probably about ninety-five-percent certain at the moment. The way I see it, I need to keep my options open and examine all possibilities. I mean, say I became an actress and then wish I'd become a riding instructor like Becky? That would be awkward – not to mention a waste of time and effort, learning all the acting stuff for nothing.

From what I've seen of it being a riding instructor is not too hard – you just stand in the middle of the riding arena and shout out what to do. That's what Becky does on my lessons. I could so do that. I mean okay, you have to know all about riding and stuff, but you learn all that when you get trained. Chesterton trains students in riding and looking after horses and teaching people to ride, and they all take exams at the end of their courses and then they are riding instructors. *Voilà!* (That's French for *there you go!*) Some students stay and take more difficult exams, and others leave to teach other people at other riding schools. Personally, I would rather work at Chesterton because that is where Silver lives.

I wish I could stay at the riding school after my lesson and learn all about how to look after horses and ponies, like my Nana Susan did when she was my age, but I can't. Once I've finished my lesson I have to go home. It's the rules – to do with Health and Safety. Boring. I mean, how can I learn how to care for a pony and get a head start in my career (assuming I do decide to be a riding instructor) if I can't spend any extra time with Silver?

Hebe rolls her eyes when I talk about Silver (Hebe rolls her eyes a lot, and she says horses are gross and that all they do is poo and fart, and I have to admit she has a point because Silver does fart a lot, and some real stinkers, too. I would advise anyone to be down-wind of him at all times).

The reason Silver is the best is because he doesn't do anything I don't want him to. He doesn't go too fast or try to eat grass when we go out on a hack – which is a ride out in the countryside – and he looks after me. Once, when he stopped quite suddenly after a canter, I slipped up onto his neck and I know some of the other ponies (Cracker and Amber, you know who you are!) would have put their heads down on purpose so I'd slide off, but Silver just stood still until I wriggled back into the saddle.

I'm not a very good rider yet, but one day I will be. Everyone has to start somewhere. I just wish I didn't have to start again every week because after six days of *not* riding I forget most of what I've learned, and it isn't until the end of my *next* lesson that I feel I'm back to where I was at the end of my *last* one. I ought to have a lesson every day (on my own pony – Silver!!!), because that's how you learn quickly – but, as you now know, Mum says we can't afford that. It's one lesson a week or nothing.

Amelia Armitage is – a good rider, I mean. I wish I could ride as well as Amelia Armitage. But then she would be. Amelia is in my class at school and she also rides in my lessons at Chesterton, although she started riding before I did. She's the best rider in our group. Amelia has long, very straight and very golden hair, and she's good at games, and she smiles a lot and the teachers like her because she pays attention and puts her hand up to answer questions, and they never have to tell her to put her mobile away or stop running in the corridor, and everyone always calls her Amelia, never Ami because, well, she's totally an Amelia, *not* an Ami. If you knew her you'd understand what I mean.

I'd do anything to have hair like Amelia Armitage, but mine will never be like hers because I've inherited my mum's jet black, very tight curls. They look good on my mum but I know they make my head look huge. Even the straighteners struggle to work on my hair. I mean, I use them, and I often think they've worked, but whenever I go out in the damp air my hair just scrunches up again like it's in pain, or (more likely) it's having a laugh at my expense. Once, in an effort to force it to cooperate, I left a lock of my hair between the straightener blades for so long, steam started coming out of them, and the hair sort of crisped up and actually crumbled away, leaving a hole in my hair (my mum went a bit bonkers when she noticed). My dad's fair but that's no help because I've not inherited his hair genes. So, no luck in the hair stakes for me. No way. Dream on Etta, dream on.

Which I do quite a lot – dream that is. I find myself drifting off all the time. I just can't help my imagination working overtime, and I suppose it's because I just want so much to be different, different to how I am. I want to be elegant and beautiful, with hair like Amelia has. But I'm not. So my mind sort of takes me places where I can be like Amelia.

Or even better than Amelia.

Like to Azbathria, which I totally made up. And other places. I don't always go to Azbathria, my imagination just goes where it wants to sometimes, without consulting me at all. I can't stop it.

In Azbathria I'm clever and sassy and the me I want to be, the me I *really* am under all the other stuff that people see. They don't see the *real* me because of the other, less interesting me that's on the outside, getting in the way. It hides the real me. It's like I'm encased in a big, fluffy bear suit from a fancy dress shop. Do you know what I mean? *Inside* I'm a different person to the one on the *outside*. Inside I am elegant and beautiful, and my hair is how I want it to be, and I am a fantastic rider with my own horse, Silverado. It's a complete pain having a not-real me on the outside of the real me, especially as the real me is so much better than the not-real me. I don't understand how that happened.

It's like some horrible cosmic joke.

Only it's not funny.

'Look at this totally cute tabby!' exclaims Hebe, shoving her mobile in my face.

'Look at Silver!' I reply, doing the same, my wonder pony smiling out of the mobile, the picture I took of him last weekend in focus for once. He tends to move his head about a bit, does Silver, which makes taking pictures of him quite hard.

'There goes the present Miss Elbridge School with her entourage,' Hebe muses, her eyes swinging from Silver on my mobile to Amelia in real life. She is passing our table with her two bezzie mates, all teeth and hair, managing to make their uniforms look like the height of fashion. I don't know how they do that. I mean, school uniforms are supposed to make us all look the same, but whereas Amelia and her mates look like they wouldn't be out of place sashaying down the catwalk, Hebe and I look like we've been kitted out by the charity shop (the daggy one down by the betting shop and the chippy, not the posh one in the high street that sells furniture that's better than we have in our house, and has proper labels on all the stuff, like a real shop). I'm sure my hair doesn't help. And the fact that my *real* self stays inside instead of making itself known.

I watch Amelia sweep through the dining hall like a princess on walkabout in front of her loyal subjects. She doesn't say anything to us, of course. It's not that she's mean to us or anything, we just don't show up very much on her radar. We're not cool enough. Hebe and I get up to go, throwing our rubbish towards the bin as we wander out.

Hebe scores a direct hit.

Mine misses the bin and slithers down the side onto the floor. One of the lunchtime supervisors throws me a look, like I'd better not leave it there *or else*. So, of course, now I'm tempted to. But I don't. I bet she wouldn't look at Amelia like that.

What am I thinking? As if Amelia would miss the bin. Isn't she captain of the netball team?

CHAPTER TWO

After dinner I go up to my bedroom and pull out my English homework. Then I realise I haven't much to go on regarding writing a story about King Arthur because, of course, I didn't pay attention in class. I was in a better place with Sir Nathan, the Black Knight. So I fire up the computer and look up *Arthurian Legends,* and realise I can probably do quite a passable story about King Arthur and his knights, especially if I pad it out with some additional material about King Arthur's horse. Only I don't know anything about King Arthur's horse, so I do a search about it. It appears that His Maj had more than one horse (so unhelpful!), so I decide to base King Arthur's horse on Silver because he's so interesting. At least I think so. And it can be called Silverado, like Silver is in Azbathria.

We're not supposed to copy things off the net, but if I don't I'll have nothing to hand in so it's the lesser of the two evils, which is something Dad is always saying whenever he has to choose between visiting Nana Iris (my mum's mum) and his own mum, Nana Susan. I used to love visiting both my nanas, but now I'm a bit older I can see Dad's point. Nana Iris (Mum's mum) isn't the best cook in the world, and Nana Susan (Dad's mum) is much more fun and would rather take us all to the pub for lunch where she will talk to me about horses, which only makes me sad because I can't spend more time with Silver. But, my Mum says, whenever Dad comes out with the lesser-of-the-two-evils thing, he shouldn't really say things like that because they're both family, and family is everything.

Personally, I'd say that having great hair is everything but what do I know? My hair is rubbish. Whenever I mention this Mum goes off on one and tells me I ought to be grateful for my beautiful hair (her words, not mine), and that some people with straight hair would love to have my curls, and that I need to remember that some people have *no hair at all!* Dad always takes exception to this as he's thinning on top and quite sensitive about it and Mum, instead of apologising, says *exactly*. She then softens the blow by saying she had in mind Mr Robinson, the plumber who lives next door to us, whose hairless head shines in the sun like a polished egg. This means we all have to avert our eyes or wear sunglasses if we want to save our eyesight. I mean, if Mr Robinson were an evil alien from outer space, I reckon he could actually use his head as his secret, alien weapon…

'Etta! Don't look at Mr Robinson!' cried Etta's mum, running down the garden path, her arms outstretched to add weight to the drama and desperation.

'Why not?' asked Etta – not only because she never looked at Mr Robinson if she could possibly help it, but because it seemed such a big deal to her mum, which was odd.

'Just do as I say!' screamed Etta's mum. 'Avert your eyes!'

But it was too late. Confused, Etta had turned towards the fence which separated their garden from the Robinsons'. As she did so, the full force of Mr Robinson's bald head, peeping up between the hollyhocks and the runner beans, and reflecting the rays of the sun, directed beams of blinding light like lasers towards its target.

'Ahhhh!' screamed Etta, the glare reducing her vision to nothingness. 'Make it stop!'

'Now you are under my influence,' growled Mr Robinson, menacingly, 'and you will do exactly what I say.'

'Noooo!' cried Etta's mum. 'Spare her!'

'Now, young lady,' began Mr Robinson, 'grab one of those plungers over there and come with me. We've a whole lot of toilets to unblock...'

Where was I?

That was it, homework! Leaving the alien and evil Mr Robinson in my imagination, and having got the main bulk of my King Arthur story sorted – including some rather good paragraphs about his horse Silverado – I decide it needs a bit more authenticity, so I go into my sister's room and ask her whether she knows anything about it all.

'I have TOLD you to KNOCK before you come in here!' Shona says loudly. She's lying on the bed twirling a lock of her attractive, wavy, dark brown hair around one finger (so, *soooo* unfair) and peering over the top of a home style magazine, her eyes like slits. My sister is going to be an interior designer and influencer when she leaves school. At least, she says she is. I think it takes more than sticking weird wallpaper up on the wall behind her bed, and different weird wallpaper up on the opposite wall, as well as painting two legs of an old chair in sludge green to be an interior designer. Shona says I know nothing about being *on trend*, which suits me.

'Why do I have to knock?' I ask her. 'What are you doing that you don't want me to know about?'

'Mind your own business!' she snaps.

I decide this probably isn't the best way to get her onside and help me. So I tell her I forgot, and that I'll remember next time.

My sister, being three years older than me, has the second biggest bedroom in our house. I have the smallest, which sucks. We live in a small house which was built ages ago in the 1960s, although mid-century everything and anything is currently very chic, according to Shona. It has a kitchen, bathroom, through-lounge, three bedrooms and a long, narrow garden, and one day when he gets around to it, Dad says he's going to get a conservatory put on the back (of the house, not the garden, because that would be weird).

It is also attached to the house next door so we can hear when Mr and Mrs Robinson have an argument – which they do, on average, twice a week. When this happens Mum flaps her hands at us like they're sea lion flippers and tells us to SHUSH so she can hear more clearly all the insults they sling at each other. So does Shona. It's like a mother-and-daughter bonding thing when the Robinsons fire up. Once, Mum and Shona actually put a couple of glasses to the wall in order to hear better. Dad shook his head and told them they ought to be ashamed of themselves, but Mum flapped one hand at him even faster and pressed a finger on her other hand to her lips to tell him to shut up – which was quite tricky as it was the hand holding the glass.

I can't help thinking that if we can hear Mr Robinson telling Mrs Robinson that she ought to go to the doctor and get something for her moods, and Mrs Robinson telling Mr Robinson that she wishes she had married Barry Carlton because at least he made something of himself instead of being a second-rate plumber (no exaggeration according to the reviews on *Checkatrade*), then maybe *they* can hear Mum telling us to *shush*, and Shona shouting down the stairs that she can't find a clean school blouse anywhere, but what do I know?

I do know that whenever we see the Robinsons in the garden or getting into their car they seem quite a unit, and they always wave cheerfully and say, 'Isn't it a lovely day?' or 'Raining again, typical!' or 'Your Shona's getting quite the young lady now, isn't she?'

They don't say anything about me.

I put this down to them being unable to find anything nice to say. Nana Iris is always telling us that if we can't think of anything nice to say about someone then we'd better not say anything. But then she contradicts herself by telling Mum how Mrs Dutty, who runs the charity shop where she volunteers (the daggy one), is a bossy old cow who isn't as clever as she likes to think herself, and ought to go on a management course. Or better still retire and leave her in charge.

Grown-ups need to listen to their own advice.

Anyway, when I ask her Shona tells me I ought to say how Sir Lancelot had a thing for King Arthur's wife Guinevere, and suggests I spice the whole story up a bit by mentioning it.

I think this sounds promising.

'When Arthur found out he went bonkers,' Shona says. 'He banished Guinevere to a convent where she spent the rest of her life with the nuns, thinking about how she had betrayed her husband, the king.'

'Why didn't they just get a divorce?' I ask.

'Wasn't done in those days,' Shona says, matter-of-factly. 'Besides, it was go into the convent or be burnt at the stake or something, as she did commit treason after all – even if it was for love.'

'Are you sure about this?' I ask, and Shona assures me she does because she saw an old film about it only a few weeks ago, no word of a lie, honest to God.

When Shona isn't banging on about interiors she's watching old films on one of those old film channels. I can't help thinking that Sir Lancelot's and Guinevere's forbidden attraction sounds like something Estra and the Black Knight should know all about, and I squirrel this information away in case I want to make use of it.

I shoehorn quite a bit about this into my story, saying Sir L and Queen G couldn't live without each other, which clearly wasn't true because they had to when Arthur's missus got dragged off to the convent. I think it makes the story more mine, you know, like putting my own spin on it – that and the bit about King Arthur's horse, Silverado. I bet nobody else has King Arthur's horse in their story. Anyway, I print it out before going downstairs to watch telly.

Wolfie comes over and leaps up on my lap. He's such a dude, despite the fact he's always scratching and wriggling about on the sofa next to us. It's like he runs on battery power and we can't find the off switch. When Dad comes home from work Wolfie dashes off to greet him like the sofa's been set alight. He loves Dad better than anyone. Dad's always saying the dog is the only one who gives him some respect in his own home.

Mum and Dad go outside and walk to the very end of the garden to look at the shed, and Wolfie deserts me to go with them. They seem to be out there a long time, and the boring news comes on the telly so I wander out to find out what they're up to.

'Shouldn't take long,' says my dad, kicking the dirt by the shed.

'Shirley says we can have them next week if we want them,' says Mum. 'Can it be ready by then?'

Dad nods his head and says something about getting some netting and wood, and Mum puts her arms around his neck and they both giggle a bit, which is embarrassing.

'What's going on?' I ask, picking up Wolfie, who squirms until I put him down again.

'We're going to keep chickens!' says Mum, beaming at me.

'Why?' I ask. I have no idea where this madcap idea came from. It's the first I've heard of it.

'Eggs of course!' exclaims Mum. 'It'll be fabulous to have lovely fresh eggs every day. Think of all the cakes I'll be able to make. You can have one for breakfast.'

'Cake?' I ask, hopefully. Chickens would be brilliant if I can have cake for breakfast.

'An egg,' says Mum, dashing my hopes.

I suppose an egg would be good, too.

A cake would be better.

I keep meaning to make a cake. I've seen cookery programmes on the telly showing you how to do it, and it looks easy enough. I just haven't got around to it yet. If we get a lot of eggs I might give it a go. I expect I'll totally make the best cakes ever. I'm probably a cake-making-goddess if truth be known…

'So now we're going to try Etta's cake,' said the celebrity judge to camera (who, if his size were anything to go by, looked like he might be the world's expert on cake). He cut a large slice and took a huge bite.

Etta stood nervously by her workstation, awaiting the verdict.

'Oh my,' drooled the celebrity judge, his face a picture of ecstasy, the effect spoilt only by the crumbs and cream clinging to the corners of his mouth. 'That, Etta, is the most perfect cake I have ever tasted. You're a genius!' He turned to the camera crew. 'You all have to try some, it's the most

wonderful cake ever. Etta, you need to write a cake-making cookbook and have your own TV series – the nation needs your expertise.'

'Oh, I don't know...' began Etta, modestly.

'You can't keep cake-making genius like this to yourself, it wouldn't be right, you'd let down so many people,' implored the celebrity judge. 'I thought I knew a lot about baking, but you've just rewritten the rule book. Please say you'll do it...'

'Technically,' says Dad, picking at the putty around the shed window, 'they'll be hens. Not chickens.'

And I'm back in the garden, wondering how a person gets to have a career baking cakes and stuff on the telly. It can't be too hard, can it? I mean, my mum makes cakes. I'll give it some thought. It could develop into Plan C.

'What's the difference?' asks Mum.

'Chickens are for the table,' Dad tells her. 'Hens lay eggs.'

'We shan't be eating our chickens,' says Mum, firmly. 'Shirley says they're all very tame, almost like pets. You might like to help look after them, Etta,' she adds, stroking my hair – at least she tries to but her fingers get caught in my mass of curls and I yelp. I can see where this is going: Mum wants hens, and I'm going to be roped into looking after them.

'They're your idea, not mine,' I mumble, to which Mum replies that if I want an egg for breakfast then it wouldn't hurt me to help with the hens, and it's not as though she's asking much and I take far too much for granted, just like my sister.

Where did that come from? The hens aren't my idea. Mum wants them, not me.

Dad says he hopes the hens aren't going to be a passing phase like my mum's exercise bike, 'cos she only had that for three weeks before the novelty wore off, and he almost did his back in lifting it up into the loft where, he adds, it is to this day, gathering dust, and why doesn't she just put it on eBay and be done with it?

Mum presses her lips together and flounces back to the house to call Shirley.

CHAPTER THREE

Becky announces to everyone on our lesson that we're going to be doing some jumping. I feel butterflies bouncing around inside my stomach at this announcement. No, wait, butterflies would fly, not bounce. So that's what they must be doing. Flying – no, not flying… *fluttering!*

Unless they've got a trampoline in there. Which I don't suppose they have. A tiny, weeny, butterfly trampoline. I can't feel a trampoline, only butterflies.

Jumping! Silver's good at jumping. He approaches the jumps calmly and never makes a fuss about it. Not like Cracker, who's a thin, creamy, off-white-coloured pony with a wispy mane that never gets tangled up in his rider's reins, and who gets a bit excited whenever we do any jumping. Amelia is riding Cracker today. She doesn't mind that he jogs a bit and canters a little bit too fast and likes to sidle up to jumps sideways. Amelia just sits there, calm and serene as a swan, and gives him a pat afterwards like it's no big deal. Which is clearly isn't – for *her*.

I give Silver's neck a rub. I want him to know he's appreciated. I feel my cantering was pretty good this morning. I hardly bounced about at all. I had the usual struggle with my hair before the lesson as I crammed it under my riding hat. I swear I could feel it lifting up again like some levitating magic trick as I fastened my chinstrap, my hair forcing it upwards like I had an inflating balloon in there. I run a finger between my chin and the strap on my hat – my hair making it feel tighter. I could be the first person ever to die because of the size of their hair…

'What have you got there, Sarge?' asked the chief superintendent as he peered over his sergeant's shoulder at the body.

'Young girl,' stated the sergeant, shaking his head sadly. 'Strangled by a lethal combination of her own hair and the chinstrap on her riding hat. That her hair is too big for the hat is obvious – look, you can see the mark under her chin where the chinstrap did for her.'

'Any sign of foul play?' asked the chief superintendent, raising his eyebrows.

'I don't think so,' sighed the sergeant. 'A classic case of death by hair that's too big for a hat. No doubt about it, Chief.'

'Shame,' said the chief superintendent, pursing his lips. 'Someone should have done something about the poor girl's hair. If only she'd had the long locks of that nice Amelia

Armitage girl, or even the smooth red hair of her friend Hebe, then this would never have happened.'
'Too right, Chief, too right...'

'Etta, are you listening? I just said I'd like you all to trot around one at a time in your jumping position,' says Becky. 'Remember to keep your weight in your heels, and to tuck a finger under your pony's neck strap if you feel insecure. Whatever you do, DON'T HANG ON YOUR REINS FOR BALANCE!'

That's telling us. When it's my turn it takes me half a circuit to find my balance, but when I do it feels great – if I don't count my legs aching.

It's also quite hard to breathe in my body protector. Whenever I moan about the tightness of my body protector Becky reminds me that it has to be fitted tightly for it to work. A *loose* body protector, Becky is always saying, is worse than *no* body protector.

If my chinstrap and hair don't get me, I might just die of shortness of breath due to an over-tightly fitted body protector...

'What about the body protector?' asked the chief superintendent, stroking his chin. 'Could that have had a hand in the poor girl's demise?'
'I don't think we can rule it out, Chief. We'll know more when the forensic report comes in, but I shouldn't be surprised if it showed a straightforward crush injury. Cause of death: big hair, chinstrap, and inability to breathe due to over-zealous fastening of a body protector...'

Silver hugs the fence surrounding the manège at a steady trot. He's such a star. I earn a *very good* from Becky. It's going well. Cracker breaks into a canter when it's Amelia's turn, but she stays in her jumping position, completely unconcerned. I think I might not look the next time it's Amelia's turn. It's too depressing. I'll look at the horses grazing in the paddock next door, instead.

'Now I want you all to watch Amelia,' says Becky. 'That's exactly the right position: legs underneath her, heels down, in balance. Well done, Amelia.'

That's that idea out of the window, then. I wonder how tight Amelia's body protector is. She doesn't seem to be having any trouble breathing.

Becky sets up a small jump by the letter E that's been painted on the school fence, and adds three trotting poles on the approach side. It's nothing we haven't tackled before and I give Silver's neck a rub, the bit where his mane flops onto the other side, above where it gets mixed up in the reins.

Amelia is first to go.

Of course she is.

She gets Cracker to go steadily over the poles and pops the jump, dead centre. Textbook.

Of course she does.

Becky tells her that was excellent!

Of course it was.

Two other pupils do the same. One has a wobble after the jump, but no harm done.

'Okay Etta, let's see you and Silver,' says Becky with a smile. 'Look where you're going, not down at the jump.'

Yeah, I think to myself as I press my heels into Silver's sides, I could totally rock as a riding instructor. Piece of cake. Oh…. unless I pursue the idea of baking cakes on the telly as a career. I feel it is a bit early to draw a line under that idea.

Silver and I set off at a steady pace and I can see Silver's beautiful little ears pricked in front of me, pointing towards the jump. Over the poles… one, two, three… then a stride… then the jump. Pop. Over. Sorted. Try to stop gasping and breathe normally.

Fail to breathe normally due to the combined efforts of the chinstrap-body-protector combo.

'Very good, Etta!' cries Becky. To be fair, she says that to everyone. She rarely says anything else, even if we're rubbish. She's very positive, is Becky. I have a feeling I may need to be like that if I want to be a riding instructor. That might be the hardest thing about the whole idea.

After we've jumped a few times Becky sets up another jump, two strides further on from the first.

'A combination,' she tells us. 'You'll need to ride on between the first jump and the second, so don't just collapse and give up when you land after the first.'

A combination. Just like they have in the big competitions at Hickstead I've seen on the telly, where the jumps are taller than the height of my dad – combinations, ditches, walls, the works. What must it be like to be a good enough rider to jump those? I'd need a bigger horse than Silver. I'd need a huge, well-bred, stonking great horse with long legs, powerful hindquarters and the courage of a lion…

The huge crowd fell silent as the commentator's voice boomed out across the famous Hickstead showjumping course.

'And last to go are Estra Marshall and her mighty grey, the partnership that helped Great Britain secure the Nations Cup at Aachen earlier this year. Can Estra and Silver-Ore-Nothing get a clear round in the fastest time to take the cup?'

The elegant rider gathered up the reins as her stunning dappled grey stallion, Silver-Ore-Nothing, cantered around the ring. Estra's striking green eyes studied the course, her smooth black hair snaking behind her in a long and elegant plait. The crowd held its breath, willing the darling of the home crowd to pull out all the stops, to gallop around the huge and terrifying course that had witnessed the downfall of so many international riders, to go faster, to jump higher than anyone else and secure the cup for Great Britain.

The first jump loomed large before them as Estra and Silver-Ore-Nothing galloped towards it, determined to beat the clock. The grey made nothing of the vast planks and they turned to the next, a wicked combination of twin oxers. Taking off for the first element too early caused the crowd to gasp – surely the distance was too much for even this plucky rider and her talented horse? But no! With a supreme effort Silver-Ore-Nothing reached for the back rail and, as the pair landed, the pole rocked in the cup... but stayed up!

They tackled the rest of the course in a similar fashion, for Estra Marshall knew that risks had to be taken – this was a win or go-home-trying round. She would take victory or come nowhere. The darling of the crowd would never settle for second place.

From the collecting ring Estra's fiancé, fellow showjumper Nathan Black, stood silent, a stray lock of hair falling over his forehead, the expression on his handsome face – the pin-up of a million horse-mad little girls – a mixture of admiration and love.

And then only the last combination stood between the pair and success. Over the first element, over the next and finally the last – with time seeming to stand still as Silver-Ore-Nothing appeared to hover over the poles – before landing with a soft thud, the crowd's cheers the only sound that followed. Their clear round was a full two seconds faster than that of their closest rival.

They had done it! They had secured the championship! Estra Marshall had become the youngest rider ever to have done so, Silver-Ore-Nothing taking the record for the fastest clear round on the course.

After a hug and a kiss from a devoted Nathan, the pair approached the rostrum. Flowers were flung from the stands by the ecstatic crowd, and the Duchess of Somewhere-or-the-other (an accomplished horsewoman and sixteenth in line to the throne), stepped forward to present the rosettes, trophy and sash. Estra, in her typical modest fashion, turned to her horse, acknowledging the debt she owed to her loyal partner.

The Duchess of Somewhere-or-the-other, in an unprecedented move, took the microphone to add her own glittering accolades, and as she opened her mouth to speak, the crowd fell silent.

'It gives me great pleasure to...'

'... aim for the centre and remember to ride to the far end.'

Whatever is the duchess talking about? I mean, I know she's a brilliant rider and all that, but...

'Etta, it's your turn. *Go!*' says someone who sounds far away, and quite like Amelia.

It *is* Amelia. And it wasn't the duchess dishing out the instruction, it was Becky. After all, it's her job.

Oh, the combination! Well that ought to be a doddle after what Silver and I have just done.

Except that we didn't actually do it....

No matter, we still smash the three trotting poles and two jumps. I don't mean literally; we leave everything as we find it. As we reach the far end of the manège my chinstrap feels really tight again. Taking a hand off the reins I shove my hat further down onto my head and as I do so, Silver turns the corner a bit sharpish, and I lurch over towards the fence.

Nearly!

At the end of the lesson I give Silver a hug to thank him, and as soon as I pull away he shakes his head and neck as though he's trying to shake my smell off him. Bit rude, I think. Leading him to the gate of the manège, one of the students takes his reins and the last I see of him for a whole week is his untidy loo-brush tail disappearing around the corner of the yard on his way to his stable. He has quite a large bum, does Silver, but it doesn't seem to matter to horses and ponies. In fact, it looks quite nice – especially with his darker grey tail standing out against his pale bottom.

On the way home in the car, with Wolfie on my lap, Mum asks what the red mark is on my neck. When I explain about my hair, my hat and my chinstrap, she suggests I try putting my hair in a plait next week – which is spooky, because that's exactly how Estra Marshall wears her hair when showjumping.

'Hmmm,' I say, gazing out of the window and remembering my meeting with the duchess, 'it worked at Hickstead...'

Mum gives me a look and murmurs, 'You're a strange one, aren't you, Etta?'

Not so much strange as a bit stupid not to think before I speak, I reckon.

CHAPTER FOUR

I AM WALKING TO school on Monday morning, trying to think of a way to get out of running the 400 metres at our end-of-term sports day (Miss Colby in PE has put my name down for it simply on a default basis because A. I'm rubbish at everything else and B. nobody else wants to do it – plus she caught me in the middle of imagining the Black Knight meeting Estra as she was taking a drink by a stream with a rather lovely waterfall as a backdrop, so I wasn't able to think of an excuse to get out of it), when I catch sight of three boys ahead of me. This makes my heart beat faster, and I slow down and hang back a bit so I don't catch them up.

I wouldn't do this normally, not for any old three boys (as if), but one of them is Nathan Black – recognisable even from the back. He and his mates are kicking a football along the pavement, and I'd rather stay behind them so that Nat can't see my horrible hair. The other two boys are his mates, and I don't know what their names are because that information is on an am-I-interested basis, and I'm not.

But Nat I *am* interested in. Nat is the second thing in my life I am totally in love with.

Because Nat is gorgeous.

No, really, he is. Like totally drop-dead, heart-a-flutter, can't stop staring gorgeous. He could be in a boy band or be an actor or model or something (I'm not joking).

He's tall.

He's dark and smouldering with melting brown eyes (a bit like Silver's).

He's athletic (he's in the school football team and is always kicking a ball about with his mates).

He's got the most amazing smile.

When he pushes his hair out of his eyes my knees turn to marshmallow. I don't want them to you understand, they just do it without consulting me at all.

Nat's in the year above me at school so I reckon he must be quite mature, not like some stupid boys I could mention, like Max Rybart in my class, for example, who won't stop telling (very bad) jokes.

Unfortunately, Nat Black doesn't know I exist. Or maybe that's fortunate because even if he did the chance of him wanting to know me better is less than zero. More like minus a hundred. More like minus a million I reckon.

Also, he did glance in my direction once and my face went all peculiar – my eyes blinked so fast I couldn't focus on anything, my face went all hot – and I couldn't move my legs and had to look in the other direction just to get control of my body back. It was not a nice experience at all. It took all of ten minutes before I felt like myself again.

Oh, and he's the inspiration for the Black Knight who pops up in my made-up life in Azbathria, as well as my showjumping boyfriend. But I expect you've guessed that bit by now, because it's blindingly obvious.

When I get to the school gates Hebe's there, and she's already clocked Nat and his ball-kicking chums.

'Look at you shuffling behind Noshus Nat like a lovesick puppy,' she grins.

'Shut up,' I say, knowing my face is turning red. I wish I'd never told Hebe how much I fancy Nat, although she probably would have guessed because I'm so transparent.

'Honestly, the way you're glowing it's a wonder Nat didn't feel the heat behind him. It must be like being followed by a dragon,' says Hebe.

A dragon? Hmmm, a dragon….

The dragon crept nearer, its eyes like glowing embers, flames darting from its lips as it drew breath, preparing to exhale a blast of fire to scorch to a crisp the damsel tied to the tree. She was the latest in a line of maidens offered up as sacrifice by the villagers in order to appease the wicked reptile, an annual ransom paid in exchange for a year of living without fear of attack from the beast.

'No, please!' cried the damsel, writhing in terror, fighting against the ropes that bound her tightly, her soft, shining

yet manageable curls tumbling around her shoulders. Miraculously, the ropes gave under her determined pressure, and as she wriggled her hands free from her bonds Lady Estra grasped a fallen tree branch, stout and true (and very handy), and prepared to defend herself with courage and resolve, causing the dragon to hesitate, unprepared for this unexpected turn of events.

'Stop where you are, foul beast of the devil!' commanded a voice, and both damsel and dragon turned to see a handsome knight on his ebony steed, a steel-tipped lance in his hand.

'Sir Nathan, the Black Knight,' gasped Lady Estra as she swept her tumbling locks from her face, relief showing on her delicate features.

Turning, the dragon switched its attention from a potential meal to its new and dangerous adversary and, with a screech of fury that shook the very leaves from the trees, dived at the wide-eyed horse and its rider. Flames erupted from the dragon's breath, spouting forth a deadly cascade of heat and smoke.

But the Black Knight was too quick – his lance found its mark on the dragon's throat. With a cry and a hiss the dragon fell, its tail thrashing, signalling its death throes.

'Forever at your service, My Lady,' declared the Black Knight, dismounting and bowing deeply. 'You are now free to return to your people,' he added, giving his restless and snorting horse a reassuring pat.

'Oh Black Knight,' Estra whispered, eternally grateful to have been rescued by one so dashing, 'goodly Black Knight, how can I ever repay you? You truly are my knight in shining armour...'

'I don't know what you see in Nathan Black,' says Hebe, driving the dragon and the Black Knight from my thoughts. But I know she does. Everyone does. You'd have to be dead or ancient not to fancy Nat.

I think Hebe might fancy Nat on the quiet, but I don't want to think about that so I don't pursue it. Some things, Nana Iris says, are better left unsaid.

I think about Nat during assembly to take my mind off double maths to follow (whoever thought up our class's timetable this term needs a stiff talking to – I mean, DOUBLE MATHS, FIRST THING MONDAY MORNING? Come ON!). He *was* going out with a girl from a neighbouring school, but I overheard some girls from his class talking in the corridor and they reckoned it was all off. Not that it will make any difference, it's not like our eyes are destined to meet across a crowded assembly, Nat will suddenly see me for what I really am (the inside, real me, not the outside, fake and not-very-funny cosmic-joke me with big hair) and, pushing everyone else aside, rush over and declare his undying love for me, is it?

Not in real life, anyway… I don't think…

Their eyes met across the school hall. Somewhere, on the stage, the head teacher's words melted away into silence. It was as though the rest of the pupils faded like mist and there existed only the two of them – Etta and Nathan. With a sigh, and without taking his eyes from her radiant face, Nat moved towards her, gaining speed with every stride. Standing still, her heart beating, her beautiful green eyes blinking in confusion and adoration, her raven-black hair tumbling around her shoulders in bouncy, yet shiny and controllable curls, Etta held her breath. As he reached her, Nat held out his arms to enfold and hold her close, the two of them becoming one as she heard his soft voice whisper...

'...pssst, Etta, sit down!'

I'm the only one still standing up. Sniggers can be heard. All the teachers on the stage are looking at me with their superior teacher faces, their raised eyebrows looking like they've asked a question and are waiting for me to answer it.

I sit down with a bump.

'If Henrietta Marshall has no objection, I'll continue,' says Mr Brampton, our head teacher. He thinks he's terribly amusing when really he's just totally boring. Just because nobody interrupts teachers it doesn't mean we're hanging on their every word. We're just not allowed to request they stop torturing us.

'Drama Club tonight,' hisses Hebe, chewing on a hangnail as Mr Brampton continues to drone on and on.

'Yep!' I reply, wondering how long I will feel as though I am on fire due to embarrassment. I didn't even need the dragon.

Ms Pertwee, who teaches drama and art, and embraces her inner-child by possessing the dress sense of a toddler whose mother used to work as a circus clown, has started an after-school drama club. Naturally, as a person who is going to be a famous actress when they leave school (possibly, pending other, alphabetically nominated career choices cropping up) I have put my name down for this. It won't hurt to get my eye in a bit.

Hebe said she would come with me as it didn't clash with her athletics practice (she yawned as she said it and rolled her eyes, so I know she's not keen), even though she has no aspirations to either tread the boards (that's acting speak for going on the stage) or see herself on the silver screen (films) in future, but I'm glad she's coming. It'll be more fun with both of us there. I'm not one of Ms Pertwee's biggest fans since she asked us all to pretend to be a cat and I asked her about my motivation (which is actor-speak for how I might get into character). The answer, *'Just use your imagination, Etta,'* was, I felt, totally inadequate.

Ms Pertwee let herself down badly there.

The day drags, as usual. FINALLY, the end-of-the-day-bell goes, and Hebe and I make our way to the big hall where Drama Club is being held. Ms Pertwee is already there, clipboard in hand, nodding to Amelia Armitage who has turned up with her bezzies.

'Oh great,' sighs Hebe, rolling her eyes and dumping her bag on the floor.

I know what she's thinking because I'm thinking the same thing: Amelia is going to dazzle Ms Pertwee and will probably be as brilliant at acting as she is at everything else.

About twelve pupils have turned up, all telling Ms Pertwee their names and standing around eyeing each other up, the younger ones looking like they wish they hadn't come and the older ones taking no notice of them. Ms Pertwee knows our names as we're both in her art and drama classes.

'Hello girls!' Ms Pertwee says, brightly. Ms Pertwee says everything brightly. If words were colours everything Ms Pertwee says would come out in pink and yellow and fluorescent green. Not like Mr Taritt, who would talk in black and navy blue. And sludge green, like pony poo. Amelia Armitage would talk in white, like freshly fallen snow. Nathan Black would emit words that were the sort of strong, traditional colours Shona is always going on about for posh interior walls, and I would talk in…

No, I have no idea, I don't know where I'm going with that.

So I'll just stop.

Suddenly, the door to the hall opens with a loud crash and Max Rybart clatters in, ripping off his tie and grinning as he sends a manic wave in our direction.

'I wouldn't have thought this was your thing,' says Hebe. She says this because Max Rybart is always clowning around in class, and never takes anything seriously.

Max Rybart runs his fingers through his (very) blonde hair and tells her he's going to be a comedian when he leaves school, so he thinks performing in front of a live audience would be beneficial.

Well, that makes sense. It also explains why Max Rybart is always telling jokes, although if he's going to be a comedian he is going to need some new (better) material if he doesn't want to risk getting heckled or pelted with rotten tomatoes.

Ms Pertwee, who is wearing a big, puffy skirt above her knees, red tights and a white blouse with red spots, says the idea of Drama Club is for everyone to have FUN! She says fun in CAPITAL LETTERS with an exclamation mark after it, in the way my dad says WALKIES! to Wolfie. This always sets Wolfie off in a frenzy of bounding around the house, running up and down the stairs and on and off the furniture, barking furiously until Mum shouts, 'Must you wind that dog up every time, Dave? It's doing my head in!'

Also, Ms Pertwee says she's been thinking it would be FUN! to put on a play at the end of term, and she hopes everyone will be up for that. She has, she tells us breathlessly, penned her own play specially for us loosely based on Shakespeare's *Romeo and Juliet* but with a modern twist, set in the present day and with up-to-date dialogue. It is, she tells us, called *A Town Divided*, and she hopes we'll all be up for performing it at the end of term because she thinks it will be tremendous FUN!, won't it.

At this bombshell, a boy and a girl from the year below ours pick up their bags and leave the hall.

'Oh,' says Ms Pertwee, clearly disappointed. 'Oh well, never mind,' she continues, even more brightly to make up for it, 'I take it everyone else is totally up for performing the play.'

Nobody says anything, they just take a sneaky look at everyone else to see what the general feeling might be.

'Well I am,' announces Amelia, and her bezzies nod furiously.

'Good, good!' says Ms Pertwee, as though Amelia speaks for everyone.

There are some further murmurings at the news of the play which could or could not – depending on your view – be taken as conformation that it might be FUN!

'That sounds pretty crap,' hisses Hebe, which I take to mean she's not totally on board.

I say nothing. My mind is just about to go into a fantasy about me playing the lead in the play that's based on *Romeo and Juliet*, but with a modern twist, when Ms Pertwee's voice swoops in and puts a stop to it. Which is a shame. It's always a shame to stifle imagination, I think, especially when the imagination in question is mine.

'Now,' continues Ms Pertwee, 'before we even think about the play I thought it would be FUN! – just to see what everyone is made of – to perform some exercises…'

Hebe groans. I know what she's thinking because whenever Ms Pertwee gives us exercises in drama class Hebe says they're stupid, and that she can't pretend to be a balloon when she's physically unable to get off the ground for longer than half-a-second.

She has a point.

'… so I'd like you all to spread out and pretend you're a tree!' concludes Ms Pertwee. 'Any tree – a willow, a graceful silver birch, a majestic oak – anything,' she adds, waving her arms about. 'This will help me when we carry out auditions for the play.'

We all shuffle into our own space, and I deliberately avoid eye contact with Hebe as I put up my arms and imagine I'm an apple tree moving in the wind, so that Ms Pertwee can totally see what I'm made of.

It is essential to do these exercises when you are going to be a famous actress when you leave school because part of being an actress is making people (the audience) believe you are someone (or something) you are not. I know all about this because of the two different people I am already – the outside one everyone sees, and the inside (real) one that keeps itself hidden. In this respect I am way ahead of everyone else in the acting stakes. I have turned a negative into a positive, as my mum is always saying I should.

I wonder whether anyone has ever been so good at pretending to be a tree, the audience actually thought they *were* a tree. That would be acting *par excellence!* (That's French for the highest quality.)

'Very good Amelia!' I hear Ms Pertwee say. She is writing something down on her clipboard. She obviously hasn't yet got around to noticing the tree masterclass I am performing.

Suddenly, the door to the hall opens and in walks a latecomer with one of his chums.

And not just any old latecomer.

'Well look what the cat dragged in,' hisses Hebe, giving me A LOOK.

I stop being an apple tree – or maybe I have turned into an apple tree which has stopped moving in the wind, a tree that is sort of surprised and delighted and gobsmacked at the same time – and I make a point of not looking at the newcomer, even though I want to.

'Oh good, Nat and Ollie, you've come,' says Ms Pertwee, writing on her clipboard. 'Perfect! We need more boys. We're just being trees.'

'I can see that,' says Nat Black, throwing Ms Pertwee a grin that makes my apple tree's trunk and roots go all wobbly.

Nathan Black is joining Drama Club (why are boys always late?).

'If that's not a drama, I don't know what is,' sniggers Hebe.

I can't talk.

There are no words.

I don't mean because I'm being an apple tree, I mean *I* have no words.

If Ms Pertwee would like us to act like jelly then I'm way ahead of her because that is exactly how my insides feel. And my legs.

I force myself not to look at Nat Black because I know what will happen if I do. It doesn't work; I can feel myself going red anyway. If Ms Pertwee says anything I shall have to say my face is an apple on my tree.

She doesn't.

Hebe does.

'You could fry an egg on your face,' she says.

'Don't be stupid!' I reply.

'You totally could,' says Hebe. 'You look like you're about to catch fire!'

I think that's daft because nobody could fry an egg on their face. Could they?

'Oh blimey, the griddle's on the blink!' cried one of the cooks in the school kitchen (the granny-type one with the faint suggestion of a moustache).

'You're joking!' exclaimed the more glamorous second cook, rolling her chewing gum around her teeth and tapping her gel nails on the counter. 'But we've got a pupil waiting for a fried-egg sandwich. Whatever shall we do?'

'Where's that girl, the one who's always got a red face?'

asked the granny-type cook, looking around the lunch hall with narrowed eyes. 'Ah, there she is in the queue.' Beckoning with one hand she shouted loudly, 'Oi Etta, do us a favour and let us fry this egg on your face, will you?'

'Shut up!' I hiss back.

Hebe just shrugs and chews her nails.

'Come along now Hebe,' trills Ms Pertwee, in words of orange and lime, 'I'm having trouble working out what sort of tree you might be.'

'I'm an oak tree that's been struck by lightning,' says Hebe. 'I'm just a trunk, no branches, no leaves. No movement. It's really difficult,' she adds, pushing it.

'Ahhhh, very imaginative,' nods Ms Pertwee. 'Original thinking, I like that!'

She hasn't even noticed my apple tree. I'm beginning to wonder just how much Ms Pertwee really knows about acting.

CHAPTER FIVE

When I get home from school, still fired up after the unexpected excitement and emotion of Drama Club, I am forced to slide around Mum's friend Shirley's massive white 4X4 that's backed onto our driveway in order to reach the front door. When I get in the house is silent. Nobody is in it, not even Wolfie.

I can hear him barking, though.

Looking out of the kitchen window I spot Mum and Shirley at the bottom of the garden, and Wolfie running up and down the new netting Dad has put up around the shed. This can only mean one thing: the hens have arrived.

'Come and look, Etta,' Mum cries as I get to the end of the garden. 'Shirley's brought the hens over. Aren't they adorable?'

I see no hens. They are obviously all in the shed.

'Come here and you can see them through the window,' says Mum, beckoning.

'I bet you can't wait to have a lovely fresh egg for breakfast, can you,' says Shirley, her earrings wobbling.

Shirley has a vast selection of earrings, all of which dangle below her ears and her hair, which is usually piled up on top of her head with a biro skewered through it as though it's a kebab. She also favours clothes inspired by the animal kingdom. Today, a leopard-skin print is stretched over her vast chest area, under which Shirley folds her arms so it looks like she's holding her top half up against gravity.

Peering through the shed window I can just make out a large mound of what looks like feathers in one corner.

'They'll soon settle, them chickens will!' says Shirley, cheerfully. 'Be laying in no time, no time at all!' Shirley likes to say things twice, as though she doubts you heard her the first time. This is weird because she talks so loudly, you'd have to deaf not to hear her. It might be difficult if a chainsaw was being used in the next garden, or a power washer or something, but usually there's nothing around to hinder her voice at all. But there, as Nana Iris is always saying, you are.

'Do they need injections or anything, like puppies?' asks my mum.

'Gawd no!' shrieks Shirley.

'How about their claws?' asks Mum. 'Will I need to get them trimmed?'

'What? 'course not!' says Shirley. 'Honestly Sam, you're a right warrior, you really are.'

I can't help it – it's like even my mind has a mind of its own…

'Etta, take this sword and follow me – we've got to repel the invaders in the garden,' cried Etta's mum, throwing open the kitchen door and rushing outside. Etta followed, wondering at her mother's choice of clothing: sandals with leather lacings up to her knees, an animal skin tunic with a burnished breastplate, her wild hair topped by a conical cap from which two large horns protruded on either side. And was that blue woad painted on her mother's face?

'Er, Mum…' said Etta, coming to a sudden halt at the sight of a whole hoard of marauding ancient tribesmen and women standing by the pear tree and wielding axes and swords, all looking menacingly in their direction.

'Come on! Don't just stand there, help me fight this battle!' cried Etta's mum, and emitting a blood-curdling battle cry, she launched herself at the hoard with all the gusto of a warrior queen…

'Worry, worry, worry! Just chill, Sam, them chickens are fine. They virtually look after 'emselves, they do. They'll be running around in no time,' finishes Shirley.

Oh, I get it. *Worrier*. Not warrior. A bit different – I suppose…

'Etta, tell me honestly,' pleaded Etta's worrier mum, 'does my bum look big in this animal skin tunic? If it does, I'll never hear the last of it from those marauding tribeswomen. And put in another order of blue woad, won't you, we're

nearly out. Oh, and I almost forgot, I think the horns on my helmet are coming loose and I can't for the life of me remember where I put the glue. Be a love and find it, will you? If one comes off in battle I'll be all lopsided and be able to do nothing but run around in circles...'

I wonder whether I ought to get my ears examined.

'I can't wait,' says Mum. Then she tells Wolfie, who is still barking, to be quiet, but he takes no notice. Mum asks Shirley what the hens are called.

'Oh call 'em what you like, darlin'!' says Shirley, waving a hand glittering with gold rings. 'It's not like they come to call is it? Call 'em whatever you like!'

For some reason Shirley thinks this is hilarious, and she and Mum laugh together. Mum tells Wolfie to shut up. He doesn't. He continues to bark. He's clearly not as keen on the hens as Mum is.

'I'm going to miss my girls, I am,' says Shirley, pressing her red lips together and shaking her head like a person overcome by tragic news. 'They're such characters Samantha, they really are, them chickens. Had me in stitches they did, running around the garden an' all. Such characters – and them eggs was to die for.'

I can't help wondering why Shirley gave 'her girls' to Mum if she was so fond of them, but grown-ups are odd like that. Dad's always telling us he could have played for Chelsea, given half the chance. I mean if he could have, why didn't he? Though we're all glad he didn't as it's bad enough him shouting at the telly when the football is on and rattling on about the game as though we're interested (which we're not).

As the chickens, hens, whatever, seem to be stuck to the floor of the shed I retreat back to the house, but not before I hear Mum tell Wolfie that if he doesn't shut it, he'll be in serious trouble.

Wolfie takes no notice. He only stops barking when Dad comes home and picks him up.

'You're still the man, Wolfie!' Dad tells him, and Wolfie wags his tail and licks Dad's face and forgets the hens in the event of his hero arriving home and taking over the responsibility of guarding the family from the aliens Shirley has dumped at the end of the garden.

The next morning before school Mum and I go and open the shed door so our new hens can go out into the pen, run around the garden like they did at Shirley's and entertain us.

Nothing happens. Even Mum throwing chicken feed on the grass and calling, '*Here chickie, chickie, chickie*,' doesn't tempt them – well, you can't blame them. They seem to be stuck together in the same corner of the shed as they were last night. I wonder if they might actually be glued to the floor. Maybe Dad spilled something sticky.

'What were they like at Shirley's?' I ask.

Mum assures me she saw them all running around and digging up the lawn with their feet.

'Why didn't Shirley want them any more? She seemed keen to sing their praises yesterday,' I say.

'Hmmm,' says Mum, screwing up her mouth and thinking. 'Maybe she didn't want them running around and digging up her lawn with their feet.'

I tell her Wolfie won't be impressed if the hens dig up the lawn because he totally has the monopoly on that activity. You can't move for piles of dirt where he's decided to excavate, like some one-dog time-team. Mum's always moaning about it, but Dad says when Wolfie unearths a Saxon hoard of gold coins worth zillions of pounds she won't give a fig about the lawn.

When that day comes I'm going to buy Silver and we'll need to move to a bigger house with a field and a stable. Come to think of it, if I'd known we could have hens in the garden I'd have made a case for buying Silver and keeping *him* in the shed. I mean, we've got quite a longish lawn, even if it is full of holes. I take heart in the thought that maybe the hens will find the Saxon hoard of gold coins. That would be a result.

'I'll give it a few more days and then I might see whether we can find a chicken whisperer,' says Mum to no-one in particular, and she goes into the shed to see whether there are any eggs.

The answer to that is no.

No eggs.

Just a pile of put-out-looking hens.

Is a chicken whisperer even a thing? I'll Google it.

Indoors, Shona is standing by the kitchen window eating toast.

'I thought you'd want to come out and see the hens with us,' says Mum.

'No thanks!' cries Shona, her face in horrified mode. 'They stink and we'll probably get rats. They totally give me the creeps with their beady eyes and their sharp beaks and their talons. They're like fat raptors. Imagine if they were as big as us – they'd peck out our eyes and eat us!'

Mum snaps, 'They're just hens – and they've got claws, not talons.'

I think the novelty of having hens might be wearing off already.

Shona and I leave for school – only we don't walk together, obviously! She meets up with her loser friends at the corner of the road, and I make my way by myself because Hebe lives across town and walks to school from the opposite direction.

I can't stop thinking about what Shona said in the kitchen, about the hens being fat raptors. She's right, it's a good job they're normal hen-size, not huge, gigantic…

As a twig snapped behind them, Estra and Wolf stopped dead. Placing a warning hand on Wolf's neck, Estra felt his hackles rise beneath her fingers, and she noticed his lips curling back to reveal white, shining teeth, weapons he wouldn't hesitate to use to protect his mistress, to defend her to the death.

Suddenly, there was a rustling in the bushes and the girl and her grey wolf turned towards the sound. Drawing her sword from its scabbard in a determined arc Estra crouched down, her beautiful long, wavy hair bouncing around her shoulders above the flattering skin-tight leather outfit which encased her lithe form. She made no sound as she strained her ears, her highly tuned survival instincts on full alert.

Wolf's amber eyes indicated the direction from whence their foe approached. Through the rustling leaves a head emerged, a huge head with beady eyes and a formidable beak: the Giant Chicken of Azbathria! The legend was true, the giant avis did exist! And there it was, come to devour its prey – unless…

Fearlessly, Estra faced the mighty bird, Wolf growling beside her. The chicken advanced, its giant head bobbing, eyes glistening in anticipation of an easy meal.

'Come then you freak of nature!' cried the girl, courageously. 'Come and meet your end!'

The chicken hesitated – and at that moment Wolf sprang, sinking his teeth into the chicken's throat. Estra leapt forward, her sword flashing like lightning, but still the giant bird pecked at the brave wolf which held it in its grasp. Suddenly, the giant chicken shook off its foe and grasped it with a mighty claw, pinning it to the ground. The girl heard a yelp as the huge beak found its mark, stabbing Wolf through the heart. The wolf fell at his mistress's feet to rise no more, a faithful servant to the end.

'Die vile creature, die!' cried Estra, as the chicken fell beneath her sword. She took no pleasure in slaying the beast, wishing only that they had never encountered the terrifying enemy, the sacrifice of her loyal companion too high a price to pay. With the foul fowl dispatched she dropped to her knees, burying her face in the fur of her dying friend, who lifted his head for a final time to lick her face in forgiveness, understanding and love.

'I have come too late!' cried a voice, and Estra turned to see through the mist of her tears Sir Nathan, the Black Knight, dismounted from his snorting ink-black stallion, his sword drawn, his eyes full of concern, sorrow and remorse.

'I have lost a true friend, a brother in arms,' cried the girl, and she allowed the Black Knight to lift her from her

fallen comrade, to envelop her in his arms and stroke her ebony hair (dark, smooth, and shining with natural health) with a tenderness she could not have imagined from his masculine, war-like countenance.

'One true knight is indeed lost to you,' he whispered, 'but let me take his place. Together we can rule Azbathria, and I and my knights shall drive out all enemies from this fine land.'

Estra heard a trumpet call, a fanfare to herald a new beginning in the history of Azbathria, even though the Black Knight had been too late to save her lupine lieutenant...

...'OI-OI! Get out of the road you idiot! You'll get yourself killed walking across the road without looking like that! I'll telephone the school, I will.'

Some people can be so rude. And a bit too handy with their car horns, too.

I look around. True, I am in the road, and it appears a car has just missed running me over, but what's that compared to the threat of having my eyes pecked out by a giant chicken, losing my loyal companion and getting it on with the Black Knight?

Then I notice three people laughing at me from the other side of the road. Nat Black and his friends! Nat Black has just seen my embarrassing episode with the car, and obviously thinks I'm some kind of weirdo – which is even *more* embarrassing when a second or two ago he was in my head as the Black Knight.

I can feel myself GOING RED again. This time, I can't pretend I'm an apple.

CHAPTER SIX

We're at Nana Iris's and she's made lunch: roast chicken, roast potatoes, stuffing, vegetables – the works. We all tuck into the food as though we haven't eaten for a week. Surprisingly, it's not bad.

'We've got chickens now, Mum,' says my mum, making a rather gruesome connection.

'Well, hens to be more precise,' Dad corrects her. 'You know Iris, for eggs.'

'Gross,' mumbles Shona.

'Why?' asks Mum.

'We're actually *eating* chicken,' Shona says, pushing a wing around her plate. 'It's enough to make me go vegan.'

Avoiding the chicken, I fill up with roast potatoes instead. I've gone right off lunch. Hebe's already totally vegan. I wonder whether I ought to be, too. I'm practically vegetarian when I can be, except that whenever I try to go fully veggie Mum dishes up sausages or pepperoni pizza for dinner and I cave.

'What's wrong with your chicken, Etta?' asks Nana Iris.

'Urrrrrm...'

I glance at Mum and her eyes widen in warning. 'You've always eaten chicken before,' she says frostily (mainly because she keeps cooking it). But before things get really awkward Dad leans over, stabs my piece of chicken with his fork and swiftly transfers it to his plate.

'Sorted!' he says, giving me a wink. Talk about take advantage of a situation. I reckon Wolfie would be proud of him.

'I don't know,' begins Nana Iris, 'kids today being picky about their food. We were glad just to have food on our plates, weren't we Henry?'

Everyone lets out a sigh. Not this again. There's nothing Nana Iris enjoys more than launching into her regular, *we had things tough, and today's generation doesn't know it's born*, routine. What's worse is that she addresses it not to us, but to the picture of Grandpa Henry encased in a silver frame on the wall above the fire, like he can hear her. Grandpa Henry has been in no position to hear Nana Iris – or anyone else – for twenty years.

If we're lucky, Nana Iris will run out of steam after putting Grandpa Henry in the picture. If we're not lucky she'll go on to include the other two men in her life whose portraits share the same wall: ageing rock musician Rocky Hazard (with his guitar) and has-been Swedish tennis legend Sven Hordvick (serving up an ace), heroes both to Nana Iris. They've been her heroes since way back when she was a girl. It's as though Nana Iris hasn't noticed anyone – or anything – else since then.

Luck is with us; Nana Iris comes to a natural stop once Grandpa Henry is up to speed on my faddy appetite.

'So what are you two girls doing at school these days?' Nana Iris asks us a bit later as she clears the plates from the table to the kitchen. We have all shed a layer or two of clothing as Nana Iris always has the heating on, whatever the weather, and we can hardly breathe. When anyone asks her about it she draws her cardigan around her and says she doesn't see why she should be cold in her own home.

'Oh, the usual,' mumbles Shona, scrolling through her mobile.

'What's the usual?' says Nana Iris. She's persistent, I'll give her that.

'Studying for exams and things,' says Shona, airily.

'And what about you, Etta? Got yourself a boyfriend yet?'

Shona snorts. 'As if!' she says. 'Who'd fancy Etta?'

'That's enough, Shona,' says Mum, stroking my hair. Her fingers get stuck near one ear. Honestly, she never learns.

'I got an A in English for my story about King Arthur and his horse,' I inform Nana Iris. (Mr Taritt wrote *Good imagination, Etta*, and *Well written!* at the bottom of my story, which was a first. I think I might tap into my made-up life more often in English. You know, make it work for me a bit.) 'Oh, and I've joined Drama Club, Nana,' I say, trying to keep her away from the subject of romance.

'We're putting on a play that's based on *Romeo and Juliet*, only with a modern twist.'

I don't know why I said that what with *Romeo and Juliet* being a full-on romance.

'Do you mean *West Side Story*?' asks Shona in a bored voice, her eyes still trained firmly on her mobile.

I look a bit blank. This is because I have no idea what she is talking about.

'*West Side Story*, you dope,' says Shona. 'It's a film based on *Romeo and Juliet*, only it's set in 1950's America. At least the original film was, I dunno about the remake.'

Shona doesn't do remakes. She's only interested in the original films, no matter how old they are. Me, I don't know anything about either version.

'Oh that's a lovely film,' says Nana Iris, and starts singing some song about someone called Maria. It goes on a bit, and Nana Iris's voice gets a bit wobbly and then stops altogether when she fails to hit a high note – which is a relief. It's a good job Wolfie isn't with us because he would have howled the place down.

'It can't be that because Ms Pertwee has written the play,' I tell them. 'It's called *A Town Divided.*'

Shona snorts. I take it she's not impressed.

Nana Iris is.

'That's wonderful, Etta. You're going to be a famous actress one day, and we'll be seeing you on the telly. Mind you, you have to keep your wits about you, there are some terrible people in that business, you mustn't believe all they say...' and she's off on another of her pet subjects, *not-knowing-what-the-world-is-coming-to*. If there is a negative spin to be milked from any subject – even one that starts off positive – Nana Iris will find it. It's a skill, and she's aced it.

Eventually, she returns to base. 'You could end up getting an Oscar or one of those other awards,' she tells me, carefully folding up the tablecloth before screwing it up into a ball and shoving it into a drawer in her sideboard.

'Don't encourage her, Mum,' says my mum, fanning her face with a place mat.

An award, I think. That might be fun...

'And the award for the best actress goes to... Henrietta Marshall!'

With a hand clasped to her throat in surprise, Etta rose to her feet and made her way to the stage, past all her fellow actors and actresses (the ones who hadn't won), with everyone around her clapping and cheering and calling out words of congratulations. Dressed in a shimmering silver dress, her long, dark, very smooth hair elegantly coiled on top of her head, diamonds twinkling at her neck, Etta graciously accepted the award and turned to face the audience. A sea of faces, all delighted for the winner, fell silent as Etta began her acceptance speech.

'My friends,' she began, 'I am so humbled by the honour you have bestowed upon me tonight. To have been voted best actress by my peers means more to me than words can say. Thank you, thank you, thank you!'

A cry of, 'Three cheers for Henietta Marshall!' could be heard, everyone thrilled at the outcome of the best actress vote. Etta Marshall was the most popular actress around, star of stage, screen and television, and universally liked and admired. She was also engaged to the popular up-and-coming English actor Nathan Black, star of the latest Hollywood blockbuster, and tipped to go places, film-wise...

'... it's bad enough we have to sit through all Etta's histrionics without you making it worse,' I hear Mum say.

I think the central heating is getting to her, and I make a mental note to look up what histrionics means.

After lunch, and in an effort to escape the fug from the radiators, I go outside with Dad who spends some time fiddling with the door to Nana Iris's car, which Nana Iris says keeps sticking. Apparently, she spent twenty minutes struggling to get it open in a car park in town last week, and was finally rescued by the parking attendant, who only got her out by putting his feet on the bodywork and hauling on the handle. Unfortunately, he then demanded she pay for the twenty minutes she'd already been parked in addition to the time she wanted, which resulted in Nana Iris writing a lengthy, very indignant letter to the council about its attitude and shocking customer service. Nobody has yet replied, which seems to confirm the point Nana Iris was making.

Dad starts by jiggling a screwdriver in the lock, and when this cuts no ice he gives the door a few hefty shoves to teach it who is boss. This seems to be the language the door understands (the parking attendant knew a thing or two) for following this treatment it opens and closes as it did some nine years ago when Nana Iris drove it gingerly off the showroom forecourt at twenty miles an hour. I don't think it's been much over that speed since. Dad grins like he's just got a fighter plane off the ground in time to win the Battle of Britain and winks at me. This is Dad speak for, *no need to explain to Nana Iris how I got it fixed.*

During this mechanical interlude, Mum and Nana Iris go through a big bag of our old clothes Mum has brought round for the charity shop where Nana Iris volunteers. The reason they go through it is because Nana Iris insists on vetting everything Mum throws out. This means we always take back half the stuff we bring round because Nana Iris says things like, *But there's plenty of wear in that,* or *Not that one Samantha, it makes you look slim,* or *Surely you're not throwing that out, the colour is so lovely.* This means we'll be stopping off at the *other* charity shop in town on the way home with all the stuff Nana Iris says we ought to take back home and wear.

Just as Nana Iris revs up to begin her, *folks have too many clothes these days, we were lucky to have a couple of dresses and our Sunday best for church when I was a girl* routine, Mum announces that we've had a lovely lunch, thank you Mum, and that we must all be going because Shona has some homework to do and we have to get back to feed the hens.

I'm beginning to see the point of the hens.

Dropping off the rejected old clothes to the *other* charity shop is not as simple as it sounds because it's on the main road, and Dad parks up with the hazard lights flashing. I sit in the back with Shona, who is still scrolling through her phone, while Mum dashes in and tries to dump the bag before dashing out again – only the volunteers who work there won't let her get away with that because they always insist on going through the bag just in case she's trying to dump something on them they don't want.

Meanwhile, in the car Dad taps the dashboard with his fingers and mutters, 'Come on, come on,' all the while looking around for any cruising parking attendants. It's as though we're gangsters sitting in a getaway car, revving the engine and waiting for our accomplice who has rushed in to rob a bank…

'Where is he? He should be out with the swag by now,' grumbled Getaway-Dave, nervously pulling down the brim of his trilby hat and giving the car engine a serious revving.

'Chill out!' snapped Etta, better known to the police as Etta-the-Hair, famous for her range of up-to-date and amazing hairstyles. Leader of the notorious Hair and Scare Gang, she flicked a bleached blonde curl back under her fashionable 1920s cloche hat. 'Nat knows what he's doing.'

'I can't do bird again,' whispered Getaway-Dave. (It is bird, isn't it? That is gangster slang for prison, isn't it? Well if it isn't, then it is here!) *'I'm never going back; I can't stand doing another stretch I tell you!'*

'Nobody's gonna be doin' bird,' snapped Etta, chewing gum. 'Nifty-Nat'll get the readies, I'm telling yer. Just keep yer head or we'll all be doin' time.'

'You're right,' said Getaway-Dave, getting a grip. 'You always were the cool one. No wonder Nat fell for you – you're both tough, cool and afraid of nuffink.'

'I know,' said Etta. It was true. She and Nifty-Nat were cut from the same cloth – they were both fearless, reckless and ruthless (that's a whole lot of lesses and could be why

they say less is more). *They made the perfect partnership, both in crime and romance.*

'Here comes Nifty-Nat now,' cried Etta, swinging open the car door. 'He's got the swag, too, just like I said. Now putcha foot down, burn some rubber and live up to your name – you need to get us out of here before the feds arrive...'

'You took your time,' says Dad, as Mum runs back to the car minus the bag.

'Just drive!' says Mum, slumping back in her seat. It must have been bad in there. Very bad.

Wolfie goes bananas when we get home, and even the hens seem pleased to see us. As least we can see some space between them now, rather than one big hen-y blob. They obviously found moving home quite stressful.

Histrionics, according to the dictionary, means *exaggerated emotional behaviour done for show or to get a reaction from someone*. I totally do not do histrionics. As if! I mean, honestly! What a cheek! I don't believe it! The injustice of it all...

CHAPTER SEVEN

I AM WAITING IN the riding school's office before my lesson on Saturday morning. I am not terribly happy, to be honest, because I see on the board that I am NOT going to be riding Silver. I am scheduled to ride Poppy.

Poppy is a brown-and-white pony (which is known as *skewbald*) who has a very thick mane and whose ankles (*fetlocks* in pony speak) are surrounded by lots of long hair (which is called *feather*). She looks less like a pony, more like a fluffy-boot-wearing cow.

Poppy is also a bit of a plod, to put it bluntly. I know I can't always ride Silver (WHY NOT!!!!!) but riding Poppy is worse than a disappointment. Riding Poppy is VERY HARD WORK! Not only is Poppy lazy and slow but she is also fat, which means I can hardly get my legs around her which, in turn, means I can hardly use them to get

Poppy going. It is, as Nana Iris might say, a downward spiral.

If I moan about riding any other pony but Silver Becky tells me a good rider has to cultivate the *right attitude* and be able to ride any horse or pony. She says this in a very brisk, very irritating voice that I can't argue with. To my way of thinking, once I can ride Silver perfectly then that will be the time to work on riding other ponies, but Becky doesn't agree. When I am a riding instructor I hope I will be more understanding, having experienced this sort of warped thinking first hand. This, I believe, will give me the edge regarding my pupils' psychology. I am sure they teach you pupil psychology when they train you to teach riding. If they don't I shall campaign to get it included on the syllabus.

Having the *right attitude* seems to be a recurring theme with Becky. I find this confusing, mainly because my dad is always shaking his head when he's reading the paper and saying things like, 'I can't keep up with all these changing attitudes,' as Mum pats his arm and gives him a bit of a look. I mean, if my dad can't keep up with all the different attitudes then how on earth am I supposed to? There is obviously more than one attitude, so how can I tell which one is the right one to have? The one I choose might be the wrong one next week! I'd hate to waste time cultivating what I think is the right attitude only to discover that it is now out of fashion, and there is a new attitude I should be working on. The way I see it, it might be better not to get involved in any attitudes to start with and avoid disappointment – not to mention a lot of work for nothing.

If you think things can't get much worse this morning then you're VERY WRONG because guess who is down to ride Silver? That's right: Amelia!

Maybe I can say I have a headache or a stomach-ache, or something. Or that I'm allergic to Poppy. Which I might well be.

Hey, wait a minute… what if I *am* actually allergic to Poppy? Or any other pony except Silver? Oh if only…

'Ahhhh!' screamed Amelia. 'Whatever is the matter with Etta?'

'What?' asked Becky, looking around. 'Oh, I see what you mean! Etta, what's happening?'

'I don't know!' cried Etta, as she felt herself swelling up like a balloon astride Poppy's saddle. Her legs grew larger like fat sausages, her arms inflated like long balloons, her face was twice its usual size and her clothes strained around her as though she were the Incredible Hulk.

'She must be allergic to Poppy!' gasped Amelia, her normal-sized hand flying to her normal-sized mouth in horror. 'Just as Etta was demonstrating the right attitude, too.'

'Get off, get off!' shouted Becky, running over to her rapidly-expanding pupil. 'You'll burst if you don't get away from Poppy!'

'I can't!' wailed Etta. Her arms and legs stuck out at right angles and, like a cork from a bottle, her hat suddenly jettisoned skyward off her swollen head with a loud ping.

'Quick, roll towards me!' called Becky, her arms outstretched towards the ever-increasing young rider. 'I'll catch you.'

'I can never ride Poppy again,' Etta mumbled between lips which resembled huge, fat, pink slugs.

'No, of course not,' agreed Becky. *'You'd better ride Silver from now on. Only Silver...'*

It could happen.

Couldn't it?

Last time I rode Poppy I couldn't get her to jump. As we approached the jump (which was tiny – I mean really *weeny*) she got slower and slower (so I realised I was on a hiding to nothing and admit I may have given up a bit), until she slithered to a halt at the last minute, her legs and body on the approach side, her head and neck stretched over the jump on the away side. If Poppy could talk she would have said, *'Somebody has put this, this...HUGE THING in my way. Whatever do you expect me to do?'*

Everyone laughed and I was HUMILIATED so you can understand why Poppy is NOT my favourite pony. It's like she goes out of her way to make me look a rubbish rider. AND, to add insult to injury, Amelia (full to bursting with the *right attitude*) got her to jump the following week. Poppy trotted up to it and sailed over as though she was some kind of champion showjumper. Double humiliation!

If I am allergic to Poppy then that might explain why I can't get her to do things.

When Amelia (of Poppy-jumping fame) arrives in the office she sits next to Kayleigh, who she is quite chummy with, and then things go – as Nana Iris is always saying – from bad to worse.

'Guess what my mum is getting me for my birthday?' Amelia says to Kayleigh.

For one horrible, terrifying, heart-stopping moment, I have the most awful feeling that Amelia is going to tell Kayleigh that her mum is buying her a pony. Not just any pony but Silver…

'Say goodbye to Silver,' said Becky. 'Amelia and her mother simply couldn't resist the lure of his USP!' and she waved as Silver turned his head in the trailer and whinnied, clearly distressed at being sold to Amelia, of all people, and desperate to be rescued.

'Nooooooo!' Etta cried, but Becky held her back. Amelia smirked as she climbed into her mum's brand new 4X4, and Etta watched helplessly as, slowly, the car pulled the trailer holding Silver captive out of the yard.

Hearing Silver whinny again, and with a desperate cry of, 'Silver, I can't let you go!' Etta wriggled out of Becky's grasp. She wasn't helpless, she decided; Silver depended on her and her alone! Running down the driveway Etta leapt up onto the back of the trailer and deftly undid the bolts. Hearing the ramp hit the ground with a crash, Amelia's mum brought the car to a halt – Etta hadn't much time!

Swiftly untying Silver's head collar rope, she vaulted lightly onto the pony's back, acknowledging his soft nicker of thanks. In a single bound the pair leapt out of the trailer and galloped – not back towards the riding school, but away across the fields, racing to find a safe place where they could be together forever, away from Amelia and her mum and the horror of being apart…

'...a side-saddle lesson at a riding school in the New Forest,' says Amelia.

'Oh you are *soooooo* lucky!' exclaims Kayleigh.

'I know!' agrees Amelia, nodding.

I feel a bit sick. With relief.

But there is still an hour of Poppy to get through.

It doesn't go well. Poppy is even slower and lazier than usual. Silver, on the other hand, with Amelia in his saddle, is promoted to leading file at the front of the ride, responsible for the pace and direction of everyone else on the lesson.

How come I never get to take leading file when I ride Silver? I could do that. I could *so* do that!

Poppy and I are positioned in the middle of the ride behind Kayleigh on Pip, a long-legged black pony who tends to look sideways and snort nervously at anything he considers to be suspicious (most things), and in front of a tall, willowy girl called Pearl who is riding Amber, a bright chestnut mare with a white blaze, four white legs and a golden mane and tail, who shows considerably more enthusiasm for lessons than Poppy.

'Can't you hurry Poppy up?' hisses Pearl, who can be a bit bossy. She always wears her long, thick brown hair in a single plait which hangs down from under her riding hat and bounces about on her back like a snake. When she's sitting to the trot, her snake-plait jiggles and twitches about like it's alive. Today, what with Pearl being behind me, I can't see the snake-plait, I can only hear Pearl moaning.

I turn around and am surprised to see Pearl much closer to me than I expected. Amber has her nose practically on Poppy's tail – which is having no influence on Poppy *whatsoever*. If anything, it is causing her to go even slower. I suspect Poppy might be trying to tell Pearl something, which has missed her brain by at least a metre.

'You're supposed to leave half a length between each pony!' I hiss back. I don't see why it is my fault Pearl is too close.

'Doh!' she snaps. 'Amber can't *go* any slower. Give Poppy a whack!'

I don't want to give Poppy a whack. I mean, all the riders carry a whip, but we are only supposed to use them lightly to reinforce our leg aids, and only then if Becky tells us to. I hardly ever use mine. Not only because I don't want to hit the ponies (and I NEVER hit Silver) but sometimes when you do use a whip – even gently – the ponies buck and I don't want to fall off. But Poppy is going so slowly I chance lifting my whip and waving it about a bit behind my leg and, of course, Poppy doesn't even notice.

Becky does, though.

'Etta, use your legs, NOT your whip,' she shouts. 'Pearl, drop back and get Amber to slow down – you're crowding Poppy. If you're not careful, Amber will step on Poppy's heels!'

'Told you!' I mutter, really cross with Pearl now because I've been told off for using my whip when it wasn't my idea, and I didn't even *actually* use it.

'Etta's going too slow,' grumbles Pearl, determined to drop me in it.

'Yes, come on Etta, wake Poppy up – use your LEGS!' shouts Becky, siding with Pearl when she should, as I see it, have stamped on her for telling tales. 'And Pearl, you need to slow Amber down; remember your half-halts!'

Amelia and Silver carry on at the head of the ride, oblivious to anyone else's problems. The only words I hear Becky say to Amelia are along the lines of, *Well done,* and *Very good,* and *Yes, yes, just like that!*

I would give anything to be able to ride better than Amelia – and for Pearl to know it…

'Amelia, if you're having trouble, watch how Etta does it,' said Becky. 'Yes, that's right, Etta, just like that – perfect! Now Pearl, see how Etta gets Poppy to canter around the school? That's because she's using her legs and her seat. Pearl, if you rode as well as Etta, and concentrated on riding your own pony instead of trying to land other riders in it, not to mention blaming them for your own shortcomings, you would be able to control Amber's pace. Also, I can see your plait bouncing about, which tells me your body is too stiff – you need to relax. Come on now, girls – especially Pearl and Amelia – just copy what Etta does and you'll all do much better. I know it's a lot to ask, Etta being such a natural rider, but do try!'

As if!

'Etta, you need to be more determined,' cries Becky. 'Poppy just doesn't respect you. Come on now, leg on like you mean it!'

I can feel my face going red and as it does, I feel myself getting cross. Nobody's going to fry an egg on my face today! So I sit down and leg on like mad and give a bit of a growl to indicate to Poppy that I REALLY mean it this time and guess what? She actually goes faster! I know, I can't believe it, either. I didn't realise I am supposed to work much harder than the pony I am riding, but it seems to work.

'Well done, Etta!' cries Becky. 'Keep Poppy going! You've got the measure of her now!'

The trouble is, after a circuit of getting the measure of Poppy my legs feel as though they're about to fall off – but I can't stop now, not now Poppy's actually paying attention to me. By the time Becky puts up a jump at the end of the lesson I feel ready for a lie-down in a darkened room. I can feel the sweat trickling down my back underneath my t-shirt and my body protector (I'm amazed there is room), and I'm panting like Wolfie does when he's round at Nana Iris's hot house.

I look at the jump and my heart sinks. I'm exhausted. I can do no more. The jump can do its worst – Poppy can do her worst. I am totally done in. I'm so exhausted my brain can't even summon an imaginary scenario whereby I rev-up Poppy and sail over the jump.

It's not happening.

Nothing is.

'Come on Etta!' cries Becky brightly, after Amelia and Kayleigh have leapt over the jump in fine style on Silver and Pip (with only a hint of a wide-eyed glance at the jump from Pip). 'Your turn!'

I take a deep breath, dig in my heels and growl at Poppy who, surprisingly (and obviously remembering that her saddle holds a person who now has the measure of her), shuffles forward to the outside track. We trot towards the jump, and the jump seems to come towards us (quite slowly) like a big joke. A big, fat, joke jump, just there to make a fool of me. I feel like I'm going to burst and, rather than face the nightmare of turning around and having to approach the jump again, I keep legging like a person possessed. If I don't get Poppy over the jump the first time I won't have any energy for a second go or – heaven forbid – a third. Instead, I know I'll just roll off her and die right there in front of everyone, and it would serve them all right.

'Oh poor Etta, we should never have made her ride Poppy,' gasped Amelia, her hand over her eyes, unable to look at the sight of her fellow rider lying prone and lifeless in the sand.

'I'm totally traumatised,' said Pearl. 'It's all my fault – I was so horrible to her. I don't think I'll ever get over it, I'm mentally scarred for life!'

'I should have been more understanding,' sniffed Becky, reaching for a tissue. 'I wish I'd let her ride Silver on every single lesson.'

'I'll never ride again!' wailed Kayleigh, throwing herself off Pip and rushing out of the school, unable to hold back the tears.

The jump looms.

I growl in a desperate, last-ditch, gasping sort of way.

I kick. And kick. And KICK.

Poppy keeps trotting and, wonder of wonders, heaves herself over the jump with a groan – like *she's* the one making all the effort!

'Well done, Etta!' shouts Becky. 'Give Poppy a big pat.'

Did I hear right? Give POPPY a big pat? I'M the one who deserves a pat!

When we have all lined up and dismounted (I almost collapse onto the sand because my legs are like jelly due to all the Poppy-kicking I've had to do), and my breathing rate is on its way back to normal (body protector permitting), Becky drops a bombshell.

A good one.

'If you've read the notice in the office, (What notice? Where? What?) you'll know that Chesterton is now an approved Pony Club Centre, so if anyone wants to become a member and attend the special Pony Club rallies we'll be organising on a regular basis, please pick up a form. Not only will we be holding rallies at the weekends but there will be special events and a chance to gain some Pony Club badges. I hope you will all join because it will be lots of fun!'

'Wow!' exclaims Amelia, running up Silver's stirrups and loosening his girth. 'I'm so up for that, aren't you Etta?'

She says this like I'm her best chum and am as good a rider as she is. I can only manage a gulp and a nod due to needing resuscitation from having been a person who has (only just) got the measure of Poppy. The Pony Club? Just try and stop me, I think. It crosses my mind that I may be dreaming, and that this day isn't actually happening, but after giving myself a good pinch (which hurts) I can confirm that it is.

Amelia and I crowd into the office with all the other pupils from our lesson and exit with the forms.

'We can try for Pony Club achievement badges,' says Amelia, flicking back her hair (which *isn't*, I notice with a sinking heart, squashed flat to her head with sweat like mine is), 'and there will be special half-day rallies and even competitions. It sounds amazing!'

It certainly does…

'Here's Henrietta Marshall on Silver, last year's winners of the silver challenge cup for dressage. Can they win again this year against stiff competition from Amelia Armitage? Let's see…'

'I've always wanted to go in for competitions, haven't you, Etta? I'd just love to win a rosette!' chimes in Amelia, interrupting my galloping thoughts…

'Oh, there's a shame! Just when it looked as though Henrietta Marshall had the challenge cup in her sights Amelia swooped in and snatched victory with an amazing score of…

(Hang on, wait a minute, I have no idea what a good dressage score is. A hundred points? A clear round? Zero penalties? Lots of penalties? Not that it matters…)

'Bad luck Henrietta. Well done, Amelia!'

I wish people would leave others to their own made-up lives instead of crashing into them and taking them over. It was going so well…

'Ah good,' says Becky, noticing the forms in our hands, 'I'm glad you're both interested in the Pony Club. It will be great fun, and will improve your riding, too! See you both next week!'

I am absolutely certain that Becky's idea of fun is going to be a huge improvement on any FUN! Ms Pertwee has dreamed up for us. It will be no contest!

CHAPTER EIGHT

As soon as I get in the car I shove the forms about the Pony Club under Mum's nose.

'What's this?' she asks, throwing the book she was reading onto the back seat and starting the engine. Amelia's mum (older version of Amelia, all blonde hair, great bone structure and oodles of confidence) watches her daughter's lessons from the tiered seating outside the riding arena. My mum watched one lesson. Well, I say *watched*. She spent most of the time on her phone and, afterwards, spent the journey home moaning about how cold she had been, and how hard the seats were. She doesn't really understand how much I love riding, and how much I love Silver. I think she'd rather I went to art classes or ballet, anything less expensive, less smelly and less outdoorsy, although she hasn't actually said so.

Ever since that first lesson she's brought a book with her, or phones her friends, or catches up with her emails in the car. Not that I mind because the one thing worse than my mum staying out of the way while I ride would be if she were to sit and have a cosy chat with Amelia's mum. I wouldn't be able to concentrate on my riding AT ALL if I had that to worry about. I mean, what on earth would they talk about? That's right. Me. And Amelia. And how different we are – and not in a good way.

I tell Mum about the Pony Club, emphasising how joining it is guaranteed to improve my riding and not to take my word for it, but that it is Becky's opinion. Mum says something about Becky knowing the best way to sell an idea to someone, especially when it involves extra expense, to which I suggest she is deliberately looking on the bleak side of things, to which she replies that if she is cynical (that's the word for it, apparently), it's because she has been caught out before, such as when I promised I'd work harder at school if I could have riding lessons and so far she has – judging by conversations at all subsequent Parents' Evenings – seen no evidence of my having come up with the goods.

I can think of no answer to this which doesn't incriminate me, so I sit in what I consider to be dignified silence. I wish I were the sort of person who had an instant reply to hand when parents trot out comments like this, but I'm not. It's very depressing. What's more depressing is that I am bound to think of the perfect answer later, when it will be too late to be of any use.

When we get home I go through the Pony Club forms like I'm examining a secret document on which my life depends. Naturally, this sets me off thinking about when and if my life might depend on a secret document and reaching the obvious conclusion that being a spy might be a rather cool career. I wonder how you get to be a spy. Go to Spy School, I suppose, where you learn all about secret codes and disguise and being brave under a lot of pressure behind enemy lines. I wonder what qualifications you need – geography, probably, so you know where you are and where you need to be. And languages so you can understand what other spies, the ones that work for The Other Side, are saying, secrets and all that.

I might look into it. I quite fancy being a spy, being brave and obtaining secrets and exposing double agents. Oooh, maybe *I* could be a double agent – you know, pretend to work for The Other Side (I'm not sure who The Other Side is right now, but they'd teach me that at Spy School) and learn all about their secret missions, but really I'd be working for Us, and gain lots of information that way. I'd probably have to dress up and disguise myself…

Etta (code name Miss White) clutched the briefcase to her chest and looked carefully around the corner of the building, her fawn mackintosh firmly belted around her waist, a black beret atop her blonde wig, dark glasses on her nose so that although she might appear to be looking straight ahead, her eyes could secretly stray left and right, scoping the scene around her. Could that be her contact, Mr Black, sitting on the bench overlooking the river, awaiting the dangerous, yet vital, handover of secret documents? The only way to find out was to make contact, using the secret code.

Taking a deep breath Etta stepped out and walked briskly – yet in an out-for-a-stroll-not-doing-anything-clandestine-that-a-watching-member-of-this-country's-secret-service-needs-to-worry-about, or-anything-out-of-the-ordinary-so-don't-even-think-about-stopping-me-and-asking-to-see-my-identity-papers sort of way – to the meeting point. Sitting casually at the other end of the bench, and resisting snatching even the merest glance at the young man beside her, Etta said the secret code in a low voice, in perfect French: 'The squirrel flies at night.'

The man continued to stare straight ahead, looking neither right nor left. Then Etta heard him say, in a low yet clear French accent, 'Yes, but the badger goes by train.'

Etta allowed herself a quick glance at his face. It was a handsome face, strong and brave – a face that, despite potential risks too awful to contemplate, belonged to a man determined to obtain secrets vital to the security of the British government. A man willing to risk his life for freedom and for the country he loved.

Suppressing the mutual physical attraction which was so obvious to them both, Etta rose gracefully to her feet and walked purposefully away from the agent she knew only as Mr Black, leaving the briefcase behind for him to take. She had completed her mission and done her duty. British national security was once again safe – for now. She would return to her digs and make radio contact with HQ to learn of her next assignment. That was, of course, she reminded herself with a small shudder, if she managed to make it out of the country alive.

'Etta! Nana Susan is here!' Mum calls up the stairs. I go downstairs, taking the Pony Club forms with me. There is a method to my madness for I have already noticed there is a cost involved in joining the Pony Club and I don't need to go through another of Mum and Dad's lectures about how money doesn't grow on trees and how, if it did, we'd have a couple of them in the garden (cue much laughter from both of them, so annoying). Now we have hens perhaps we'll have some extra cash because of all the money we'll be saving by not buying eggs.

Nana Susan is sitting in the kitchen. Nana Susan is as different from Nana Iris as Silver is to Poppy. Nana Iris is all doom and gloom, be careful, take no risks, nothing good, everything bad; Nana Susan is the complete opposite and always very positive. She never suggests NOT doing things, she only thinks of ways to make things happen. Nana Susan is always saying things that make me think anything is possible, or that there is a way – or lots of ways – of getting things done. Nana Susan, I believe, definitely has the *right attitude*. But then, of course, Nana Susan never has to ride Poppy, or put up with watching Amelia doing things perfectly.

The only thing Nana Susan does have in common with Nana Iris is that she, too, lives alone. Granddad Peter, her ex-husband and my dad's father, now lives in New Zealand with his new wife Griselda, whom no-one has ever seen. I mean that none of the *family* has seen her, what with Granddad Peter having met Griselda in New Zealand. I expect other people in New Zealand have seen her, obviously. I mean, she's not invisible. At least everyone assumes she isn't. Maybe she is. Maybe she's imaginary. Maybe she's just a figment of Granddad Peter's imagination.

'Come along, Griselda,' said Granddad Peter, *'and meet the family. This is Dave, my son, and his wife Samantha. Dave, Samantha, meet Griselda.'*

'Er, Dad, there's nobody there,' said Etta's dad, *looking bewildered.*

'Don't talk daft, lad,' said Granddad Peter, *waving an arm towards nothing at all.* *'There she is, as plain as the nose on your face!'*

'Er, why don't you come and sit down over here, Peter,' said Etta's mum, *patting the chair beside her as she gave her husband a wide-eyed look.*

'But there's no room for Griselda there,' said Granddad Peter, *shaking his head.* *'Whatever's the matter with the pair of you? Can't you see her?'*

'Well, that's just it, Dad...' said Etta's dad, *'...we can't!'*

'You two need your eyes examined,' said Granddad Peter, *angrily.* *'Don't think I don't know you're trying to make out I'm mad...'*

Well, if we ever go to New Zealand to meet them it might just go like that I suppose. I don't think Nana Susan is at all bothered about whether anyone can see Griselda or not. She goes to lots of clubs and societies round at the library, and is always being asked out by widowers and divorced *gentlemen callers*, as my dad likes to call them (that's boyfriends to you and me – although I can see why Dad doesn't call them that because they're old, they're hardly *boys*). They never last long, though, because Nana Susan values her independence and dumps them whenever they get a bit clingy (her words) or start thinking they know what's best for Nana Susan (which, roughly translated, means they start telling her what to do).

Whenever Nana Susan tells us she is no longer seeing Gerald/Thomas/Jeffrey, and Mum or Dad express disappointment, she shoots me a wink and says she doesn't need anyone organising her life, *thank* you, and that there are plenty more fish in the sea. She did say once that she's too long in the tooth for any knights in shining armour, and that armour seems to tarnish quicker than ever these days.

This made me wonder whether that made us more alike or less alike, what with the Black Knight and everything, but I wasn't sure what she meant by the armour quickly tarnishing, or her teeth being too long, and I didn't want to reveal anything about the Black Knight, so I didn't say anything.

Personally, I think the value Nana Susan puts on her independence is another example of having the *right attitude* (and so would you if you'd ever met Gerald/Thomas/Jeffrey), but my parents don't agree, and are always whispering to each other that they think Nana Susan is too picky. I think Nana Susan can be as picky as she wants. She seems happy enough.

Another example of how Nana Susan definitely has the *right attitude* is that she never bangs on about money not growing on trees, but often comes up with the odd handy contribution to the Etta's-riding-and-other-expenses-fund even without being asked, which is what all nana's should be like. I mean, it's a real plus, as I am sure you will agree.

'What have you got there, Etta?' asks Nana Susan (see what I mean, she doesn't even need a hint to take the bait).

So I show her the forms and tell her all about the Pony Club. Nana Susan sympathises with my love for Silver because was in love with a bay pony called Mr Pepperpot when she was my age. I've seen old, curly photographs of her riding him, in which she was wearing a riding hat with an elastic chin strap, no body protector and short boots with a strap around them instead of the elastic-sided ones we have now. Mr Pepperpot was wearing a funny-looking bridle without a noseband, with yellow plaited reins and a shiny yellow-and-white browband under his bushy forelock.

Nana Susan was sooo lucky because she used to spend all her spare time at the riding school near where she lived, grooming the ponies and tacking them up and stuff, and even getting free rides in return for helping out. You could do that in the old days. Not like now, worse luck.

Looking through the forms Nana Susan throws a wink in my direction and reaches for her handbag – which looks like an expensive designer one but is just a copy from the market. 'Let me treat you,' she says, pressing several twenty-pound notes into my hand. 'The Pony Club is fabulous, go and enjoy yourself.'

Mum swoops in like she's got antennas tuned in to our conversation (I hope I've inherited that trait because it will come in very handy if I decide to become a spy). 'Etta,' she says, 'I hope you're not pestering Nana Susan for money!'

'Of course she isn't, leave the girl alone,' says Nana Susan, totally on my side.

It's about time somebody is.

'Oh Susan,' says Mum (she would have to notice the cash), 'you shouldn't!'

Don't discourage her, I think – I mean it's not like my mum was offering.

'Say thank you to Nana Susan,' says Mum unnecessarily, like I'm a toddler. I'm already giving her a big thank-you hug.

'You make sure you enjoy yourself – and I want to know all about it!' says Nana Susan, brushing a smear of a vivid shade of crimson lipstick off my cheek. Nana Susan always wears lipstick. And mascara. And trendy clothes in bright colours. I have noticed my mum and dad exchanging looks and shaking their heads sometimes when Nana Susan has gone, and I've heard Mum saying something about her needing to act her age, but I don't really see what it has to do with them. If Nana Susan wants to wear a red jump suit or white skinny jeans, and she doesn't look a fright then I don't see why she shouldn't. I don't see why anyone else would care.

It seems to me that grown-ups are always telling other people what they should do. Or not do. They just can't help themselves – they tell young people what to do, and they tell old people what to do. Why do they think they are the only ones who know things?

In contrast to Nana Susan, Nana Iris only ever wears pale clothes in beige or lilac or lemon. Sometimes, it's difficult to see that she is actually there, she just sort of blends in with her surroundings. Like those lizards I can't remember the name of right now. It's as though Nana Iris doesn't want anyone to notice her.

Odd.

And boring.

Unless Nana Iris is an actual spy, and has strict instructions not to draw attention to herself.

Doubtful.

'When I was your age,' says Nana Susan, 'I spent every spare moment at the riding school with my friends. We mucked out, groomed, rode the ponies bareback down to the field – we did everything we could to help. I know it's not like that now, though.'

'We're not allowed to stay behind after our lesson,' I tell her, thinking how unfair it all is. I wonder what it would be like to ride Silver bareback...

Vaulting lightly onto the mustang's grey-and-white back, the young daughter of Chief Running Bull pressed her moccasins to the pony's sides, feeling the warmth of his hide beneath her. The pair galloped on as one, the girl's black braids matching the angle of her pony's tail as they streamed out behind her in the wind, the flying eagle above them throwing a shadow on the dusty land below.

'You are wild as the sun and the stars above us,' whispered the young girl, leaning over her pony's shoulder and hearing his unshod hooves beat a rhythm on the ground. 'Surely no-one ever had such a wonderful pony as you, Silver Cloud. You are swift like the wolf, strong like the bear, as much part of this landscape as the buffalo.'

Suddenly, the girl leant back and the pony came to a halt, half-rearing as he did so (which the young girl sat with ease), and they looked down the hill to the flat lands below where dust clouds rose to the sky. A wagon train was approaching, rumbling across the prairie and led by a handsome young cowboy on a dark cowpony. Despite the attractiveness of the cowboy leader the young girl frowned. White settlers! She had to warn her tribe. Turning her pony, the girl urged Silver Cloud to gallop back to the encampment so she could tell her father the news. She knew the settlers meant nothing but trouble for her people – unless, somehow, an alliance could be formed between Running Bull's daughter and the handsome leader of the wagon train.

'Well, if you join the Pony Club at least you'll be able to spend some time around the stables and learn stable management. You'll love it!' says Nana Susan with a smile.

I tell her I can't wait, because I can't.

Anyway, I skip back upstairs and look up the Pony Club's website. It's full of very experienced and determined-looking riders on very whizzy and dangerous-looking ponies doing very difficult and dangerous-looking things (like jumping huge jumps and leaping on and off their ponies in gymkhanas without the ponies stopping, or even slowing down but going really fast – I mean *cantering*) which puts me off a bit. I mean, I get the heebie-jeebies whenever I head Silver towards a tiny-weeny jump, and I've only ever mounted from the mounting block. This is why I need my own pony because you get to learn these things when you can ride all the time.

But then I think that maybe if I join the Pony Club I could become one of those riders who can ride those sorts of ponies and do all those very difficult things. That's what the Pony Club is for, isn't it? I remember reading somewhere once that practically everyone who has ever represented us at the Olympic Games in any equestrian events used to be members of the Pony Club. Maybe the Pony Club is just waiting for me to join and fill a gap in the market, so to speak, a void only I can fill…

'Where's Etta?' asked the District Commissioner, looking at her watch.

'She's just warming up over the Olympic-size cross-country course,' replied Amelia, unable to keep the envy from her voice.

'I don't know where that young girl finds her courage,' said the District Commissioner, in tones of admiration. 'Mark my words, she'll be short-listed for our next Olympic Games or I'll eat my hat, so I will! She's the rider we've been waiting for, the rider to lead our team to gold medals and glory!'

'I'd do anything to have Etta's talent,' sighed Amelia. 'She's always riding the whizzy and dangerous-looking ponies and doing very difficult things. I wouldn't have the nerve.'

'I know, Amelia, I know,' said the District Commissioner, patting Amelia's arm in commiseration and throwing her a small smile of encouragement. 'We can't all be blessed with greatness like Etta. She's an inspiration to us all – even though a talent like hers is such a rarity…'

Then I realise I'm on the wrong part of the website, and that I am going to be joining something called *Centre Membership*, based at riding schools for people *without* their own whizzy and dangerous-looking ponies, and who *can't* do dangerous things like leaping on and off their ponies while they're cantering – at least they can't *yet*. Clicking on that part of the website I notice it all seems a lot more do-able, and most of the pictures are of members grooming, saddling up and leading ponies at riding schools, all grinning and having a good time. Fun, if you like – sorry, I mean FUN!

I take a look at the achievement badges members can work towards. I'm totally up for taking some tests. Becky will teach us. Oh, and I can ask Nana Susan for help, too. She's bound to know lots.

Yeah, I'll take some tests. Surely that will show that I have the *right attitude*. I'll take them with Silver, with any luck. It would be pretty cool to get badges, evidence to show my skills…

*'Don't tell me that's **another** certificate, Etta?' gasped her mum.*

'I'm afraid it is,' said Etta, with a modest smile.

'What's this one for?' her mum asked, unable to keep the pride out of her voice. 'Dave,' she called out, 'Etta's won another certificate! Can you frame it for her?'

'I'll have to order some more frames,' Etta's dad shouted back from the sitting room. 'I've used up the last lot.'

'I thought you were getting the economy pack with dozens in it?' said Etta's mum, frowning.

'That's right! I've used them all. You'll have to stop achieving things, Etta,' said her dad. *'I can't keep up with you!'*

'Sorry!' exclaimed Etta. *'I just don't seem to be able to stop the Pony Club awarding me certificates.'*

'Gosh Etta,' said Shona, arriving home from school, *'that's never **another** certificate, is it? I wish I were as clever as you.'*

'Etta!' shouts Mum from the kitchen. 'Dinner's ready! Don't forget to wash your hands!'

She doesn't realise I'm destined for equestrian glory.

Nobody does.

Oooh! Remember when Mum said about me having shown no evidence of having made much effort with my schoolwork, you know, after she'd agreed I could have riding lessons? Well I should have replied – in a very dignified way – that I can't help it if all my hard efforts are not appreciated by people who insist on concentrating on the negative. I knew I'd think of an answer when it was too late. I'll squirrel it away for later – it's bound to come up again sometime.

CHAPTER NINE

It's Drama Club night, which explains why I've been walking around all day like a quivering jelly, chewing my nails (because Nat will be there, obviously). Hebe freaks me out at lunchtime by telling me, in a very bored voice, that she doesn't think she is cut out for drama, and it might be better if I go without her, seeing as I am the one destined for the silver screen and all, and that she already stays behind two nights a week for athletics practice and is getting a bit fed up with being at school so much. Personally, I can't help thinking that her melodramatic act proves she is more than cut out for drama.

'So you're going to give up, just like that? You're going to be a quitter?' I say in a disappointed voice, hoping to shame her into changing her mind. I need Hebe with me, I don't think I can cope with how Nat makes me feel without having someone else to talk to and distract me. And hide behind.

'Yeah,' Hebe says, twirling a lock of her red hair around one finger, obviously neither shamed nor bothered.

'Oh come on Heeb,' I say, noticing that my voice has adopted a bit of a whiney tone. It's very unattractive but could be passed off as acting, if challenged. 'You *promised* you'd go with me.'

'I didn't *promise*,' says Hebe (she didn't, I just made that up hoping she wouldn't remember), 'but I'll come tonight if you insist. But if Pertwee has us all pretending we're lighthouses or ducks or something, I'm done.'

I can't imagine Ms Pertwee would want us to be lighthouses or ducks, but I can't be certain so I mentally prepare, just in case. You never know with Ms Pertwee, and I only realise I am talking my prep a little too far when Madame Carter, our French teacher (who *isn't* French, but still insists on us calling her *Madame*, but I can forgive her that because even though I don't know any French people to talk French to it does mean I have picked up a few useful French phrases, which makes me appear quite *cosmopolitan*) asks me, as I walk past her into class, '*Tu veux aller auz toilettes, Etta?*' (or something like that), because I didn't realise that mentally preparing to be a duck meant I was walking like a duck.

When Hebe and I arrive at the big hall after lessons there seems to be a lot more pupils than last time cluttering up the space. They are all from the year below ours, and they are all GIRLS. They also appear to be rather over-excited – giggling and whispering to each other behind their hands and glancing at the door.

Ms Pertwee is clearly made-up that our numbers have swelled, attributing the influx to all the newbies wishing to star in her play.

'How wonderful!' she enthuses, telling them all how the aim of Drama Club is not only to put on her play, but to have FUN! The newbies continue to alternate between glancing at Ms Pertwee and staring at the hall doors. When Nat and his mate Ollie appear the newbies all flutter about like poppies in the wind, and there are quite a lot of red faces and more giggling.

'If I'm not very much mistaken,' says Hebe, rolling her eyes, 'Drama Club has been overtaken by Nat's fan club.'

I am agog (I have never been agog before but have always wondered what it might be like, having read in books about people being it. It turns out to be quite disturbing and I wouldn't recommend it). 'I don't do all that stupid fawning and giggling and whispering stuff, do I?' I manage to ask Hebe behind my hand.

Hebe raises her eyebrows as she shoots me and my hand a look – totally NOT the reaction I was hoping for. I decide I need to watch my step – not to mention my hand.

Ms Pertwee has evidently decided she has seen enough of what we're made of because she makes no mention of lighthouses or ducks. This evening she looks like an over-enthusiastic children's TV presenter, dressed as she is in a frilly orange blouse and a green-and-orange checked skirt. She is sporting a floppy, crocheted daffodil on her blouse which wobbles as she talks, and her shoes are also orange. She is so bright I can still see her when I close my eyes.

'Now!' she begins, in a firm, dark crimson voice. 'Those of you who would like to be considered for the major parts in my new play, *A Town Divided*, please take a script from Mrs Harris, and we'll begin auditions.'

Mrs Harris is a volunteer teaching assistant who must be at least a hundred years old and never misses a Monday, Wednesday and Friday. Wisps of her long, grey hair are always escaping from the bun she has fixed at the top of her head, and they waft about her face and shoulders in slow motion, making her look like she's under water. The effect is most strange and a little bit mesmerising – particularly when she pushes her tiny glasses back up to the bridge of her nose and the light catches them. It's like she has lasers coming out of her eyeballs. Freaky!

This evening, Mrs Harris smiles vacantly as she sits at a table, on which a pile of scripts awaits us. Several of the less confident pupils (and a number of Nat's fan club) shake their heads and tell Ms Pertwee they are perfectly happy with a non-speaking part or doing things behind the scenes while others – like me – step forward and pluck a script from under Mrs Harris's wafting locks.

Amelia does the same and her bezzies follow her lead. So does Nat, his chum Ollie and Max Rybart – and several other people who fancy their chances at stardom.

'Okay, who would like to go first?' asks Ms Pertwee. 'Amelia?'

Amelia escorts her perfect hair up onto the stage in a confident manner and reads through the part of Juliet-with-a-modern-twist. I appraise her with the critical eye of the rival actress.

'You can't say no-one will be able to hear her at the back of the hall,' hisses Hebe.

Hebe is right. Amelia's voice is very clear and very loud. This is called 'projecting your voice'.

'She's not very subtle,' I hiss back, noticing how Amelia opens her eyes wide when she is reading bits where Juliet-with-a-modern-twist is anguished, and throws her free arm around when she is supposed to be angry or upset.

'She's got great hair though,' sighs Hebe. 'She looks the part.'

I have no answer to this because of course it is true. Amelia looks the part of a heroine, even one with a modern twist. I suck in my cheeks. How many heroines have black, curly – okay, *fuzzy*, especially when wet – hair? That's right, you are spot on: none.

Amelia finishes, flashes Ms Pertwee a winning smile and vacates the stage. It is my turn, and as I look out from the stage I can see everyone looking at me. Well, not everyone – Nat and his friend Ollie are deep in conversation, Amelia is being congratulated by her bezzies, and Hebe is scrolling though her phone, probably looking at cat videos, but it's still an audience – of sorts. Ms Pertwee, of course, is beaming at me in encouragement and so I begin ACTING! Naturally, I am all over it.

'How did I do?' I ask Hebe, when Ms Pertwee has thanked me for my efforts and called the next wannabe to the stage.

'What? Oh, um, fabulous!' says Hebe. 'So much better than Amelia. You know, professional!'

I throw her a look. She looks sheepish. Cat videos, defo.

We mooch about while everyone who wants to takes a turn at auditioning. When Max Rybart reads, he gives me a wide-eyed look and puts on a funny voice in a totally inappropriate place, which has a few people laughing but causes Ms Pertwee to frown and shake her head.

'There's no need for any individual interpretation, thank you Max!' she says. 'You really need to choose your moments more carefully!'

Max just grins and winks at me, like I'm an accomplice and in on the joke. I don't think he can help himself, really. At least, as Hebe says, he's cheerful, and sometimes we can do with a laugh.

I try not to look too intently at Nat when he reads for the part of Romeo-with-a-modern-twist. The fan club has no such restraint and heads swivel towards the stage, all its members staring in rapt attention, punctuated by several sighs. Of course, Nat is really good, and I can see from Ms Pertwee's face that he has the part. Of course he has, he's a born hero. He also has the audience in the palm of his hand due to his smouldering good looks and the fact that most of them are fully paid-up members of the Nat Black fan club. A better Romeo-with-a-modern-twist you would be hard pushed to find.

I hope I will be able to keep a professional distance when we are cast as the main leads in *A Town Divided*.

But will Nat...?

'Etta!' gasped Nat, gripping her arm as soon as the curtain fell after the first act. 'Tell me you weren't acting just

then. Tell me you really meant those words, those words of adoration you uttered.'

'Nat, please, we have to stay professional about this!' exclaimed Etta, pulling away, her eyes pleading. 'How can we continue with the play if we allow our own feelings to overwhelm us?'

'But I can't go on like this, Etta!' cried Nat, his voice full of anguish. 'Saying these words and not knowing whether you feel the same as I do. Please, Etta, tell me now, put me out of my misery, I have to know!'

'Nat…' Etta whispered, breathlessly, '… you must know I feel the same way…'

'Okay, gather round everyone,' says Ms Pertwee, notes in her hand, when everyone has finished their audition and she has had a conflab with Mrs Harris which involved much shuffling of papers and copious note-taking. 'I have decided that today's auditions will be sufficient for our purposes.'

And that's not all she's decided.

'With the invaluable help of Mrs Harris, whose observations regarding the auditions today have been most insightful, I can now announce the cast,' Ms Pertwee continues.

'I bet you anything you like Amelia is Ms Pertwee's Juliet-with-a-modern-twist,' whispers Hebe.

I have a sinking feeling she might be right, even though I know the part of Juliet-with-a-modern-twist is destined to be MINE. It has my name all over it.

Hebe *is* right.

'Amelia is to be our LEADING LADY,' says Ms Pertwee. 'You will play Julia, our heroine.' Ms Pertwee says this in shades of red and orange, which is just about right because the colours of red and orange totally match my outrage. I bet it was Amelia's hair that swung it. I mean, she totally has leading lady hair – long, blonde, bouncy. If I had hair like Amelia's I would so have been Ms Pertwee's first choice for Julia.

I am beyond miffed. I mean, there are always wigs. Could I get a wig to stay on over my hair? Or might it be destined, in the middle of a tender and passionate scene with Nat, to gradually lift up from my voluminous curls and sit on the top of my head like some kind of hairy hat…

'Oh my, whatever is going on with your hair?' asked Amelia, her eyes wide in horror, and drawing everyone's attention to Etta.

'What?' asked Etta, her hand flying up to her head. The wig she had carefully fitted over her own hair, which had looked so beautiful in the dressing room, was now sitting atop her own curls like a big, yellow, hairy tam-o'-shanter. Glancing at her reflection in one of the hall's windows, Etta realised she looked as though she had two heads, one on top of the other.

'That's hilarious!' chuckled Amelia. 'Here, tie it on with this belt, that'll sort it!'

Etta jammed the wig back on, buckling Amelia's belt under her chin. 'Is that better?' she asked.

Amelia shook her head, trying to suppress a loud snigger. 'You'd be better off tying a couple of locks of it under your chin. Oh no,' she added, as Etta struggled to do just that, 'my mistake. It looks terrible whatever you do with it.'

'I'm sorry Etta, your hair has just lost you the part of Julia,' interrupted Ms Pertwee. 'Come along Amelia, you'd better do it, your locks are much better behaved. I'll never forgive you for this, Etta, my play isn't supposed to be a comedy, you know!'

Well that wouldn't work, would it? This is NOT turning out as I expected. I didn't join Drama Club to be one of the also-rans at the back of the stage. I mean, I am the one destined to be an actress when I leave school (if I don't become a riding instructor, or a much-adored TV baking expert with my own series and a book deal or, as a last resort, a spy), and yet Ms Pertwee seems blind to my obvious talent.

'You know who is going to be Romeo-with-a-modern-twist, don't you?' hisses Hebe. I am now wishing I hadn't persuaded her to come with me. I am now wishing she had persuaded me to opt out of Drama Club with her, instead.

'Nat, you will be our LEADING MAN,' says Ms Pertwee in words dripping with green and blue, and with a winning smile that makes her look a bit mad. I think she might be. Cue appreciative murmurs from the fan club – like it was ever going to be anyone but Nat.

I daren't look at Hebe. I look instead at Nat because nobody will notice as everyone else is looking at him. Nat nods, but he doesn't look terribly happy about playing the lead. Amelia, on the other hand, looks thrilled. No wonder. I'd be thrilled. Who wouldn't be thrilled? This is another reason why the part of the leading lady should be MINE!

'You will play Ricky, a-boy-from-the-wrong-side-of-town,' says Ms Pertwee (cue more squeals and claps from the fan club).

All I can say is that if Ricky, a-boy-from-the-wrong-side-of-town, looked anything like Nat, everyone would be moving there, and property prices would soar.

'Why is there tumbleweed bowling along our road?' asked Etta, throwing her school bag on the kitchen table.

'All the houses are empty,' replied her mum, her eyes red from crying.

'What! You mean we're the only family left here?'

'That's right, the Robinsons went yesterday!'

'But why?' wailed Etta.

*'Everyone's moved to the wrong side of town,' her mum replied, as two removal lorries raced each other along the road, swaying from side to side, the sound of antique furniture crashing about inside clearly audible above the noise of their engines. 'Haven't you heard? That devilishly handsome boy who lives there has created a demand – all the girls in town have made their parents buy property there. If only we'd moved there sooner! Now we've missed out, and nobody wants to live here any more. Now **this** is the wrong side of town! We'll never sell this house...'*

I am more than disappointed. I am a mixture of despair and fury! Plus, I'm not sure what makes the-wrong-side-of-town the-wrong-side-of-town, and Ms Pertwee isn't saying and I'm not going to look stupid and ask. However...

'Miss,' I say, raising my hand. Hebe gives me a wide-eyed stare as if she's scared I might be about to put Ms Pertwee straight – about me being the natural choice for the part of Julia.

'Yes, Etta?' beams Ms Pertwee.

'Wasn't the film *West Side Story* based on *Romeo and Juliet?* That had a modern twist, didn't it?'

Ms Pertwee's lips pucker, which makes her look as though she's sucking a lemon. '*West Side Story* is a film, not a play,' she says, 'and besides, my story is COMPLETELY DIFFERENT.' She sounds a bit cross, like she's speaking in tones of grey and brown, which makes a change. I've never heard her talk in anything but a rainbow before. My knowledge of *West Side Story* has hit home.

Ms Pertwee knows I'm on to her.

Hebe and I are given minor roles – friends of Julia, just a couple of lines.

Also-rans.

Hebe pulls a face at me and shakes her head. I take this to mean that for Hebe, Drama Club may just be old news and if I want to keep coming, I could be on my own. Max Rybart is going to play Julia's father, who disapproves of Ricky, a-boy-from-the-wrong-side-of-town, which seems like a big ask.

Ms Pertwee flutters about directing us here and there as we do something called a 'read through,' where we all stand around on the stage and read our lines. I manage to wrangle my way next to Nat, but Ms Pertwee sends me to the other side of the stage. Of course Amelia and Nat have most of the lines, and all the remaining members of the cast have to stand around waiting for their cues. We stand around for so long I get totally bored and wonder whether the present situation (disappointing though it is) might yet work to my advantage...

'Etta, can I have a word?' said Nat.

'Of course, what is it?' replied Etta, graciously flicking back a lock of her long, luscious black hair that flowed around her shoulders like a glorious dark waterfall.

'You should have got the lead part, not Amelia. You're much more talented than she is, not to mention more beautiful – and your hair is better, too.'

Etta blushed, attractively. 'Oh Nat, I don't know...'

'It's true!' exploded Nat. 'You're far too modest, everyone else can see it – why can't you?'

'ETTA!'

That's my name – only I'm in the big hall and all the members of Drama Club are looking at me. The expressions on their faces couldn't look less like an adoring crowd.

I have to stop doing this...

'It's YOUR LINE!' says Ms Pertwee in accusing tones of dark pink, with an additional warning touch of grey with black around the edges.

I haven't a clue where we are in the script and glancing around I know I can't expect any help from Hebe who just looks at me expectantly, totally getting me back for making her come to Drama Club.

'Er...' I say, rustling the papers in an effort to look like I'm totally on it.

'Page six,' says Ms Pertwee, her hands on her hips. It looks as though FUN! isn't on the agenda today.

Everyone else is sighing and groaning like I've committed murder instead of just losing my way, and I know I am going red. Even all the fan club members look as though I have personally insulted them, which I don't take kindly to – they're only here to fawn at Nat. I'm a serious actress! I daren't look at Nat. Whenever I'm around Nat I'm supposed to be projecting an image of confidence and capability, not convincing everyone I'm dim-witted.

I think Hebe may have the right idea about not coming back to Drama Club. I'm not sure I will after this. And then I remember that it isn't just about the drama (although there is plenty of that) but that Nat is here. So maybe I'll just suck it up and come again anyway. How else can I get to know him? How else will he ever notice me (especially with the fan club now crowding me) and realise we are destined to be together, just like Ricky and Julia?

This totally isn't how Drama Club was supposed to pan out.

Eventually Ms Pertwee declares the rehearsal to be over.

'Well done everyone,' she says. 'The play is going to be a huge success!'

But there's more – our drama teacher hasn't quite done torturing me yet.

'Now before you all toddle off there is just one more thing,' says Ms Pertwee. 'The major roles will, of course, need understudies – just in case a major player is ill or indisposed on the night of the performance. It will require those chosen to learn the lines of their leading characters and be prepared to step in, should the need arise.'

I have switched off a bit by now, wallowing in a pit of injustice, so Ms Pertwee has to say my name twice, and Hebe nudges me in the ribs before I take in what's being said.

'I would *really* like Max Rybart and Etta Marshall to be Nat and Amelia's understudies.' Ms Pertwee is talking about me. Me. ME who should be playing the part of Juliet-with-a-modern-twist. She's asking me to understudy Amelia! AMELIA SHOULD BE MY UNDERSTUDY!

Though wait a minute, it might just be the opportunity I have been waiting for…

'Etta, thank GOODNESS you're here!' gasped Ms Pertwee, her eyes like saucers. 'Amelia is ill, she can't go on. I need you to play the part of Julia. Only you can do it, nobody else can take on the role – it's too demanding. Say you'll do it, Etta, I know you can, you're my last hope!'

'But, but…' Etta stammered, '… I'm not sure I'm totally familiar with the script, Ms Pertwee.'

'Don't be modest, Etta, I know you can recite it with your eyes shut – and Nat will help you, won't you, Nat?'

Nat stepped forward and took Etta's hand in his. 'Of course I will. You have to say yes, Etta, I implore you.'

'Well…' Etta murmured, coyly lowering her chin, her eyelashes a-flutter as Nat's burning gaze melted her heart. '… I suppose I can try!'

'Atta girl!' cried Nat. 'Quick, get changed, the curtain is about to go up and we can't keep the audience waiting. I

knew you wouldn't let us all down – didn't I say she'd do it, Ms Pertwee? She's such a star!'

Ms Pertwee dabbed at her eyes with a huge, red-spotted handkerchief before thrusting it into the oversize pocket on her blue-and-pink striped dungarees. 'Thank you, Etta,' she said. 'Thank you for saving my play.'

Later, when the play had finished (Etta was word-perfect), and as Etta and Nat took yet another curtain call, the crowd unwilling to allow them to leave the stage, the applause ringing in their ears, a huge bouquet in Etta's arms, Nat turned to his co-star and lifted her hand.

'You shall always be my leading lady,' he whispered, lowering his head in order to brush her knuckles with his lips.

'Et-ta! Et-ta!' cried the crowd (even the fan club have realised their quest is hopeless and just want the best for their hero). 'Et-ta! Et-ta…!'

'Etta!' says Ms Pertwee, snapping me back into the hall. 'You will need to pay more attention than you have tonight if you want to be Amelia's understudy. Do you?'

'Do I what?' I ask, applause still ringing in my ears.

'Want to be Amelia's understudy?' says Ms Pertwee.

'Oh!' I say, imagining Amelia stricken in bed with flu, or hobbling about in a huge body cast, or held up in traffic with her mother who just had to go shopping for a new pair of shoes and forgot the time.

'Of course!'

'Oh thank you Etta!' cries Amelia, clasping her hands together as though my agreeing is a personal favour to her.

Little does she know that Ms Pertwee's decision to make me her understudy has put her first choice of leading lady in serious jeopardy.

I could be playing the heroine yet…

CHAPTER TEN

'Are you ready, Etta?' asks Mum. I am. I have never been readier. I've been ready since six o'clock this morning because today I am attending my first Pony Club rally at Chesterton. It's scheduled for the whole morning and will include my usual lesson. I'm not sure who is going to be there and I'm both excited and nervous at the same time. I know this because not only have the butterflies started up in my stomach again (I think they're having a party in there) but I've been to the loo three times in the last hour. By the time I get home tonight I will have learned something about stable management and stuff, will actually have been on the yard with Silver, and be much more knowledgeable about ponies. I can't wait. If my present loo habit continues all morning, I may also be several kilos lighter.

When we get to the riding school I can see that Amelia, Kayleigh and Pearl are already there. I don't know why I am surprised by this as they are all on my lesson every week.

'Hi Etta!' cries Amelia, waving. She has new navy jodhpurs with paler blue strappings at the knees, and these are topped by her new Pony Club sweatshirt. Her gleaming blonde hair is tied back with a yellow ribbon under her navy-blue riding hat, and her boots shine as though she's spent all night polishing them. She looks not only full-on navy but frighteningly efficient, like she has her own pony – one of those whizzy and dangerous ones I saw on the Pony Club website.

I have teamed my new Pony Club sweatshirt (we all have to wear these, it's the rules – almost twenty quid of Nana Susan's money gone in a blink of an eye) with my usual beige jodhpurs and black hat. Our body protectors are stacked at the back of the office ready for our ride. I am afraid that I do not look frighteningly efficient but rather nervous. Then it occurs to me that I might employ my acting skills and act confident. This is harder than you might think – especially as I am getting precious little practice at Drama Club, what with Amelia having stolen the part destined to be mine.

I wonder, though, whether a nice new navy riding hat, like the one Amelia has, would help. Possibly. Although I expect it will have the same battle against my hair as my black hat. The other new Pony Club members are all my fellow pupils on my lesson, as well as all the pupils from the lesson after ours, so there are twelve of us in total.

The first thing Becky says when she sees us all isn't, *A big welcome to all you new Pony Clubbers,* or even, *We're all going to have such a fabulous time.* You might think it would be, but you'd be wrong. Instead she says, 'How did you get on riding side-saddle on your birthday, Amelia?' dealing my confident act a severe blow. More crushing it, actually.

'I had the most wonderful time,' replies Amelia, smiling angelically under the luxurious velvet pile of her navy hat.

'Oh, do tell us all about it,' says Becky.

Yes, I think, do. Or don't…

'Oh, you don't want to hear about my silly old side-saddle lesson!' cried Amelia, waving her hand in a gesture of modesty. 'There's nothing to tell really, and I don't want to bore you all. Besides,' she added, 'I fell off three times and the instructor told me that I'm so useless at riding, I might as well give it up altogether.'

'Oh dear,' said Becky. 'What a shame. Off you go then and take up something safer, like knitting or crochet or learning to play the tambourine.'

Well, we all know that's never going to happen.

'I rode a *beautiful* palomino pony with the most *amazing* snowy-white mane and tail called Golden Nugget,' begins Amelia. I want to shut my ears and float away, but I stay stuck with all my fellow Pony Club members, forced to listen to Amelia regaling tales of her amazing side-saddle adventure. How come she lives such a glamorous life? I mean isn't having the lead in Ms Pertwee's play opposite Nat, the part I was destined to play, ENOUGH? Amelia has no need to make up a life for herself, she lives her (and my) made-up life EVERY DAY.

'Oooooo, was it difficult sitting sideways?' asks Pearl.

'Not really,' says Amelia. 'You see the saddle has two pommels that stick up on the nearside, and by wrapping my legs around them and keeping my right shoulder back I felt really secure. It was easy, really.'

'What was it like trotting?' asks a girl on the other lesson who's called Emma. I know this because we are all wearing name badges so everyone can make friends.

'It was all right,' Amelia tells her, 'but cantering was better.'

A murmur of great impressiveness can be heard from everyone.

'Wow, cantering!' says Becky. 'I *am* impressed, Amelia,' she says.

Told you. Amelia was obviously born to ride side-saddle. I'm not surprised. I mean it's so fairy-tale – even the pony she rode was a palomino. Why couldn't she have ridden a fat, lazy, slow, dirty-brown cobby pony with a badly hogged mane and warts on its muzzle called Brian? It's the perfect way to be up on everyone else. Talk about trumps, it just about trumps everything else you can think or dream of.

Oh, hold on – except for…

Estra sat easily on the bare back of the snowy-white unicorn, its pearlescent coat glinting in the pale moonlight, the barley-

twist horn beneath its long, flowing forelock glistening as though sprinkled with fairy dust...

Really... a unicorn?

Oh, why not? I mean the unicorn is the bit you don't believe? Seriously?

... 'Steady now Silver Light,' whispered the girl, running a slight hand along the unicorn's neck as its long mane entwined around her legs. She was clad in the pale blue garments of her tribe: a close-fitting tunic, leggings, soft shoes and a silver cape. Her long, shining ebony hair tumbled around her shoulders as her beguiling emerald-green eyes searched the moonlit woodland for signs of her enemies. The girl's loyal servant Wolf, wary of the unicorn's hooves, walked beside them...

*(*Yes, I know Wolf met his untimely demise fighting the Giant Chicken of Azbathria, but it's *my* made-up life and he's far too good a character to lose at the drop of a hat – or even a chicken. He stays!*)*

... Wolf's ears acted as the girl's ears, twitching to-and-fro, anxious to pick up any sounds that were not of the woodland. They were far from home and knew not what this part of Azbathria held hidden within its depths.

Suddenly the wolf growled, and he turned to face the tightly-packed trees, one front paw lifted as his eyes searched for the origins of the unknown sound. Estra wound one hand around the unicorn's long, silver mane, while the other reached into her tunic for the dagger she knew to be there.

A horse approached, golden in colour with a long, silver mane and tail, its rider sitting elegantly on the side-saddle upon its back, her crimson velvet skirt reaching almost to her horse's knees. The jewel-encrusted saddle emitted sparks of light in the moonlight and the girl's hair, like the horse's coat beneath her, shone like spun gold under a diamond-encrusted coronet of silver and rubies.

'I am Princess Amelia,' called the girl. 'What brings you to this fair land?'

'I flee the savage Heratos tribe, headed by the evil Tarituss,' Estra explained. 'Can you offer me and my companions safe haven for the night?'

'Of course,' replied the princess, graciously. 'Come, follow me for the Black Knight is my protector, and he shall protect you, also.'

'The Black Knight?' enquired Estra, a tightness in her chest revealing her surprise.

'Oh yes,' Princess Amelia said, beckoning to Estra and Wolf. 'Sir Nathan and I are betrothed and shall wed at the next full moon. I beseech you to stay for the wedding and be our honoured guest. Our alliance shall make this part of Azbathria the strongest in the land, and our greatest wish is to free those tribes under the tyranny of the Heratos and unite all our people. Gods willing, we shall bring peace and harmony to all Azbathria.'

Estra's expression gave nothing away as she wrestled with her feelings. Was she not ruler of one of the tribes of Azbathria? Hadn't Princess Amelia described a dream for so long akin to her own? Had she not wished for the very same outcome – to free Azbathria with the Black Knight at her side, partners and rulers together? She could not find room in her heart to wish Princess Amelia's dream to fail – she cared too much for Azbathria for that. She would need to put her own feelings aside for the sake of the land she loved, and for the people of her tribe.

The girl, the unicorn and the wolf followed the golden pair, but it was with a heavy heart that Estra entered the beautiful, fairytale-like castle of Princess Amelia, knowing she would soon be seeing the man her hostess was to marry, the man she had grown to admire, the man with whom she had for so long fought side-by-side against the evil Heratos: the handsome and kindly Black Knight.

'Here, hand your unicorn's reins to my jester, the hilarious Maximus,' said Princess Amelia, as a brightly-clad man with a mop of hair the colour of ripened corn came forward to help Estra dismount. 'He will see that your mount is well cared for.'

'Be kind to my Silver Light, good jester,' ordered Estra, 'for he is as the wind and the stars and the sun; he is everything to me.'

'Fear not My Lady,' the jester replied with a wink and a bow, 'for I shall guard this magical creature with my life. In the meantime,' he added, 'might My Lady grant me licence to entertain her with a riddle or two, and maybe a mesmerising magic trick?'

'Not now, Maximus,' ordered Princess Amelia. 'Honestly,' she said in a confidential tone to Estra, 'he is a talented jester, and he has the court in good spirits when times are *tough, but he has little sense of occasion and knows not when to rein it in.'*

'… and I finished the lesson with a couple of jumps,' Amelia says, her riding hat bobbing in time with her words rather than a regal, ruby-encrusted silver coronet.

'Jumping? Side-saddle? Wow, that's amazing!' cries Becky.

We all put aside the image of Amelia leaping over huge, Hickstead-sized jumps side-saddle (and I put aside the images of Princess Amelia and the Black Knight, as well as the unexpected vision of Max Rybart popping up in Azbathria in the guise of a jester – typecasting at its best) and move on to the pony yard.

This is where Silver lives, as well as Poppy and Cracker and Amber and all the other ponies. I can feel my heart beating faster because I am in the stable yard AT LAST, and the ponies are all looking out over their half-doors at us – except for Pip, the tall black pony who suffers from his nerves. Pip is tied up outside his stable, and as we all crowd in through the gate he turns his head and looks at us all wide-eyed, his head on the wonk, his lower lip trembling at this unexpected turn of events – twelve would-be riders all in a huddle. He's probably wondering whether we've all come to ride him at once. He must know by now he only ever has one rider at a time…

'Move up a bit, Pearl,' ordered Becky. 'There's room for one more.'

'I'm on Pip's neck already,' moaned Pearl. *'I'm almost being cut in half.'*

'Stop wobbling,' said the girl called Emma who was up behind Amelia, who was behind Kayleigh, who was behind Pearl. *'When you wobble, we all wobble.'*

'Come on Etta, hurry up and get on,' said Becky, bending down to give Etta a leg-up.

'Isn't five too many?' asked Etta, putting her knee into Becky's hand, despite her misgivings.

'Nah! Once you're on I'll vault up behind you,' said Becky. *'Make it an even half-dozen.'*

'I think I can feel Pip's legs buckling under the strain,' said Amelia.

'Okay, I'm on. Come on Becky!' cried Etta.

As Becky vaulted up onto Pip's rump, the pony's legs did indeed buckle, and everyone fell down in a heap.

'Oh,' said Becky.

'Told you!' said Amelia, picking herself up and dusting down her navy-blue riding hat.

'...how to handle a pony correctly and safely,' I hear Becky say. Jade, one of the students, stands by Pip's head and grins at us.

'You know how to lead a pony, you've all led the ponies you ride in the arena,' begins Becky. 'But now we're going to handle them in the stable and the yard so you all need to pay VERY STRICT ATTENTION because although ponies don't want to hurt us, they are very big, and very heavy, and some ponies who are NOT used to working in a riding school can be quite nervous. That is why you need to develop good habits with our lovely, very forgiving, school ponies.'

Okay, I think, wondering what terrors unforgiving ponies might unleash upon us were we foolish enough to develop bad habits.

'We must always talk in low voices – never shout – and move very deliberately around ponies so we don't startle them,' continues Becky. 'I don't mean move in slow motion, just make sure you don't make any sudden or jerky movements,' she explains. She also points out how ponies' eyes are positioned at the side of their heads, which is why we should always approach them from the side so they can clearly see us. Oh, and we have to take care not to get our toes trodden on.

'You probably will get trodden on at some point,' says Becky. 'When you do, you won't want it to happen again. Ponies are heavy!'

Well, I thought, some are heavier than others. I mean, Poppy is well chunky whereas Silver isn't, so if I am going to be trodden on, I hope it will be Silver doing the treading, not lardy Poppy.

I can see Silver looking over his stable door in the corner of the yard, and I feel my heart lift. He's so gorgeous, and from where I'm standing it looks as though he is gazing at me, just waiting for me to saddle him up (if I knew how!) and go for a ride in Azbathria with Wolf, where we'd be totally in tune with each other and have some amazing adventures. As Silverado he would do anything he could to keep me from harm and save me from danger. There is always plenty of danger lurking in Azbathria – not only from the horrible Tarituss and the rest of the Heratos, but other dangers from which only my loyal companions could save me…

'Silverado, help me!' cried Estra, already up to her knees in quicksand, pockets of which still existed in Azbathria to trip up the unwary. 'I'm sinking, Silverado, help!'

(I'm not really sure about the unicorn. I think I'll stick with Silverado, he's much more like the real Silver.)

With his mistress in trouble, and without a thought for his own safety, the beautiful horse didn't hesitate. He leapt forward, Wolf at his side, determined to do what he could, even though he knew that the quicksand could pull him into its murky depths and drag him down, with Estra, to their shared fate. Wolf stepped in front of him to halt his progress, howling in distress as the two creatures stood at the edge of the hateful and deadly shifting sands, both desperate to help, and knowing that life without their mistress would not be worth living.

'Your reins, quickly!' gasped Estra, as she sank lower into the mire. Silverado knew what to do. Tossing his head, the reins were flung over his neck…

(You see, a unicorn horn would just get in the way. It's a liability, to be honest – it could have someone's eye out if things were to get a bit hectic.)

…and he nodded his head up and down in an effort to throw them to within Estra's reach. Wolf growled encouragingly

as Estra leaned forward and stretched out her hands. Miraculously, she managed to grasp the very end of the reins, and she held on tightly.

'Now my wonderful Silverado, pull back!' Estra gasped, and the brave horse took strong and sure steps backwards, pulling Estra from the deadly sands. Before long she was on firm ground again, her arms around her faithful mount's neck, a hand caressing Wolf's head, and together the trio stood in silent and grateful thanks for Estra's lucky escape…

'… and the other group is with Jade,' says Becky.

I have no idea which of the two groups I am supposed to be in, I was too busy being rescued in Azbathria by my loyal friends, so I dither about a bit until Jade throws me a puzzled look and beckons me over.

'Nothing to be nervous about,' she reassures me.

I am not nervous. I wasn't nervous when I was disappearing in quicksand and I'm not nervous now, but I understand why Jade might believe I am.

I do not want to be the person at Pony Club who everyone thinks is nervous. I need to PAY ATTENTION!!!

We are in two groups because we are all going to learn how to put a head collar on a pony and lead them in and out of the stable (our group has Amber, the other group has Pip, who still looks very uncertain about it all). Jade reminds us to talk in low tones and, before she even opens Amber's stable door, she tells us we must never, EVER, wind the lead rope around our hand whenever we lead a pony. This is because if our pony takes fright and runs off, the rope could tighten, and we would not be able to let go.

I am beginning to realise why we have not been allowed on the yard before now. What with the possibility of being trodden on and of being dragged – not to mention incidents too terrible to imagine that could arise due to us developing bad habits – the yard is looking a decidedly dodgy place to be. I make a mental note to keep this information to myself when Mum or Dad ask me about what I've learned. Otherwise, I think my Pony Club career could be over before it has barely begun.

Once we have watched Jade put a head collar on Amber she announces that we should form pairs so we can work more closely together. Before I have time to think I hear a familiar voice say, 'Hey Etta, shall we pair up?'

It is Amelia. She's being very friendly so I feel I can hardly refuse. I don't know how I feel about it because I suspect that Amelia is going to be much better at everything than me, and I wonder whether she might take over, leaving me trailing in her wake and doing the donkey work. Plus, I'm having trouble moving on from the whole leading lady thing at Drama Club, even though I know it isn't Amelia's fault she got MY part (not to mention the whole Black Knight betrothal, which I acknowledge is unreasonable, seeing as I made it up in my head). But it's too late. We're standing together like a good pair should, and everyone else has paired off.

Each pair has one of the students to help them, and Amelia and I stay with Amber while the others are dispatched to various stables and ponies around the yard. Our student is called Lucy, and she watches closely as Amelia has a go at fitting a head collar around Amber's head, which she does quite easily.

Then it's my turn. When Amelia hands over the head collar and it's in my hands it looks completely different to when it was in hers – and when Lucy had it. Then it looked like a head collar. In my hands it looks like random bits of purple nylon and brass buckles, all tangled up like nothing I've ever seen before. I turn it over and try to make sense of it. I fail.

'Here,' says Lucy, taking it from me, 'I'll sort it out for you. There.'

It looks no different – oh, wait a minute, I recognise the noseband. So, forgetting what I've just been told, I stand in front of Amber and try to force the noseband over her nose – only she's having none of it (probably because she's had it on twice, and is now pretty fed up with it all).

'Stand at her shoulder and face the same way as Amber is facing,' says Lucy, kindly. 'If you approach Amber from the front she's bound to back away. She thinks you're up to no good.'

I have another go; snaggle Amber's nose; can't get the long strap thing over her head. Amelia goes around the other side and helps me. I buckle it up. It is on. I have (sort of) put on the head collar. My feeling is one of anti-climax. It was much more difficult than Lucy made it look. And Amelia. Of course, it would be. That's the trouble with anything to do with ponies I have found, it all looks simple when other people do anything but when you have a go yourself it isn't easy AT ALL!

'It needs to be a bit tighter,' says Lucy. 'Look, it's very low on Amber's nose. Pull it up a few holes.'

As I adjust the head collar, Amber gives me a very unimpressed look before emitting a very long (suffering) sigh.

Pony Club, she seems to say, isn't her idea of fun.

Eventually, the head collar is on to Lucy's satisfaction and Amelia and I take turns leading Amber out of her stable (I have to open the door wide, go in front of Amber, look back and keep her body straight so she doesn't knock her hips on the door frame, and only turn her when she is TOTALLY clear of the door – phew, there is such a lot to remember!).

This all takes ages because everyone has a go, but watching everyone else do it helps me to get my head around the head collar thing and, hopefully, this will help me get it around a pony's head next time. With the ponies back in their stables Jade shows us how to tie a quick-release knot because if you ever tie up a pony inside or outside his or her stable, you have to use one of these. This is so you can quickly untie the rope with a sharp yank on the free end if the pony gets scared and pulls back or has a nut-do or something. Jade tells us the riding school ponies hardly ever have a nut-do, but we still have to use a quick-release knot anyway, EVERY SINGLE TIME!

After all this activity and information we had to stuff into our brains and keep there we have a bit of a break – and so do the ponies.

CHAPTER ELEVEN

During break (we all sit in the lecture room, which is full of charts and bits of saddlery and things which I don't recognise and have no idea about – yet) Pearl plonks herself down on a bench by the table next to Amelia and makes like her bezzie mate. Kayleigh and Emma sit themselves around the same table, and I squeeze myself on the end, opposite a girl called Olivia, who has only been coming to our Saturday lesson for a few weeks and is very quiet.

Becky suggests we all have a drink and one of the snacks we've brought with us, so I pull out a couple of Jaffa Cakes and start munching. Amelia and Pearl both have matching muesli bars from Waitrose (which makes me suspicious that they've been texting each other between lessons and are, actually, already best buds), and Pearl gives my Jaffas a bit of a sniffy look which plainly says, *junk food!* I don't care because everyone knows Jaffa Cakes taste better than some old muesli bar any day of the week, and I don't know why Pearl should look so superior about a bar full of old bits of breakfast cereal. I decide to rise above Pearl's disapproval, which is something Shona is always saying whenever I moan about her. When she says it she sticks her nose in the air like she has a bad smell under it. I try doing that but I'm not sure I pull it off. I suspect it may just look like I've got a sore neck.

'Who's your favourite pony?' Olivia asks me.

'Silver,' say, warming to her because her question allows me to talk about him.

'Oh, I love Silver, too...' Olivia begins.

Any warm feelings I have about her instantly freeze. Olivia is not allowed to love Silver. Silver is MY FAVOURITE! I can see that Olivia and I could fall out BIG TIME unless she backs off and gets herself another favourite pony.

'... but my *favourite* pony is Cracker,' she continues.

I relax. Olivia can have Cracker any day of the week and all day Sunday as far as I'm concerned. I agree that Cracker is a very nice pony (he is. He's a pale creamy, off-white colour – which I suppose is why they called him Cracker – and although he's a bit whizzier than Silver and therefore a bit of a stressful ride, I can see he has qualities). Because the others are all talking quite loudly amongst themselves (mainly about Amelia's side-saddle lesson, again), Olivia and I shift away a bit and talk more about ponies and the Pony Club. It turns out we are both excited to be members because we both want to learn how to care for ponies, and are looking forward to spending more time with our favourites.

'I hope I ride Cracker on our hack this afternoon,' says Olivia. That I hope to ride Silver is, of course, a foregone conclusion (which means already sorted, like it's in the bag which, of course, it isn't). I hope I don't get Amber because she is always trying to munch grass, and the last time I rode her on a hack she put her head down to eat so suddenly I slipped over her neck and onto the grass she was busy stuffing into her mouth. I wasn't hurt but I was pretty embarrassed, and Amber gave me a look which plainly said, '*Do you mind not sitting on the grass when I'm trying to eat it!*' which I thought was a bit much, as she made me.

Before we can go on a hack, Becky tells us we are all going to learn how to tack up.

I am beyond excited! I have always wanted to know how to put Silver's saddle and bridle on him and now I am going to do it! No, really, I am because when I look at the board my name is chalked up next to Silver's, which means I am going to ride him on the hack!

But first we all watch Becky tack up Poppy. Then we fetch our ponies' saddles and bridles and go to the stable of our allocated pony, where a student is waiting to help us.

I'm not going to lie, tacking up is DIFFICULT. I mean, fitting a head collar was bad enough but the bridle has a bit which goes in the pony's mouth (Silver's bit is called a snaffle, apparently), and the thought crosses my mind that it might be tricky to get the bit in Silver's mouth without being bitten, even by accident. Jade, who is helping me, gets Silver to open his mouth to show me he has no teeth where the bit goes – but from what I can see he has lots all around where his muzzle is, and masses more HUGE ONES the back of his mouth, so there are plenty of opportunities to get chewed.

As it turns out I don't, but the point is I could.

With the bridle on I have to make sure Silver's forelock and mane aren't all bunched up under the browband and the headpiece of the bridle (they're the parts in front and behind his ears), and that his noseband is straight. Phew!

The saddle is even tricker. Standing on Silver's nearside (his left), I have to put the saddle on the lower end of Silver's neck, before sliding it back in place so his coat lies flat underneath it. I then have to go around to Silver's offside (around the front, not behind) and check everything is all flat and comfortable before pulling the front of Silver's saddle cloth up into the arch of the saddle (so it doesn't press on his withers). I then have to go back to the nearside where I started and tighten the girth. Only not too much – that comes later, just before I mount.

I don't think I'll ever remember it all. I think learning to be a riding instructor might be a lot harder than I first thought and I shall need to study for ages. It is a good job I am now in the Pony Club as this will considerably cut down the time I need to study. For example, I now know how to tack up.

Eventually (it takes a long time for everyone to tack up their ponies, even with help) we are all mounted in the yard and Becky, Jade and two other students are also mounted on school horses. Making sure we are all ready, Becky heads her horse towards the bridle path next to the riding school, and we all follow in a line.

We don't hack out very much – I've only been on three hacks during the summer, and we never hack out in winter – so this is a real treat. I see that Amelia is mounted on Cracker and Olivia is on Pip. I bet she wishes she was on Cracker. The bridle paths are not very wide so we all ride in single file, Becky at the front and the students spaced out between riders. I lean down to give Silver an appreciative pat.

'I'm so glad I've got you, Silver,' I tell him, and he wiggles his ears back and forth, which I take to mean that he is glad he has got me, too. It is a warm day; I can hear Silver and the other ponies' hoof beats on the track, and occasionally a pony sneezes as there is quite a lot of dust being kicked up by all the hooves.

It is like being a cowgirl on a trail in the Old Wild West, where danger lurked behind every bush, where girls were expected to wear skirts and be ladylike, cowboys were heroes, and outlaws and natives threatened law and order...

Estra adjusted her Stetson and peered at the trail ahead. Getting the herd across the prairie was her top priority – a hundred head of longhorns on a cattle trail was no job for a girl – or so everyone back at the ranch had said. But Estra was determined to prove them wrong. She would see that the cattle made it to the town in the east. She would battle rustlers and hostile natives, the heat and the dust, the cold and the snow, to get her cattle through.

Suddenly, she heard gunshots, and from behind some rocks a group of rustlers burst out at a gallop – to the terror of the cattle. Leaping into a frenzied stampede, the cattle raced blindly along the trail. Cramming her Stetson down onto her dark, shining and bouncing curls, Estra urged her cowpony, the nimble and willing Silver Dollar, into a gallop. Looking ahead she could see her foreman, Nat-the-kid-Black, trying desperately to head off the lead cattle, to turn them away from the path leading to the edge of a deep ravine where the herd, racing blindly, would fall to certain death.

'Turn them, Nat,' Estra muttered to herself, leaning low over Silver Dollar's already sweating neck. Her brave and willing cowpony was galloping his heart out – but could he keep up the relentless pace? Behind her, Estra could hear the rustlers' whoops and jeers; ahead she could see Nat-the-kid doing his best, the wide ravine already in sight, the yawning gap which heralded certain death to the cattle and a disastrous end to Estra's cattle drive looming closer and closer with every stride.

And then, miraculously, the lead cattle turned away from Nat-the-kid's waving Stetson and slowed down, no longer running in blind panic. Estra caught her breath as Nat drew his pistol and she heard shots. The rustlers, realising their plan hadn't worked, and seeing who the rider ahead was (Nat-the-kid-Black had a reputation for being quick on the draw and deadly in aim), hastily pulled up their horses, turned around and rode off into the scrubland in a cloud of dust.

When Estra caught up with him Nat sat easily on his sweating cowpony, a grin on his face as he raised the brow of his Stetson with the barrel of his Colt 45.

'Crisis over, Miss Estra,' he drawled, giving his pony a pat. 'Ain't nobody gonna get one over on you and your cattle drive ma'am. Not while I'm around, I do declare. No sireee.'

'Thanks Nat, I'm mighty obliged to you,' said Estra, reining in Silver Dollar, wiping sweat from her brow and taking a swig of water from the canteen wrapped around her saddle horn.

'Now let's get these 'ere critters to where they're supposed to be at!' said Nat, and the pair of them turned their ponies toward the longhorns, rounding up strays as, together, they headed onward to their destination...

'Etta, I asked whether you were ready to canter,' says Becky.

I look around me. All the riders in front of me are turning in their saddles and giving me evils. I am sure I can feel the same stares boring into my back from the riders behind. Becky's eyebrows are raised – she must have asked me that question more than once.

'You look as though you're somewhere else,' Becky says, and I hear a snigger from Pearl.

'Oh no,' I assure her, gathering up Silver's reins, disentangling my hands from his mane and wriggling deeper into his saddle which isn't, I notice, the nice, deep, comfortable western saddle he was wearing when he was Silver Dollar. 'I'm totally up for a canter, thank you.'

The rest of the hack passes uneventfully, but by the time we get back to the yard and are all taught how to unsaddle our ponies I am more in love with Silver than ever – although I'm sure I'll never remember everything I've been taught today. Silver is so gentle, and he even opens his mouth for me to lower the bit out of his mouth. Before we learn how to clean tack I manage to sneak back to his stable for a hug over the half-door.

'You are the best pony in the whole world,' I tell him, my mouth close to his ear. And by the way he looks at me with his big brown eyes, I believe Silver thinks I'm pretty cool, too.

CHAPTER TWELVE

It is Drama Club again tonight, our first proper rehearsal of *A Town Divided* – even though Ms Pertwee is allowing us our scripts as insurance against forgetting our lines. We've spent several weeks playing separate scenes but tonight we're going to string all the acts together and see – according to Ms Pertwee – how the land lies!

'*Do* try to do *without* your scripts if you *can*!' Ms Pertwee emphasises in words of orange and purple. A touch of fluorescent green has crept back in today, possibly due to anxiety on her part. 'Only resort to the script if you *really* have trouble,' she adds. 'Mrs Harris is in the prompt box to help you, so make full use of her.'

All heads swivel to look at the prompt box, set slap-bang in the middle of the stage, right at the front. I don't think all school stages have a prompt box, but ours does.

Don't ask me why, I don't know. To my mind, it's a bit up-itself. Maybe our school had a grant from *The Arts*, hoping to foster the next generation of actors and actresses. Like ME, an ambition Ms Pertwee is doing her best to thwart.

In the gloom of the prompt box the top of Mrs Harris can just be seen, her grey hair and specs catching the light like she's signalling for help in Morse code: L E T M E O U T L E T M E O U T. Grinning manically, she gives us all the thumbs-up sign. Mrs Harris may not possess the advantage of youth, but she is nothing if not enthusiastic.

Today, Ms Pertwee is wearing a long, swirly skirt in several different shades of pink, and a short-sleeved top in clashing scarlet (nobody can see what Mrs Harris is wearing as we can only see her head – probably something grey and woolly that matches her hair, as usual). When Ms Pertwee stretches her arms out towards Amelia in order to make a point about the way she is supposed to say a line, I notice with a start that her upper arm, emerging from a scarlet sleeve, is smothered in green and blue ink: a tattoo! I can't see what it is, but it looks pretty large, like it might extend over her whole shoulder. I can't make up my mind whether being tattooed is, or isn't, cool.

Firstly, I think fancy Ms Pertwee having a tattoo! Secondly, I wonder whether Ms Pertwee has any more. Thirdly, I wonder whether she has any piercings (I don't spend long wondering about that because, frankly, the image that pops into my mind is TOO GROSS), and fourthly, I wonder what it is like to be inked, and what tattoos I might have if I decided they *were* cool…

'Oh wow, I can't see where your t-shirt ends and you begin!' exclaimed Hebe, her eyes wide. 'Very cool,' she added, nodding in approval.

'I'm covered in them,' Etta said, lifting her jeans to reveal two tattooed legs, her whole calves awash with beautiful images of Silver and all the other ponies at the riding school.

'And what's this?' asked Hebe, lifting a sleeve.

'Oh, that's nothing,' said Etta, blushing furiously.

'It most certainly IS something!' cried Hebe, looking at it closely. 'It's a heart pierced with an arrow and the words "Etta and Nat forever" inked boldly on a band below!'

'Nat has one exactly the same,' Etta admitted, shyly. 'He is so romantic, and I didn't like to say no – he seemed so set on it.'

'He really must be mad about you,' said Hebe, solemnly. 'It's a declaration of his undying love for you – and only you.'

'I know,' said Etta, lowering her eyelashes...

'I don't know why I'm still coming to this poxy club,' whispers Hebe. 'I have hardly any lines,' she adds, not bothering to stifle a yawn.

'Shhhh,' I hiss back, 'we're starting the rehearsal.'

'If lover boy wasn't here you'd have copped out weeks ago,' is Hebe's parting shot, knowing I can't reply because Amelia is in full flow, going on and on about Ricky, the-boy-from-the-wrong-side-of-town, of whom her parents disapprove.

'Are you sure of your feelings for him?' I ask Amelia/Julia (it's my first line – my first of three, pathetic lines throughout the entire play – and someone else is learning them, too, for when I have to step in to fill Amelia's shoes due to some unforeseen catastrophe to Amelia that propels me into the limelight and stardom, relegating the original leading lady to oblivion).

'Oh yes,' gasps Amelia/Julia, her hands clasped over her heart in a demonstration of her commitment to Ricky, as directed by Ms Pertwee. (I think she's overacting, to be honest. When I am called in as understudy, Ms Pertwee will see my much more subtle performance which I feel will benefit the character and engage the audience more.)

'But he's from the wrong side of town,' says Hebe, in a bored voice. I can see Ms Pertwee waving her arms about off-stage, which is her way of telling Hebe she needs to ramp it up and inject a bit of drama into her lines. Milk it, in other words. Not that it cuts any ice with Hebe.

'But I love him!' cries Amelia/Julia, gazing towards the back of the hall, as per more of Ms Pertwee's directions. She is still overdoing it, in my opinion. *Hammy*, is the word I'd use. At this rate they'll be rolling in the aisles, and not in a good way. Besides, she's saying all MY lines, the ones I should be saying to Nat (in real life, as well as in the play). There really is no justice in this world – nor, it appears, at Drama Club.

The play rambles on. Hebe and I recite our short, insignificant lines, feeding all the best ones to Amelia/Julia. In scene two we're not needed, so we sit down on a couple of chairs and watch as Amelia and Nat meet in secret, the rest of the world unaware of their undying love. The fan club has fizzled out a bit – only three diehards have bothered to attend after the first, frenzied appearance, the rest put off by having to learn lines or apply themselves helping with wardrobe or scenery instead of just gazing moronically at Nat.

'This script is pants,' mutters Hebe, rolling up her copy and gently bashing it against her chin.

I can't help thinking she's right. The dialogue is laborious, clunky, and very unlike anything true to life. Just saying the words when I practise the Julia part is irritating.

'It's supposed to be modern – but Pertwee might as well stick a few *thees* and *thous* in it for all the up-to-date feel it has,' Hebe continues, swiping a passing fly with her script roll. She's really got it in for Ms Pertwee and the play tonight.

I feel… glum. Glum is the right word. Glum about the fact I'm not playing the lead (bad dialogue and all – I know I could work it better than Amelia and make the character of Julia much more sympathetic), glum about Amelia getting all the stage time with Nat, and glum that Hebe has such a downer on the whole thing. I am beginning to wish we hadn't signed up for Drama Club. But here we are, stuck. Ms Pertwee would probably weep if we told her we weren't coming again. I wonder what colour weeping might take.

'Can we just try to get through this?' I ask Hebe, worn out by my friend's negativity, and cross that she is right.

'Never again,' she mutters darkly, folding her arms across her chest with a loud huffing noise which reminds me of something… Oh I know what it is – Silver makes a similar noise when he gets dust from the outdoor arena up his nostrils, and he is revving up to sneeze. I don't tell Hebe this as I don't think she is in the right frame of mind to appreciate it.

Half-way through the play Ms Pertwee declares that we should all take a break. Somehow (miracles do happen), Nat finds his way to the seats near to where we are sitting, and flops down on one beside us opposite his mate Ollie, who is playing Ricky's chum Algernon (who's called Algernon, for heaven's sake? Hebe says it is probably the name of some past boyfriend of Ms Pertwee's, which is something I don't want to think about). Hebe shoots me a look, her eyebrows lifted so high, I can't see them for red fringe.

'So what do you think of the play?' Hebe asks them, dead casual. She's a cool one. I say nothing. I am rigid in the presence of Nat, all ability to speak totally lost.

'Not much,' sniffs Ollie, before scrolling through his mobile and totally blanking us. 'Dunno why you persuaded me to do this, Nat.'

'Got a bad report last term, my folks are kicking up. They insisted I volunteer for something,' Nat tells him. He stares morosely into the distance and grunts, 'Did you see the match?'

'Yeah, 'course,' replies Ollie. 'Great pass by Milton, only to be dropped by that muppet Kennit – how he missed that goal in the first half I'll never know.'

'He needs glasses,' says Nat. 'He's not worth the fortune the club paid for him, that's for sure. Money down the drain – he's yet to score this season.'

'We'll be relegated,' sniffs Ollie, still staring intently at his phone.

'Oh don't,' groans Nat, putting his head in his hands like it's the end of the world. 'That would be just the worst…'

At least I think that's how the conversation went. There was quite a lot of *blah, blah, blah, blah, blah*, for all I understood of it.

Hebe isn't giving up, though. 'How do you think rehearsals are going?' she asks, brightly. She might as well be talking to herself.

'If only we hadn't given that penalty away in the match against Tottenham,' moans Ollie, shaking his head.

'Honestly, *I* could have done better than that – I mean, so much at stake and he puts it over the bar. What was he thinking?' says Nat, angrily.

'They should never have let him take it. Johnson has a much better record at penalties, so why they didn't let him step up I'll never know,' says Ollie.

'Total madness!' agrees Nat.

See? More *blah, blah, blah*.

'Nat,' cries Ms Pertwee, in big yellow letters edged in gold, 'could I trouble you for a few moments of your time to go through this scene with Amelia?'

As Nat trundles off Ollie looks up, glances at us as if seeing us for the first time, gives a small shake of his head and takes himself off to chat with one of his other mates. Snatches of more football talk waft over and reach our ears before they both meander over to the back of the hall and out of hearing.

Hebe gives me a look. 'Well,' she says, sarcastically, 'Nat's quite the conversationalist!'

I have no words. I am beyond words. Not only do I feel glum, but I now feel crushed. Nat is a total, crashing, dreary, football *bore*.

Now *I* feel like weeping, and any words I might utter would be black as black can be.

CHAPTER THIRTEEN

We don't have a Pony Club rally every week, but I still have my Saturday morning lesson. It is weird getting there just a few minutes before, as I would love to be able to tack up Silver (or whichever other pony I am scheduled to ride) and lead him from the yard to the outdoor school, but we're still not allowed to do that if it's just a lesson.

I NEED MORE EXPERIENCE! But it's no good, I can't have it. IT'S THE RULES! Arriving a bit late (Mum couldn't find the car keys – even though they were in her bag all the time), I haven't time to look at the board in the office, and Becky is already issuing instructions in the school. The ponies are all lined up and the students are waiting with them to help the riders. The trouble is I can't see Silver anywhere. Maybe he's late because I'm late.

'Let's all mount up and get this lesson going,' says Becky, rubbing her hands together as though that will make us go faster. 'Amelia, you're riding Amber today. Pearl, you're on Cracker and Etta…'

Please let it be Silver, *please* let it be Silver, *please* let it be Silver…

'… Etta, you're riding Silver.'

YES!!!

'Oh no, wait a minute…'

My heart has just stopped. Honest to God, stopped. Just like that. Becky holds the power of life and death over me.

'… I forgot; Silver's lost a shoe. I'd like you to ride Dixie this week.'

Dixie? My face does that thing it does when I'm faced with something I have no idea about. It sort of contorts, like someone has hold of it and is squishing it about like a rubber ball. I make a huge effort to stop doing it because Hebe tells me it is totally not a good look – and she should know because she can see it.

'Dixie is our new pony,' says Becky. 'She's only young so you will need to sit still and be very clear with your aids, Etta. I know you can do it.'

Me? *Me* ride a *new* pony? A new, *young* pony? ME??? Whatever is going on? Why isn't perfect Amelia riding Dixie?

I sneak a quick glance at Amelia to see whether she is thinking the same thing. Is that a flash of disappointment and envy flickering across her face?

'I should be the one to ride the new pony, not you,' hissed Amelia, her face contorted with envy and rage (not at all like my contorting-face thing, but just as off-putting – no, actually I think it should be WORSE).

'Maybe not, but I can try,' Etta said bravely, her heart pounding. She wasn't sure whether she was experienced enough to ride Dixie, but she knew one thing: she was going to do her best, and that was all anyone could do, whatever the circumstances. It was simply a matter of having the right attitude – which she definitely had buckets of.

'You'll fail!' cried Amelia. 'If Becky hasn't asked me to ride her, you certainly won't be able to!'

Etta could see Amelia looking at her with pure hatred. Through no fault of her own she had made an enemy for life…

Actually, I don't think Amelia's face is showing any negative emotion at all. It's obvious she doesn't care one way or the other who I am riding, and she looks perfectly content on Amber.

Becky points me towards Dixie who I would (eventually) have realised was new because she is the only pony I don't recognise. She is dark bay – brown with black mane, tail and legs – with a narrow, white stripe down her face and a mane that sticks up like a brush, which makes her look surprised. She doesn't look like the sort of pony to gallop off or buck or throw me to the ground and stamp on me – but you never know with ponies. Jade is holding her, and she helps me to mount and adjust my stirrups.

'Now,' Jade begins, fixing me with a steely gaze, 'sit quietly on her, don't fidget and give your aids softly but clearly. She's a nice pony but she's not used to working with the others yet.' She swaps her steely gaze for a cheesy grin. 'She's very responsive so just enjoy it!' she adds with a wink. 'You'll be fine!'

I feel better after Jade's encouragement. Maybe I *will* be fine.

'Etta, just pop Dixie in behind Amelia on Amber,' instructs Becky. 'Amelia, you have a very important role to play today because you need to give Etta and Dixie a really good, solid lead at a regular pace. I know you can do it. Right now, whole ride walk on!'

Well that's taken the shine off my day. I thought it was going to be about me, but it seems Amelia will be riding Dixie for me.

I sit very still. On Silver I can wriggle about a bit and fiddle with things, like the length of my reins, and sometimes where I sit in the saddle because I don't know how or why but I often find myself sitting a bit too far back and have to worm my way forward into the right place. I didn't ask Jade what might happen if I *didn't* sit still on Dixie. I don't think I want to know – I certainly don't want to try it out so I sit like I'm starched. Dixie is what Nana Iris would call an *unknown quantity*.

'Relax Etta,' instructs Becky.

I don't.

I daren't. I think it might be best not to relax too soon on an unknown quantity. I want to give Dixie an encouraging pat on the neck, or rub my hand up and down her strange, brush-like mane but I daren't chance putting my reins in one hand.

I offer Becky a smile, hoping she might interpret it as me relaxing.

Amelia, of course, is sitting upright ahead of me, totally relaxed because she's ridden Amber masses of times. Amber's golden tail swishes to and fro like a pendulum on the grandfather clock Nana Iris has in her sitting room. Tick-tock. Tick-tock. Tick-tock. I tear my gaze away from it because I'm starting to feel a bit strange, and wonder whether it might be hypnotising me…

'Etta! Etta!' cried Becky.

'It's no use,' said Jade, with a shake of her head, 'she's totally under the spell of Amber's tail. I told you it would happen – that tail is just so rhythmic and mesmerising!'

'Better not wake her,' said Amelia, turning around in the saddle. 'I know someone who was woken up from a hypnotic trance once and she went ballistic – shouting, waving her arms around, the works.'

'Why?' asked Jade.

Amelia just shrugged. 'No idea,' she said, 'but she was never the same again!'

'I should have put her in behind Cracker,' said Becky. 'His creamy, off-white tail doesn't swing from side-to-side like Amber's…'

'Well done, Etta,' cries Becky. 'Dixie looks very happy with you. You're doing everything right.'

Did I hear correctly? Maybe, just maybe, I'm getting better at riding – or I really am hypnotised. Maybe I'm even getting better than Amelia; after all, she's not riding Dixie, is she?

It's about time. I wonder what other ponies and horses I might do everything right on…

'Help, help!' The terrified cries penetrated the dense forest as a horse and rider burst through the trees. The whites of the horse's eyes were showing, the fear on its face plain for all to see as the rider hauled in vain at the reins. Seeing a whole class of pupils on a school trip in the clearing the horse slowed to a halt and its rider, the beautiful blonde Amelia (her face red, her eyes puffy from crying, her blonde hair in a dull and tangled mess beneath her riding hat) flung herself from the saddle in terror.

'What the…?' stammered Nat, taking the reins from the terrified girl as she collapsed on a fallen log.

'He bolted,' cried Amelia, dropping her face into her hands and sobbing loudly. 'He's not safe to ride. He'll have to be shot!'

'No, he's as scared as you are,' said Etta quietly, stepping forward to take the reins from Nat. She stroked the face of the big, chestnut horse, speaking in soothing tones to calm it.

'He'll have to be put down, he's dangerous. Nobody can ride him,' screamed Amelia. 'Nobody, I tell you!'

'He's just sensitive – and frightened,' said Etta, putting one foot in the stirrup.

Nat laid a concerned hand on her arm. 'Whatever are you doing?' he asked, his face a mixture of fear and admiration. 'You can't possibly ride this terrifying horse, nobody can.'

'Nat's right,' said Mr Taritt (well, it is a school field trip). 'It would be madness to try. Besides, the school has a duty of care and I'll be out on my ear if I allow it.'

Etta smiled back at Nat. 'Don't worry,' she whispered, 'I know what I'm doing. And Mr Taritt's job is safe, I promise.'

Landing lightly in the saddle Etta took up the reins, running a hand down the horse's trembling neck while Mr Taritt jumped up and down in agitation, biting his nails. Sensing that he was in the hands of an experienced and sympathetic rider the horse relaxed, and after a few moments Etta had him walking, trotting and cantering around the glade like a top dressage horse, both horse and rider in total harmony that was a joy to behold.

'Gosh Etta, you're such a brilliant rider,' sniffed Amelia, unable to keep the admiration from her voice. Her eyes were still puffy and her hair, now she had taken off her riding hat, was squashed flat to her head. She looked anything but glamorous as she watched Mr Taritt drop in a dead faint by her side in relief.

The look Nat gave Etta was one of admiration. 'Your riding talent has saved that horse's life,' he told her. 'Without you he would have been destroyed. How amazing you are. Now, be a love and throw a couple of balls this way, will you? I have a match tomorrow, and I need to get my eye in...'

Dixie shies away from the letter B on the wall and I'm back in the school. I may not be quite *amazing*, but although I have lost a stirrup I am still in the saddle and not in the sand which earns me a, 'Well sat Etta!' from Becky, and a bit of a mental pat on the back from me. I have no time to dwell on the fact that my latest fantasy about Nat has been hijacked by football talk. I'll think about that later when I haven't got my hands full.

By the end of the lesson I'm feeling more positive. I got Dixie to do everything we were supposed to do – we walked at a good pace, we trotted when we were supposed to, and I managed to prevent her from cantering when we weren't. I even got her cantering on the correct lead, first time, yay! Jade was right, Dixie is very responsive – not lazy like Poppy. She is, I hate to say it, even more responsive than Silver. After a while I did relax long enough to put my reins in one hand and give her neck a pat, and I think I got praised more throughout the whole lesson than Amelia.

As we line up and wait for Becky to tell us to dismount I ease my feet out of the stirrups very, *very* quietly so as not to startle Dixie. Despite not being on Silver this has been an amazing lesson! I feel a bit like a traitor. I mean Silver still has my heart and I would hate for him to think otherwise.

Talking of my heart, only when I am dismounted and standing next to Dixie do I allow my mind to wander back to what happened in the latest instalment of my made-up life, and how Nat seems no longer under my control.

That's not good. It's bad enough living my real life with all its disappointments (apart from today's lesson, obviously) without the wheels coming off my alternative life in spectacular fashion. Maybe it will be different in Azbathria, where Nat is the Black Knight…

'Lady Estra, would you honour me with your favour,' asked the Black Knight, reining in his restless black stallion below the raised wooden seating where Estra and other members of the court were seated and looking forward to the spectacle of the joust. As the crowd waited, the colourfully clad jester, Maximus, juggled lighted torches and performed acrobatics, delighting all who saw him, and he accepted coins flung from laughing courtiers who appreciated his mastery of the performing arts.

'Of course, brave knight,' replied Estra, leaning forward to twirl her golden-and-pale-blue scarf around Sir Nathan's lance while his horse, impatient at being asked to stand still, pawed at the ground, snorting loudly.

Estra was aware that Princess Amelia, at the far end of the tilt, was favouring the Black Knight's opponent with her own ruby-and-silver coloured scarf. Sir Oliver, known to one and all as the Off-white Knight, sat easily astride his own pale cream horse, which was famous for galloping sideways throughout any joust.

Estra paused only for a moment to wonder why the Black Knight had asked not for his betrothed's favour. Could it be that he really did hold feelings for her, the raven-haired Estra, whose rescue and safety he had so often secured? Surely the feelings she had held in check for so long could not be so easily dismissed? Could the Black Knight be torn between the two beautiful maidens of Azbathria? And could Princess Amelia, even now, harbour feelings of her own for Sir Oliver, the Off-white Knight? Estra's head was awhirl with questions.

'The honour is all mine,' continued Estra to the Black Knight, lowering her eyes modestly, *'for you are my true*

champion and I am certain you will overcome all adversaries in the joust on this fair day.'

'My Lady,' acknowledged Sir Nathan, bowing deeply as he backed his powerful horse away. He then turned, riding to the end of the tilt where the Black Knight's squire stood to assist his master.

Estra felt someone at her elbow and was surprised to see Maximus, the jester who, with a glance into her eyes that seemed to penetrate her very soul, leant forward to whisper in her ear, 'You know it is hopeless. The Black Knight is not for you. Why torture yourself? For you know this to be true.'

'You are mistaken, Maximus,' Estra whispered back, aware that she was blushing. 'I know not of what you speak, and it is treason to even think such things.'

'The Black Knight is for the princess, it is decreed,' murmured the jester. 'No good can come of this longing – yours and his. It will bring only heartache and pain for all.'

Turning from the jester with a heavy heart Estra gazed at the spectacle before her, casting all other thoughts from her mind in order to compose herself.

At one end of the tilt, with Princess Amelia's favour fluttering from his lance, Sir Oliver the Off-white Knight waited astride his horse. Its cream-coloured legs showed under its brightly coloured caparison, and it snorted restlessly, keen to commence with the bout. At the opposite end of the tilt, Sir Oliver's opponent silently and purposely lowered the visor to his helmet, and as the Black Knight grasped his lance, his ink-black stallion reared in anticipation. Suddenly, both horses leapt forward at the gallop, and the two knights focused only on each other as the sound of hoof beats filled the air.

Estra caught her breath as the Black Knight's lance found its target, and the Off-white Knight was catapulted from his horse. Dismounting, and exchanging his shattered lance for a sword thrown to him by his squire, the Black Knight ran to where Sir Oliver stood waiting, eager to engage in combat, each knight's honour at stake.

'Never mind the sword,' cried Sir Oliver, heading a ball towards his opponent. 'Let's have a kick-around instead and try a few keepie-uppies!'

'Great idea!' cried Sir Nathan, casting aside his own weapon. 'Come on, kick it over here and I'll show you how it's done!'

No, no difference at all. It seems that football has crept into my Azbathria fantasies, too. Now what am I going to do?

'Okay, Etta, I've got Dixie from here,' says Becky, prising the reins out of my hands. 'Where do you go when you drift off like that?' she asks me.

'Er, nowhere,' I tell her. I am mortified. I had no idea anyone even notices that I drift off!

CHAPTER FOURTEEN

There has been a breakthrough, hen-wise, in that for some weeks now they have no longer been moving as one but have ventured out of the shed – sorry, *coop*, as Dad insists on calling it – into the garden. Well maybe not so much a break*through* as a break*out*. And now they're out, there's no stopping them. They've pecked the low-lying buds from all the flowers around the lawn and in the tubs, made super-hen-highways through the borders and have scraped an area the size of a doormat in the very middle of the lawn, reducing it to dust so they can all take turns to lie down, flap their wings and enjoy a dust bath. There isn't a part of the garden they don't call their own – even the patio. Mum caught one in the kitchen the other day – it just wandered in, bold as brass like it owned the place, and pecked at the toast crumbs we'd all dropped on the floor which had been missed by Wolfie.

Wolfie, fine guard dog that he *isn't*, fled to the safety of the sofa, whimpering. He was just about okay with the hens being imprisoned, like avian felons doing time, but now they've ventured beyond their dedicated hen-boundary he has taken offence, sitting on the patio by the French doors and watching them from a safe distance. He throws the occasional aggrieved glance over his shoulder at us and grasses them up with growls, drawing Mum's attention to the fact that they've *escaped*. It's as though he's assumed the role of prison guard.

'Aren't they sweet?' asks Mum, throwing a handful of chicken feed onto the lawn for them, all anxieties she displayed when the hens first arrived and refused to be prised apart forgotten and forgiven. Indignation overcoming his fear, Wolfie beats them to anything edible, considering he has first dibs, and he hoovers up the meal in three gulps, throwing in another growl for good measure.

'Oh Wolfie, that wasn't for you!' says Mum. 'You'll be ill.'

Wolfie just licks his lips. I can imagine his thoughts on the subject…

'Wolfie, the meal was for the hens,' reproached Etta's Mum.

Swallowing the last crumb Wolfie narrowed his eyes. 'I'm top dog in this household, and no feathered upstarts are going to eat any thrown treats, not while I'm here, not on my watch, not while there's breath left in my body. No way!'

'But Wolfie, I've got a nice biscuit here for you.'
'Okay chuck it over, I've got room for that, too.'
'But what about the hens?'
'I've told you – this is my patch. They'll have to wait their turn. It's only right and proper, it's only fair. No chickens get my pickings.'

The doorbell goes. It's Nana Iris, fresh from her stint at the charity shop, moaning about Mrs Dutty and her inability to manage the shop as she thinks it ought to be run. She has come over to see the hens she has heard so much about.

'So what do you think?' asks Mum as we all step out into the garden. The sun is streaming down, causing us to screw up our eyes against the glare. 'That one over there we've called Mrs Brown – or is it that one, or the one by the delphiniums? Anyway, we've called one of them Mrs Brown and the others are Dame Vera, Miss Piggy – she's the greediest – Countess Feathers, Lady Peckeridge and Madge. Only it's really difficult to tell them apart…'

Nana Iris wrinkles her nose and pulls her beige-coloured cardi around her tightly as though Mrs Brown (or Madge and co) might pull it from her shoulders and try it on for size.

'They might just as well all be called Mrs Brown, they all look the same,' she sniffs. 'I don't really see why you want to keep chickens, Samantha. You can get a dozen eggs from the supermarket any day of the week without all this fuss and mess.'

'But that's not really the point, Mum,' says my mum. 'And the eggs are much nicer than the supermarket ones, and fresher – you got a double-yolker the other day, didn't you Etta?'

I nod, but even I can see that it will take more than a double yolk to impress Nana Iris.

'You'll get rats,' Nana Iris says darkly, causing me to wonder whether she's in league with Shona in some kind of *Down with Hens* campaign. Mum rolls her eyes. I can't help wondering why she's bothering to show Nana Iris the hens when she knows she never sees the good side of anything.

'We won't get rats!' Mum says, firmly. 'Shirley never got rats. Do you really need that big cardigan on, Mum? It's sweltering today. You're making me feel hot.'

'I'm cold,' says Nana Iris, shivering theatrically. She's quite the actress, is Nana Iris. Maybe that's where I get it from. 'It's because of the wolverine,' she adds, like that explains everything.

Mum and I exchange glances. Neither of us has a clue.

'Wolverine?' asks Mum, frowning. Quite daring of her, I think. I can't imagine where we are going with this.

'It's a new prescription,' says Nana Iris, matter-of-factly, as though this explains it. 'You'll need to get some when you get rats. Sorts rats out, wolverine does.'

I can't stop myself…

'Got anything for rats?' Etta asked the pharmacist.

'What, like a harness, or rat toys or something?' asked the pharmacist, frowning. 'The pet shop's probably your best bet.'

'No, you don't understand,' said Etta. 'I want something that gets RID of rats.'

'Well, you should have said,' the pharmacist replied rudely, with an impatient tut-tut. She looked along the shelves of pills and potions, running her finger along the labels and pursing her lips.

'Hang on a minute,' she said. 'I think we've got something out the back.'

Etta waited, eyeing up the incontinence pads and corn plasters, and hoping she would never need either.

'Here, I thought we had one left,' puffed the pharmacist, emerging from the swinging door with her arms full of a big, brown bear-like creature with huge paws and claws like knives. 'This'll sort out your rats.'

'What is it?' asked Etta, eyeing up the claws and doubting it would fit in her bag for life. The creature lifted its upper lip in a snarl, revealing a set of very sharp teeth. A menacing growl could be heard gurgling deep in its throat.

'A wolverine,' said the pharmacist, heaving it up onto the counter with a gasp. 'Your rats won't know what's hit 'em. Bring it back when you're done with it – it's the last one and somebody else might need it.'

'You mean *warfarin!*' says my mum, a look of relief on her face. 'It's medication that thins the blood, Mum – no wonder you feel the cold.'

They've lost me. I can't help feeling disappointed. I mean, how cool would it be if Nana Iris had an *actual* wolverine? On *prescription!* Except I don't think they're very medicinal or make very good pets. It would probably shred her sofa to ribbons and make a terrible mess on her carpet. But then she might like that, having a downer on everything.

'That's what I said,' says Nana Iris, stubbornly. 'Wolverine. It kills rats!'

'Not the stuff you take,' my mum assures her.

They both meander back to the house, Nana Iris drawing her cardi around her against the side-effects of the wolverine and leaving me and Wolfie in the garden with the hens, one of which is called Mrs Brown, we just can't remember which.

Suddenly, a head pops up above the fence which separates our garden from the Robinsons'. It's Mr. Robinson (not much of a surprise there, I mean it was fifty-fifty between Mr and Mrs), all beady-eyed, his head tipped to one side, looking remarkably like one of the hens. Scary!

'Got chickens I see,' states Mr Robinson, sun-induced glare bouncing off his bald head and almost blinding me.

Just for a second I consider denying it wondering what reaction I might get, but as there are clearly half-a-dozen hens in sight, all clucking their way around the lawn, I decide against it. I can't resist telling him they're hens, not chickens, though.

'Same thing,' says Mr Robinson.

I say nothing, even though I could totally put him straight.

'Lovely legs, I suppose?' says Mr Robinson, smiling. It is not a pretty sight, a smiling Mr Robinson.

I take another look at the hens. I'd never noticed their legs being particularly lovely. I mean, they're all yellow and pimply and claw-y. Lovely wouldn't be the word I'd use; more sort of, well, hen-y.

'Much nicer than the supermarket ones,' says Mr Robinson.

It takes another three seconds for the penny to drop. Not *legs*. EGGS! I really think I ought to get my ears checked out.

'Yes,' I tell him, relieved Mr Robinson doesn't appear to have some chicken-leg fetish going on. 'I got one with a double yolk the other day,' I add, simply for something to say.

'Oh, very nice,' nods Mr Robinson. 'I expect, um, you get more eggs than, er, you know what to do with?' He says this like it's a question, which I don't think it is, which makes him sound like he's from Australia which, as far as I know, he isn't.

'Not really,' I say. 'Mum uses them for cakes and stuff.'

'Oh,' says Mr Robinson. He sounds disappointed. I can't think why.

We both stand there for a while, saying nothing. A big bumble bee buzzes by and breaks the silence.

'Well, I must go, I can't stand about here chatting,' says Mr Robinson, like I'm keeping him from something important.

Thank goodness for that, I think. When I go back indoors and tell Mum about Mr Robinson she tut-tuts like the pharmacist in my made-up life.

'Cheeky old thing,' she says, 'dropping hints.'

'About what?'

'Wants some freebie eggs,' says Nana Iris, winking.

I sigh. Even Nana Iris is way ahead of me when it comes to the motives of Mr Robinson. I wonder what she would say if I were to tell her Mr Robinson is a great admirer of our hens' legs. Only he isn't – at least as far as I know. I expect that's how rumours start.

Shona comes into the kitchen and opens the fridge door. 'God,' she sighs, like it's the end of the world, 'there's never *anything* to eat in this house.'

'Make yourself a sandwich,' says Mum.

'And *egg* sandwich,' I add, pulling a face at my sister.

'I thought you were going to make cakes all day long when we got these egg-laying raptors,' says Shona, sticking her tongue out at me.

'I can't spend all my days baking cakes,' says Mum (which isn't how I remember her selling the idea of having hens to us). 'Here,' she says, raiding one of the kitchen cupboards, 'have some crispbreads with cheese.'

'What about me?' I ask.

'What about Wolfie?' asks Nana Iris, looking down at Wolfie, who is looking up at Mum, his expression a mixture of anticipation and dread of being left out.

'You've just had some chicken meal which wasn't yours,' Mum tells Wolfie, who continues to dribble on the tiles and gaze at her with big, sad eyes, the stolen chicken meal but a distant memory.

'You're growing out of those jeans,' Mum says accusingly, looking me up and down. 'Honestly Etta, you're turning into a right beanpole, nothing in your wardrobe will fit you soon. I've noticed your school uniform is looking too tight and too short. That's more money!'

'I can hardly stop growing,' I tell her, because I can't. It's something my body does without any input from me.

I'm not doing it on purpose, just to annoy. Besides, if I grow too tall I won't be able to ride Silver (disaster!), so if I could stop myself growing, I would.

'You're such a loser,' says Shona, drifting out of the kitchen and back upstairs.

'Etta's the understudy for the leading lady in the school play,' Mum tells Nana Iris. She says it like I've got the lead part, like I'm the star in a major Hollywood blockbuster instead of someone who might just do to stand in for the real star of the show.

'Why aren't you playing the lead?' asks Nana Iris, cutting to the chase.

'Because I've got rubbish hair,' I tell her.

'No you haven't, Etta!' cries Mum, all affronted on my behalf. 'That isn't the reason!'

'What is it, then?' I ask.

'It's just not your time, that's all. You'll get to play the lead one day, I know you will.'

She doesn't. She's just saying it to make me feel better. Like that's going to work.

'Besides,' adds Mum, 'you may yet get to play the lead if something happens to the leading lady. You never know.'

I stare into the distance, her words buzzing around my head like flies do around the food bin we put out every week for recycling.

'If you're growing out of all your clothes, I'll keep an eye out in the shop for things that will fit you,' offers Nana Iris.

Now this might work should Nana Iris have an eye for vintage chic but, of course, she hasn't. Also, the daggy charity shop isn't where people with vintage chic recycle their clothes, they use the posh one.

'Er, no, you're all right, Nana,' I say, hastily.

'Yes, I know *I'm* all right,' replies Nana Iris, 'it's *you* I'm talking about.'

I need time to think. 'Actually, I'd better go over my lines,' I say, and after giving Nana Iris a goodbye hug I retreat to my room with Wolfie, who snuggles up next to me on my bed while I read through the part Amelia's been given instead of me, trying to remember and say the words before checking the script.

You never know, Mum had said, but they aren't the words which have ignited a fire of ideas in my head. Her words merely echo my own internal voice which, lately, has been suggesting ideas I've been trying to ignore. Ideas my better self knows it should shun. Actually, I'm not trying to dodge responsibility, but I think the voice isn't really mine. I think it might belong instead to some evil creature that inhabits my brain...

The hamster raced inside its wheel, inside Etta's head, exhausting itself, running round and round, going nowhere.

'You know what you want to do!' it cried, its eyes glinting red in the darkness, revealing itself to be the hamster from hell, the very devil hamster. 'You know what you NEED to do to achieve your ambitions,' devil hamster continued, bossily. 'You KNOW ways to achieve your destiny! Do you want to be the sort of person who just accepts fate? Do you want to just stand back and let others – like Amelia Armitage – achieve YOUR goals? Or do you want to seize the day, to

grasp the nettle, to stand up for yourself and claim what is rightfully yours?'

See? I have no idea where this devil hamster, egging me on to do BAD THINGS, comes from, but it popped up recently and now it's hanging around, refusing to go away. Because (devil hamster keeps saying) if something were to happen to Amelia then who would have to step up and take the lead in *A Town Divided*? Yep, you've got it, her understudy: ME. That's the point of an understudy; that's what they're for.

I couldn't help noticing (with devil hamster at my elbow – or rather, in my head) that at Pony Club, opportunities to initiate a not-very-serious accident to SOMEONE seem to crop up on an hourly basis. It's almost as though it would be easier to arrange an incident than not, quite frankly. There are so many ways…

'Ouch!' cried Amelia, her hand over her nose. 'What did you do that for?'

'What?' asked Etta, looking back over her shoulder.

'You kicked the stable door open just as I was bending down to pick up my riding crop,' said Amelia, her voice all thick and wooden-sounding.

'Oh dear, did I?' said Etta, her voice full of remorse (well, I am an actress, after all*). 'I'm so sorry!'*

'Let me look,' said Becky, peeling Amelia's hand away from her nose.

'Euuw!' gasped Pearl. 'Your nose is a right mess. Can you breathe properly?'

'No, I can't, and I'm going to have a big bruise and a couple of black eyes. I can't possibly play Julia looking like this!'

'Oh, do you think?' asked Etta, innocently.

'You'll have to do it, Etta,' said Pearl.

'Oh... well... all right then, if you think so,' said Etta, stepping up.

Would that be a bit obvious? The thoughts roll on and I'm powerless to stop them – devil hamster is up and running...

'I'm going to make sure Amber's tack is the cleanest it has ever been,' said Amelia, walking into the tack room with Amber's saddle over her arm, which prevented her from seeing the floor.

'Take care!' shouted Etta – but it was too late. Stepping on a slither of saddle soap someone had dropped Amelia slid across the tack room before landing slap, bang, upended on the floor, the saddle landing next to her with a thud.

'Oh my goodness, are you all right?' asked Pearl, her voice full of concern as she bent over her friend to help her up.

'Is the saddle damaged?' asked Etta. 'Only they're really expensive.'

'I've put something out,' said Amelia, grimacing. 'I won't be able to do the play now, I can only hobble. You'll have to do it for me, Etta, I know you'll be brilliant.'

'Oh, well, I'll do my best,' agreed Etta, shyly.

These thoughts won't do. I'm supposed to be a heroine, and heroines don't do the dirty on other heroines, do they? (Amelia has never done anything to me, not intentionally. She's actually been very friendly at Pony Club.) Even so, the possibilities are endless, and they keep on coming…

'Oops, I'm so sorry, Amelia, Silver just pushed me with his nose!' exclaimed Etta, cannoning into Amelia as she led Amber out of her stable.

'Ouch, my toe!' cried Amelia, limping across the yard. 'Amber just trod on it, really hard. My foot went under her hoof when Etta crashed into me, and Amber sort of ground it into the concrete.'

'Let me see,' said Becky, pulling off Amelia's boot as Amelia wailed in agony. 'However did this happen?' she asked, looking at Amelia's throbbing, bluing and rapidly expanding foot.

'I told you, Etta pushed me!'

'It was an accident,' said Etta, apologetically. 'It looks really painful, by the way.'

'It is!' said Amelia. 'I won't be able to be in the play now. Good job you know the lines, Etta, you'll have to do it.'

'Well, I suppose I could,' said Etta, in a martyred voice. 'If you insist…'

Could happen.

As an actress I bet I could make any scenario work.

'What do you think, Wolfie?' I ask, my imagination running full pelt as I (or rather devil hamster) engineer some mild peril. 'What would be the best way for an understudy to arrange a small yet significant accident that puts a leading lady out of action for a strategic couple of days, and lets the rightful actress take the part she was destined for?'

Wolfie sticks one leg in the air and gives his under parts a good raking with his teeth, pulling out a twig his coat has swept up in the garden before spitting it out on the duvet.

'Do you mind?' I ask him, gingerly picking up the Wolfie-saliva-soaked twig from the bed and flicking it in the bin.

Wolfie looks at me and gulps. It seems he doesn't. He doesn't mind at all.

It seems I don't, either, for it is obvious that my better self is losing. I appear – with the assistance of devil hamster (who, I would say, definitely *doesn't* have the *right attitude*) – to have gone to the dark side.

CHAPTER FIFTEEN

Two things of note happened this past week.

One: at Drama Club, Ms Pertwee had Max Rybart and me playing the leads in a full rehearsal of *A Town Divided*, to make sure we are fully familiar with our parts. This meant that although everyone else was involved Nat and Amelia (of course) were not, so they sat watching the whole production from the seats below the stage. This put me off a bit because instead of Nat having Ollie to talk to about football he talked to Amelia. They didn't actually watch the play at all. I don't think they talked about football, either.

Between my lines (which I totally remembered, by the way, despite the distraction), I could see Amelia doing these things, lots of times:

1. Chewing her hair and twisting locks of golden strands around her fingers.

2. Throwing back her head and laughing like Nat had said the *funniest* thing.
3. Pushing her hand against Nat's shoulder as though he had said something slightly daring that might make a person blush.

Between all this nonsense Nat kept on:

1. Leaning forward and saying stuff to Amelia like he didn't want anyone else to hear (which he didn't need to do, frankly, because everyone else was performing the play, NOT listening to him).
2. Leaning back in his chair and pushing his hair off his face.
3. Grinning broadly at Amelia, nodding his head and raising his eyebrows.

It's a wonder I could say my lines, quite honestly, but I managed. That's how much of a professional I am. Except when Max Rybart pulled a face at me during a particularly soppy scene and I almost laughed. Then again when he blew a sarcastic kiss at me (totally NOT in the script, thank goodness) I choked a bit and managed to turn it into a cough – even though I was dying inside thinking about Nat and Amelia having a cosy little chat below us all. If Amelia had been MY understudy, as she should have been, I would have been the one having the cosy little chat with Nat, laughing, pushing my hand against his shoulder, and twirling locks of my hair around my finger.

Well, maybe not that last one.

Life is so unfair sometimes I want to scream.

Anyway, Max and I did fine (Max is actually quite a good actor when he isn't telling jokes, and Hebe said we were much better than Amelia and Nat, although she might just have wanted to be supportive), and Ms Pertwee seemed relieved, like she had been worried we weren't going to nail it. It's a strange feeling when people don't believe in you, not to say a bit rude. But I know she is now reassured, and I expect she might be having second thoughts about casting Nat and Amelia because Max and I totally carried it off, big time. Next time Ms Pertwee puts on a play, I expect my mobile to be ringing!

The other thing that happened is that at Pony Club we are all going to take some tests. The Pony Club has these achievement badges you can get for passing tests on different subjects, pony-care and horse-knowledge wise. When you pass you get an embroidered badge to sew on to your Pony Club sweatshirt. The idea is to get them all so your sweatshirt resembles one of those old VW camper vans you see smothered in badges which say, *We've Seen the Squirrels of Shortleet*, and *Yes to Yorkshire!* and *Surfers Rock, Dude*, and you look a total know-all – as well as a been-everywhere-done-everything-and-I'm-rubbing-your-nose-in-it-'cos-you-haven't sort of person. I'm up for that. Of course, the Pony Club badges will be totally different and say horsy things like *Grooming a Pony, First Aid,* and *Saddles and Bridles,* and stuff like that.

Becky said she wanted us all to try for the *Grooming a Pony* badge first, so we concentrated on learning about grooming, and took home notes about it so we could study and learn the theory behind it all. I so wanted to learn to groom with Silver but I, together with Amelia, Pearl and Olivia, all learnt on Poppy, who stood like a rock. The reason she stood like a rock was because she went to sleep. Clearly, Poppy is specifically designed to do things that require her to remain immobile for long periods of time rather than move. This proves what Nana Susan is always telling me: that everyone has their own particular *forte*, which is Latin for being good at something. I now know what she means.

The hardest part about grooming, to my mind, is picking out hooves. You have to do this because not only do you need to clean all the mud and stones out of a pony's hooves so they don't go lame, but you also need to check their shoes are on tight, and that they don't need new ones (which is way more difficult than it sounds). Oh, and you also make sure the hooves are in good health. What they don't tell you in the notes is that pony hooves are REALLY heavy. They weigh a TONNE!

That's another reason why I wanted Silver – he has nice, neat little hooves. Poppy hasn't. Poppy's hooves are bigger than the red-and-gold place mats my mum puts under our dinner plates at Christmas, and a good deal heavier.

Pearl went first and managed to get Poppy to pick up one of her front hooves so she could clean it. Then it was Amelia's turn, then Olivia's. Finally, it was mine.

I need to push myself to the front in future because I have reached the conclusion (it's taken me long enough) that going last doesn't improve my chances of doing well, even though you would think it would because (and this was my original plan) I have time to see how everyone else copes and can avoid their mistakes. However, by the time it was my turn to ask Poppy to lift the place mats she has on the end of her legs instead of hooves she'd had enough and had decided on strike action. No amount of pulling and heaving and trying to haul one of her hooves up made the slightest impression on Poppy, who put all her weight on it and nodded off like I wasn't there. I was sure at one point I could hear her snoring.

'Here, lean against her so she transfers all her weight over to her other side,' suggested Jade, giving Poppy a bit of a shove.

Still nothing. I was starting to puff a bit and feel silly. I mean, Poppy had done it for the others. Poppy, I have decided, HATES ME.

'Push the back of her knee,' Jade said.

I did that and – miraculously – Poppy's leg bent in the middle, causing her hoof to lift up on to her toe.

'Quick!' said Jade. 'Lift it up and grab hold!'

Finally, I held Poppy's hoof in my hands. Poppy then decided that as I had forced her to lift her leg, the least I could do was to hold her up and so she put all her weight back onto it, causing me to let go again. I couldn't help it. I am not designed to hold up a pony. They are too heavy.

This went on for a while – I shan't bore you with the full story. By the time we'd finished I was exhausted.

After that, using the brushes on the furry bits was a doddle. I am sure I will have nightmares involving gigantic hooves, Poppy leaning on me until I am driven into the ground like a garden cane, and Amelia picking out all four of Poppy's hooves in the time it takes me to lift a single hoof up into the air. I wouldn't put it past Amelia to be able to pick out all Poppy's hooves at the same time, with Poppy lying on her back in an obliging way, waggling her legs in the air like a puppy.

So you can understand, what with one thing and another, why absolutely no opportunities to ensure Amelia never gets to play Julia in *A Town Divided* presented themselves at Pony Club – which is disappointing.

You would think, wouldn't you, with all the fuss Becky and the other staff and students at Chesterton make about Health and Safety, all the warnings and dire tales of what might happen if we so much as forget to aim a water bucket handle towards the wall, or leave a hay net in the yard, or approach a pony from any direction other than his shoulder, that there would be ample opportunities for causing a mild accident. But *because* of all the Health and Safety and the diligence of the staff, no such opportunities occur which, I suppose, is the point. It really is most annoying to a person who is missing their destiny to play the lead in *A Town Divided*.

But Amelia *is* going to play Julia. It is inevitable. I have no plan that will nobble her, no plan that will see Amelia relegated to the sidelines. I am, in Nat-speak, still on the bench awaiting substitution and we're a week closer to putting on the play.

What am I going to do? (I can cut out all that football-speak, for a start!)

CHAPTER SIXTEEN

Mum and Shirley are at the bottom of the garden, bending over and gazing intently at something by the edge of the hen house.

'What are you doing?' I ask.

Mum jumps like I've caught her doing something she shouldn't. 'Nothing you need to worry about,' she says, throwing the stick she was poking around the bottom of the hen house away like it is red hot. Shirley presses her lips together and looks at me all wide-eyed and innocent, the piled-up hair on top of her head wobbling in solidarity with Mum.

Something is going on.

'What's that hole?' I ask, noticing a place where it looks like Wolfie has been digging, in exactly the area my mum was poking with a stick.

'What hole?' Mum asks airily, smiling and running her fingers through her hair. I wish I could do that with my hair.

'*That* hole,' I say, pointing. It isn't a big hole, but it is a hole all the same. 'Maybe Dad can see it,' I add. This suggestion produces a rather odd reaction.

'Now there's no need to bother your father about it,' says Mum, hastily.

'Honestly, Etta darlin',' says Shirley, pulling her leopard-print top further down over her hips and smoothing it over her zebra-print leggings, 'you're imagining things, you are. Honestly, Sam, your girls have such imagination, they really do. Vivid!'

They sidle up together, blocking my view of the hole, Shirley's earrings jangling like wind chimes. To be honest, whether a hole really exists or is merely a figment of my imagination isn't the most exciting thing in the world, so I turn around and go back into the house. When I look out of the kitchen window Mum and Shirley have resumed their positions bending over the hole – the hole that may or may not be there. Shirley's backside is enormous. It looks even bigger than Silver's from where I'm standing, and she only needs a tail to complete the picture. The zebra print isn't doing it any favours…

'What's that in the garden?' asked Etta's dad, peering out of the kitchen window. 'That thing that's blocking all the light?'

'Er…' said Etta, uncertain exactly what her dad was looking at.

'It's a zebra!' shouted her father, excitedly. 'Quick, where's my phone? It isn't every day you see a zebra in a suburban back garden!'

'Are you going to call it up for a chat?' asked Etta, puzzled.

'Of course not!' snorted her dad. 'We can sell it to the papers!'

'Sell the zebra?' asked Etta, frowning.

'No, silly!' replied her dad, aiming his mobile out of the window. 'We can sell pictures of it, of course.'

'Er, Dad...' began Etta, unwilling to burst her father's bubble, '...I think you'll find that zebra... well, it isn't.'

'Eh? Isn't what?' asked her dad, still snapping away.

'A zebra,' said Etta, sighing. 'It's Shirley, Dad. She's bending over. Why do you think the zebra HAS NO TAIL?'

'Crikey!' exclaimed her father, examining the images on his mobile. 'You're right! Come to think of it, no zebra would have a backside as big as that – even if it does look as though a leopard has devoured its entire front end. What was I thinking?'

'What are they doing out there?' asks Shona on her way to the cupboard where the biscuits are kept.

'Poking some hole with a stick,' I tell her.

'I told you we'd get rats,' Shona mutters, cramming a ginger nut in her mouth and sticking the packet under her arm. 'Gross!' she adds for good measure, as she heads back upstairs to her room.

Rats, I think. I mean, RATS! I wonder how many rats we might have. I remember a teacher at school saying that rats are prolific breeders. How long before we are overrun by rats? How long before there are rats streaming down the garden towards the house, a carpet of rats, a rat river, until we can't move for rats?

'Quick!' cried Etta, leaning all her weight against the back door. 'They're trying to get in, help me close it!'

Shona leapt forward to help, and together the sisters closed and locked the door against the mountain of rats piling up against it. Rats scrambled and climbed over each other to reach the windows, working relentlessly to gain access to the house, to take over the whole property, to raid all the cupboards, the fridge, the freezer, to clear the human inhabitants out of every available morsel of food, right down to the last crumb.

'They're not getting the ginger nuts!' shouted Shona, shovelling biscuits into her mouth like there was no tomorrow, her eyes wide.

'Throw them out of the window!' cried Etta, trying to wrestle the packet from her sister's grasp. 'If we give them something, maybe they'll leave us alone! Quick, before it's too late!'

'Don't be ridiculous!' screamed Shona, beyond all reason. 'It will just make them more determined. Besides,' she added, her face distorting horribly with hysteria, losing her grip on sanity in the face of such terrible odds and clutching the packet to her chest, 'these ginger nuts are mine, MINE, I TELL YOU!'

The room grew dark as more rats piled up against the windows, blocking the light. It was too late to do anything, the girls were doomed. Etta froze as she heard the splintering sound of the back door giving way under the weight and determination of the rodents. The rats had breached the door! All hope was gone…

'Cup of tea, Shirley?' asks my mum, opening the back door and wiping her feet on the mat.

'Ohh, that'll be lovely, darlin', just lovely – two sugars!' Shirley replies, before turning to me. 'I hear you're in the school play, understudying for the lead,' she says, wobbling her earrings in my direction.

I nod, because I am.

'You'll need to know the words. Know all the words, do you?' Shirley asks.

I nod again, because I do.

'Why aren't you playing the lead, then?'

I shrug – I mean, what sort of question is that? It's like me asking why she thinks teaming two different animal prints is a good look. It isn't, it just looks like some Frankenstein interspecies experiment that's gone bananas.

'Cat got your tongue?' asks Shirley.

I am so tempted to tell her it looks like the cat has got her, what with the leopard print and everything. Instead, I just arrange my mouth into a wide, closed-lip smile.

'There you go, Shirl,' says Mum, placing a mug of steaming tea down on the kitchen worktop. 'You said you had something to tell me. What's up?'

I'm not listening, you understand, it's just that I can't shut it out.

'Ooooo Sam,' says Shirley, her earrings going bonkers, 'it's my 'arry...'

(Harry, in case you are remotely interested, is Shirley's long-suffering husband.)

'...eee's gone and booked us on a trip to Lake Windermere, no word of a lie! Booked it months ago, he did! We've off tomorrow!'

'You're joking!' says my mum. I don't know why she says this. It's hardly funny.

'Straight up!' declares Shirley, nodding.

'Why didn't you say something sooner?' asks my mum.

'That's what I says to 'arry,' says Shirley. 'Why didn't you say somethin' sooner, I says to him.'

'So why didn't he?' asks my mum, like it's interesting.

'Told me he didn't want to spoil the elephant of surprise!' says Shirley.

Which threw me...

'Erm, dare I ask what that is out on the driveway?' asked Etta's dad. 'Wolfie won't stop barking at it.'

Etta's mum glanced out of the window. 'Oh that,' she said, airily. 'It's Harry's elephant of surprise. Be quiet Wolfie!' she added.

'Let me see!' exclaimed Etta, pushing past her mum to take a look.

An elephant stood on the drive, its trunk entwined around the string of a huge, inflated balloon, upon which was scrawled the word SURPRISE! Behind, a uniformed brass band played a fanfare in the road, and cheerleaders twirled pom-poms, flashing white teeth as they danced. The whole entourage was causing traffic to screech to a halt, and for drivers to wave their fists in the elephant's direction.

'Well,' said Etta, her eyes wide, 'it certainly is a surprise!'

'Yes, that's what I told you,' said her mum. 'It's the elephant of surprise. You must have heard of it...'

What with one thing and another it's getting like an African safari round at our place.

'Oh Shirl, you are a one!' says my mum, doing that sea-lion flap with her hand she does. 'You mean the *element* of surprise!'

'What?' asks Shirley, looking puzzled. 'What did I say?'

'Elephant!' gasps my mum – and they both double up with laughter, Shirley clutching her stomach and Mum doing the sea-lion flap at double speed.

'Oh gawd!' shrieks Shirley. 'What am I like?'

For a second or two I wonder whether there was some almighty mix-up at the hospital when my mum was born, and Nana Iris might just be *Shirley's* mother, what with their shared tendency to replace certain words with animals and confuse the heck out of everyone around them. Maybe Max Rybart might appreciate some new material – it seems to have tickled my mum and Shirley, even though I'm unaffected.

Is it me? I have a nasty feeling it might be and so, leaving my mum and Shirley still doubled up and crying with laughter, I slip out of the kitchen and go to my room where I dig out my Pony Club grooming notes and knuckle down to some serious revision. After all, I don't want to let Silver down.

CHAPTER SEVENTEEN

THE COUNTDOWN TO THE actual performance, in front of an actual audience, of *A Town Divided* has begun, and peeping between the closed curtains on the stage I can see parents and pupils filing in and filling up the seats, as well as opening bags of sweets some enterprising teacher with an eye for profit has put on sale at the box office (which is just a desk in the corner of the hall with a sign on it which says *Box Office*). Behind me, and in honour of the occasion, Ms Pertwee is dressed in hurts-your-eyes yellow – big fluffy jumper, wide canary trousers and matching trainers with white soles that make no noise as she walks, which is worrying as she could creep up on a person at any time (like me). Even Mrs Harris has forsaken her usual grey in favour of a washed-out floral print dress that used to be blue – or possibly purple – although her hair is still making a desperate run for it, drooping around her face like thin, Medusa-like snakes which can't be bothered to look menacing but have elected instead to go with *chilled*.

'Thank goodness I have only four lines,' says Hebe, pulling at the dress Ms Pertwee has furnished her from wardrobe, which is a size too small for her. Either that or she's a size too big for it.

I am beyond nervous. I expect you are waiting for me to tell you that, with the help of devil hamster, I formed a last-minute plan and am about to step up and play the lead in *A Town Divided*.

But I haven't.

As far as I know Amelia – who I can't see but is no doubt around somewhere – still hasn't contracted some terrible disease, and has yet to be the target of some debilitating-yet-not-very-serious injury that would mean that she CANNOT GO ON. Time is running out!

I take my mind off this depressing thought by looking at the programme Ms Pertwee has got one of her art classes to produce. It is available from the *Box Office* with the sweets and has the cast list on the inside front cover. I am in it twice: once billed as Corrine (which is the name of my also-ran), and again at the very bottom of all the names, sharing a credit with Max Rybart, where we are listed as understudies to Amelia and Nat (with special thanks to us both). You can keep your special thanks, I think, because in no way do thanks, special or otherwise, compensate for NOT playing the lead. Special thanks just add insult to injury in my book.

The week before, Mrs Harris was tasked with making certain she spelt all our names correctly, which took ages. Despite this I see from the programme that she's spelt Hebe with two Es, so it reads Hebee. Well, that's actually three Es if you count the first one. I can't wait to see how Hebe takes it. There are going to be ructions.

Told you! She's just spotted her name in the programme and she is not happy.

'Mrs Harris is so dozy!' Hebe says, tugging at the hem of her dress again. 'Everyone gets my name wrong.'

'Like when you were down as *Herbe* on the list for the long jump team?' I ask.

'Oh don't remind me!' she says. 'Max Rybart thought it was hilarious and wouldn't stop calling me *Basil* for ages.'

'Which do you think is worse?' I ask. 'Hebee or Herbe?'

'Can we just change the subject?' asks Hebe, looking glum.

'It's my nerves,' I tell her, chewing my thumb nail. 'I'm trying to think about anything but how time is running out for my big chance because nothing yet has happened to Amelia to prevent her from performing.'

I get a sympathetic head bob from my friend, who understands.

'Where's Amelia?' I hear Ms Pertwee ask, in anxious shades of mauve. My heart leaps, and Hebe and I dare to exchange glances of hope. My dream is still alive! Amelia isn't here.

'Miss, Miss!' shouted Nat Black.
'Yes, whatever is it, Nat?' asked Ms Pertwee.

'It's Amelia, Miss, she's texted me.'

'What's happened?'

'She's not going to make it, Miss. She's stuck on the main road. Her dad's car has got a puncture and he's taking ages to change the wheel. Amelia says to go on without her, Miss. She says...'

'Oh no!' exclaimed Ms Pertwee, slapping her hands to either side of her face in an impressive impersonation of Edvard Munch's famous painting, The Scream *(only wearing a big yellow jumper, and looking scarier and more deranged). 'Thank goodness we have Etta to take over the lead – and,' she added in a confidential whisper, 'between you and me, Nat, she'll be much better in the role than Amelia could ever have been.'*

Nat nodded. 'That's what Amelia rather generously admits in her text,' he told her, grinning, 'and I agree with her. Only I feel the need to point out that Etta is pretty rubbish at football – not only is she a lousy kicker, but she doesn't even understand the offside rule.'

'She's over there,' says Max Rybart, pointing to where Amelia and her bezzies are all in a huddle. 'Nat's here, too, so despite all the work we've put in, despite all the effort, it looks like Etta and I are surplus to requirements,' he adds with a wink, before shovelling a marshmallow he's nicked from the *Box Office* into his mouth and chewing, his face suddenly putting me in mind of a washing machine. He is wearing a false moustache which is supposed to make him look older and more like Amelia/Julia's father, but instead he just looks like a boy wearing a false moustache. And a bit weird. To his credit he offers me a marshmallow, but my heart is sinking, and I am too sick with anxiety and disappointment to eat anything. I can't even comment on the moustache.

Amelia IS here. Also, I don't like the idea of being surplus to requirements. Being surplus to requirements is another way of saying I am of NO IMPORTANCE, that should I leave the hall now, nobody would miss me and that I am NOTHING! Being surplus to requirements sucks, and I bet Max isn't the only one who has noticed…

'Where's Etta?' asked Ms Pertwee.

'Who cares?' replied Nat Black in a bored voice, scrolling through his phone at the latest football scores. 'She's totally unimportant and unnecessary. I mean, it's not like she's in the Premier League, or even a physiotherapist that can be useful if a player sustains an injury before half-time…'

I pull myself together and watch as Ms Pertwee bowls over to Amelia like a big, fluffy lemon, her hands fluttering, clipboard all aquiver. Ms Pertwee is in a right old state. Putting on a play is obviously very stressful. Good job she has me she can fall back on – or would have if Amelia hadn't turned up.

'Can you see my underwear through this dress?' asks Hebe, giving it another tug.

'No,' I tell her, not even bothering to look. She should have sorted all that out at rehearsals. It's a bit late now when I have more important and pressing things on my mind, like stardom slipping through my fingers.

'Oh, hello,' says Hebe, inclining her head towards Amelia, her bezzies and Ms Pertwee. 'Something is AMISS.'

I turn my head so fast I get a crick in my neck. Amelia seems to be having a bit of a moment, clutching at her throat and shaking her head, her eyes wide. Ms Pertwee looks stricken.

Trying to look as though we are anything but interested in what is going on, Hebe and I shuffle our way across the stage sideways in a subtle attempt to hear what's going down.

'... but Amelia, you're so good at your part,' I hear Ms Pertwee say (she isn't, but I let it slide).

'I can't remember my lines!' wails Amelia, shaking her head.

'You will once you get started, it's just a little stage fright,' soothes Ms Pertwee, stroking Amelia's hair as though she's a frightened kitten (she couldn't do that with my hair). 'Besides,' she adds, waving her clipboard in the direction of the prompt box, 'Mrs Harris is there to help you if you do forget the odd line. And, of course, we are all behind you, every single one of us, aren't we girls?' (Not all of us are, but Ms Pertwee doesn't know that, and Amelia's bezzies nod like their heads are on springs.)

From the prompt box Mrs Harris grins manically and waves her script in an ineffectual way. She wouldn't give me confidence. I consider this a plus as the same thought must have occurred to Amelia.

'I can't!' wails Amelia again, as though the weight of the world is on her shoulders. I can't help thinking that if she had shown the same emotion throughout rehearsals then she might have made a much better impression in the play and therefore be more confident now, but I can't think much about that because it looks like a miracle might be happening. Amelia's stage fright is the answer to my prayer, and it could result in MY BIG CHANCE (and I had never considered stage fright a possibility! I haven't even had to endanger Amelia's life. Result! Maybe devil hamster did it all by himself).

Hebe digs me in the ribs. 'Looks like your big chance,' she hisses, echoing my own thoughts…

'Etta! Etta! You **have** *to go on, Amelia is worse than useless!' screamed Ms Pertwee, hysterically. 'She's locked herself in the toilets and is sobbing uncontrollably. I wouldn't mind but she never was much good as Julia – this may be a blessing in disguise!'*

'No problem, Ms Pertwee,' said Etta, standing on the stage and gathering her thoughts as the drama teacher counted her down in the wings. The curtains swished open and there, in front of her, a thousand (well, a couple of hundred or so, tops) *eyes stared up towards the stage, all waiting for Etta (as Julia) to say her first line, to stroll across the stage, to gaze into the eyes of Nat (as Ricky, the boy-from-the-wrong-side-of-town), and to wow them with her amazing acting ability and make a dodgy play come alive.*

'Hurry up!' said Nat (as Ricky, the boy-from-the-wrong-side-of-town), looking at his watch. 'I've got an important football match tonight so I can't be late. Get a wiggle on!'

Amelia's having a meltdown – this really could be my BIG CHANCE. But something rather odd is happening: my mouth feels suddenly dry, my knees are trembling, my heart starts to thud in my chest at double its usual rate and my hands feel all clammy. With the real possibility that I could be about to take on the starring role in *A Town Divided* I realise something:

I CAN'T DO IT!

No, really, I can't. How can I stand up on the stage and say those lines in front of everybody – all those parents, siblings, fellow pupils, Nat's fan club? It won't be like the rehearsal; it will be FOR REAL. How can I play opposite Nat – Nat, who I can't even talk to about mundane, everyday things in real life, let alone say all those soppy lines Ms Pertwee has written? I can't. I JUST CAN'T. It was easy with Max Rybart but it won't be with Nat because, actually, *this* is my real life. It's not my made-up life, the imaginary life I thought contained the real me, where I can be anything, say anything and do anything – and not just be and say and do, but be and say and do everything REALLY WELL! In this life I'm not so hot, am I?

I feel sick. How will I ever live this down? How can I explain to Ms Pertwee, to Hebe, to my family (I've spotted my mum and dad sitting in the third row in the audience with Nana Susan and Nana Iris – no Shona, of course) that I feel the same way as Amelia feels right now? The thought makes me go cold – and then hot – and then cold again.

I wonder whether anyone would notice if I just ran away and hid for a couple of hours. I could go to Chesterton on the bus, I could sneak onto the yard and tell Silver all about it – he'd never judge me, he'd totally understand. *I should have had an understudy. I'm* the one who needs someone who can go on for *me* when *I'm* ill (for ill, read petrified). What an oversight!

'Oh, hold on… not so fast…' says Hebe.

I take another look. Everything has changed. Amelia is nodding bravely, Ms Pertwee is smiling, Amelia's bezzies are all looking their usual supportive selves and clapping Amelia on the back.

'She's pulled herself together,' says Hebe. 'What a trooper,' she adds sarcastically, shooting me a sympathetic smile and an eye roll. 'Your BIG CHANCE dashed, just like that. Are you all right?'

I nod, unable to speak. The relief is overwhelming.

'Cheer up! We all know you'd have been much better in the part than Amelia,' Hebe says supportively, totally misreading my relief for disappointment.

I gulp, my heart rate slowing. 'Thanks, Heeb,' I say. I decide she's such a good friend I ought to step up a bit – not to mention the need to talk about something else right now. 'Actually, you *can* see your underwear under that dress, especially when the light is behind it. Do you want to go to wardrobe and see if there's anything else?'

'Oh God, yes!' cries Hebe, scuttling off the stage towards the rack of costumes like she's being chased by Nana Iris's wolverine. I follow at a more leisurely pace, waiting for my breathing to return to normal, rubbing my sweaty palms on my own dress, trying to cope with my own disappointment – the disappointment I feel in myself.

That's Plan A out of the window, then. Looks like Plan

B is on the cards – I'd better be a riding instructor, or a celebrity TV baker, or something else because if I can't hack a piddling little school play with terrible dialogue and a dodgy plot how on earth would I sparkle in a real play, or TV soap, or film? I wouldn't, would I?

I feel like part of my life is over. But it's no good dwelling on it. Time to start the next instalment, I suppose.

***

'Thank goodness THAT'S done,' says Hebe, unaware that for once, her sentiment totally matches my own.

'Amelia was all right,' I say, hating to admit it. She was. She remembered all her lines; she spoke up; she never missed a cue. She totally aced it – even if she was a bit hammy.

'Nat was okay, too,' Hebe says.

'Yeah,' I agree, 'he was.' Because he was. He even stuck to the script instead of talking about football – oh, hold on a minute, that only happens in my head because, of course, there is nothing about football in *A Town Divided*. The lines are beginning to blur, the lines between what happens in the here and now and what happens in my head. It's probably shock due to the realisation that I am not the actress I always thought I was. Although, actually, I am. I mean I'm acting now, in front of Hebe, pretending everything is exactly how it was before my terrible pre-play ordeal. I just don't think I can act in front of an audience, which is quite a serious oversight.

I need to get a grip.

CHAPTER EIGHTEEN

Today is a VERY IMPORTANT DAY. Most of us at Pony Club are taking our *Grooming a Pony* achievement badge. This means we shall be tested in a practical way (grooming a pony for real), as well as answering questions about how and why we clean ponies, and grooming brushes and stuff. All the Chesterton staff and students avoid using the word *test*, but we all know that's what it is. They can call it a *badge* until they're blue in the face, but everyone else calls them tests because that is what they are.

I hope Silver won't take this the wrong way but I really hope I won't get him for the practical grooming. Silver, as you know, is almost white, so getting a pony like Pip, who is black and therefore less likely to show the dirt, would be an advantage. Also, Pip's hooves are as neat as Silver's, and although he has a long mane it all falls obligingly on the offside of his neck instead of dithering about, unable to choose a side. This means grooming Pip not only takes less effort, but he also looks neater and more finished even before anyone has approached him with a brush.

I suppose this could work against a test candidate, when I think about it – although I really ought NOT to think about it…

'Has somebody already groomed this pony?' asked Becky, frowning. 'He looks very clean.'

'Um, no, I don't think so,' replied Etta.

'Hmmm. This isn't really much of a test, is it?' said Becky, disregarding the fact that the word test was not to be uttered at any cost. 'I know! We'll get you a real challenge. You want to earn that badge, don't you? You don't want to just coast along and get something for nothing!'

'Um, don't I?' mumbled Etta, as Becky led the way to Silver's stable.

'There, that's better!' Becky cried triumphantly, flinging open the stable door and inclining her head towards Silver. 'Get stuck into that!' she added. 'Much more like it!'

Etta caught her breath as Silver stopped tugging at his hay net and turned to gaze at her, chewing rhythmically. That he had been rolling in the field was evident by the thick layer of brown mud which completely obliterated his own colour. He had also dug up his bed and rolled in his stable so that straw clung to his coat, as well as to his mane and his tail which were matted and tangled. A smear of wet manure coated one flank and he looked several centimetres taller than usual, owing to all the mud and filth in his hooves – hooves which seemed to have swollen to four times their usual size, hooves that were now the size of Poppy's hooves, the size of dinner plates – and then some.

'But I've only got ten minutes!' Etta gasped.

'Best you get started then!' snapped Becky, lifting her clipboard, her pen poised above it.

I am, as I expect you can tell, proper nervous. Also, I cannot get the fact that I am no longer actress material out of my mind. It is dragging me down. I mean, it's like I have to completely re-write my entire life. Good job I have my baking-and-writing-about-baking career to fall back on, not to mention instructing in riding – although if I fail to achieve this grooming badge even that could be in jeopardy. Too much hangs on what happens today. Talk about pressure!

When I get to Chesterton, everyone else is looking nervous, too – even Amelia.

'I'm bound to do it all wrong,' Amelia says, her mouth turned down like a horseshoe.

My nerves are too shredded to reply but Pearl and Kayleigh go into a huddle with Amelia to compare notes and ask each other questions.

Olivia doesn't look nervous at all. 'Oh I am!' she cries, when I tell her. 'I can never remember whether it's the body brush or the dandy brush that you use on a pony's face. I'm bound to get it wrong.'

'It's the soft one,' I tell her. 'The body brush.'

'See!' Olivia says accusingly, as though I'm to blame for her nerves. '*You* know. *You'll* be fine.'

Maybe I will. Maybe I just need to believe I know the answers to all the questions Becky is going to ask me. Maybe…

We get right to it, no messing about. Jade takes us all into the lecture room to talk about pony breeds (which I bet everyone is too nervous to take in) and, one by one, we are called to take our test – I mean *badge*.

Both Amelia and Pearl come back with smiles on their faces, so we all know they think they did all right. I don't know whether this is a good omen or a bad one. I mean, I don't know whether they know more than I do, or they found it easy, or they're hysterical with grief.

'Okay Etta,' says Becky, with a big, encouraging smile, 'it's your turn.'

As I follow her out to the yard I feel just as I did when I thought I was going to have to be in Ms Pertwee's play, understudying for Amelia: my hands are trembling, my heart is racing and everything I know about grooming ponies seems to have flown out of my head and buried itself in the muck heap (although that didn't actually happen before the play, of course).

Amber is waiting for me in her stable. Not Silver. Not Pip. Amber has a well-behaved mane so I feel I've dipped in. I have to go into the stable and put a head collar on Amber and tie her up. I've had quite a few goes at this since my first head collar fumblings so I get it right – quick-release knot and everything. Amber twists her head and looks at me in an obvious effort to shake me, but I give her a reassuring pat, fetch the grooming kit and take a deep breath.

Becky asks me to give her five reasons why we groom ponies, and to explain about the brushes and tools as I use them, so I do. It's almost as though I am combining my acting ability (strictly amateur status now) with my instructing potential. Amber is always very good about her hooves being picked out (she picks each one up politely, never acts as though they are stuck to the ground, and she doesn't expect me to hold her up), and I do this without getting anything wrong. I think. This gives me a bit of a confidence boost, and I even remember to stand at the side of Amber when I am grooming her tail, rather than behind her.

I think Becky looks impressed, which increases my confidence even more. I remember to untie the lead rope from the ring in the wall before I take Amber's head collar off and fasten it around her neck so I can carefully brush her face. There's a bit of a wobble when Amber puts her nose in the air to avoid her head collar going back on again, but after an undignified sort of scuffle I manage to sort it out without too much bother.

Becky writes something on her clipboard. I hope it is *ten-out-of-ten*, rather than *hopeless*. Eventually, I declare Amber to be groomed and Becky then asks me some questions about the grooming kit, which I manage to answer without too much trouble. Becky nods and smiles, and then asks me to untie Amber and lead her out onto the yard and walk and trot her up and down, to show I know how to do that, and to check that I turn her away from me rather than towards me when we turn around (to avoid Amber treading on my toes). I do this and return Amber to the stable and take off her head collar. When I come out, I even remember to slide the bottom bolt on her stable door with my foot (because I'm always forgetting and bending down to work it with my hands, which is WRONG!).

And that was that. I think I did okay. It must have been all that revising I did. I go back to the lecture room smiling with relief and give Olivia a thumbs-up, but then she is up and away because it is her turn – she is the last to go.

It's funny about tests, even when they're not supposed to be tests. Even though I think I've done all right there is still a big fat doubt lurking in my mind, like I might have got it all wrong, and that I'll be the ONLY person in the whole group to have messed up and failed. I mean, how awful would that be? To be the only one without a badge at the end of the day to say I've passed…

'Okay, gather round,' said Becky. 'Here are the results. I'm thrilled to tell you that everyone has passed…'

The whole room erupted as all the Pony Clubbers leapt up and down and hugged each other in relief and congratulation.

'Not so fast!' said Becky, holding up a hand in warning. 'I haven't finished. Everyone has passed… EXCEPT FOR ETTA!'

You could hear a pin drop as everyone stopped hugging each other and stood silently. Heads swivelled as all eyes turned to Etta. Etta felt her face turn puce. It was bad enough to have failed without having all her fellow Pony Club members staring at her, their expressions a mixture of horror and pity.

'Oh Etta,' gasped Pearl, one hand clutched to the side of her face in a sympathetic gesture of despair, 'you poor thing, how perfectly awful for you!'

'Yes, Etta,' added Amelia, 'you must feel absolutely gutted – particularly as the test wasn't really that hard, and everyone else passed it easily. I mean, you must have been totally USELESS!'

'Yes,' agreed Becky, 'she was. Who would like to see Etta's marks? They're really horrendous, and some of the answers to the questions are quite hilarious. You'll die laughing, you really will!'

'Here are the badges for you to sew onto your Pony Club sweatshirts,' said Jade, handing them out to everyone – everyone except Etta.

'Oh wonderful!' said Amelia. 'We'll all wear them to the next rally – oh, except for you of course, Etta. And you'll have to re-sit the test. How HUMILIATING for you.'

'Phew, that wasn't so bad!' says Olivia, sliding onto the seat beside me and jerking me out of my nightmare fantasy.

I feel a bit sick.

Becky arrives with her clipboard, and I feel even sicker. She's going to tell me I've failed. She's going to tell everyone else that they've passed.

She doesn't. I have passed. I am SUCCESSFUL! I get my badge – a circular badge embroidered with a brush and a hoof pick – to sew on to my sweatshirt like everyone else because everyone else has passed, too. That bit I did get right. I give my badge a long look because I can't quite believe it is mine, and that I earned it, and that I have *proof* that I know about grooming – about looking after a pony. One of my possible career choices is still on track.

After all this excitement, and when we have calmed down and had a snack (more Jaffa cakes, I don't care about the healthy-option snootiness from the other side of the table because I am too made up about passing the test – that isn't a test – and getting a badge), Becky says that as we've all worked so hard, we're going out to the field behind the outdoor school to have a go over the cross-country jumps.

At first, I think she means we'll be doing it on our own two feet, without the ponies, but she doesn't mean that. We are going to do it ON the ponies, like top-class eventers who jump around Badminton and Burghley over ENORMOUS jumps that are bigger than Mr Robinson's van which has the words *Plumb Perfect* written on the side and over the doors at the back in aqua blue, because that's what his plumbing business is called (a bit ambitious, but aim for the stars and all that, as Nana Susan might say).

I am quite nervous (I am getting a bit fed up with feeling nervous – what with Ms Pertwee's play, and the grooming badge and now this, it's exhausting), but Becky insists we won't be jumping anything big, just the tiny jumps at the side of the big ones. My nerves calm down a bit at this news, and then they calm down even more when Becky tells me I'm riding Silver!

I tack up Silver, and Jade checks I've done it right, which I have, so I mount up and try to push Silver's mane over to one side of his neck while the others adjust their stirrups and tighten their girths. Olivia is riding her favourite pony, Cracker, so we give each other the thumbs-up sign and my nerves seem to disappear altogether. I feel I can do anything because I have passed my *Grooming a Pony* achievement badge, and I am riding Silver and I know he will look after me. It might also be because he is always in my made-up life as Silverado so I feel we have come through a lot together, even though we haven't really, not in this life.

We ride out to the field. All the ponies are wearing neck straps we can hold on to if we want to, and we riders have our body protectors on (I bet no-one is feeling as crushed as I am. I know exactly how walnuts and almonds feel at Christmas just before my dad uses the nutcracker on them and makes them explode, and Mum gets out the mini-vacuum and sucks up all the bits off the carpet before they get stuck between Wolfie's toes, causing him to yelp).

I am glad to see that Becky is right and there are small jumps next to the big ones. Actually, they aren't so much small as *tiny* – a telegraph pole, a fallen log, a few bits of hedging stuck between some sticks. There is also a log to jump as we go into the woods, and Becky tells us there are some step jumps in there that we can ride up or down, depending on which direction we approach them from. I'm not moaning, you understand, I'm *glad* all the jumps are tiny.

Becky tells us we are NOT to just go as fast as we can at each jump (which I thought we did have to – they go really fast at the big events), but instead we need to keep to a controlled canter between each obstacle, slowing down on the approach before riding forward for the last three strides. If we want to, she adds, we can trot up to the jumps – they are so small – the ponies will easily be able to jump them from a trot.

I really want to canter. You don't see the eventers on the telly trotting up to a vast ditch or a couple of Land Rovers, do you?

'We'll do each jump one-by-one,' Becky says, 'and then if that goes well, we can all have a go at stringing several jumps together.'

I am pretty made up at this news. I am going to ride across country! On Silver! At this rate, I may make being an equestrian a career and go to the Olympic Games!

We all jump the telegraph pole, and I have to say I feel quite sorry for Amelia because she is riding Poppy who, as you know, isn't the most forward-going pony in the world, and Amelia has to kick like crazy to get her to canter. But she does go over the pole, even if it looks like she's doing it in slow motion. Amelia really can get her going so hats off to her I say. As I watch Olivia turn Cracker towards the jump I look down at Silver's mane (half one side of his neck, half the other again), and suddenly we're at Badminton…

'And here come Etta Marshall and Quicksilver, leading after the dressage, approaching another of these huge jumps,' announced the commentator.

Etta Marshall leant forward, whispering encouragement to her noble steed. 'Come on now Quicksilver, you can do it, I know you can.'

As the huge ditch – where so many other top riders had faltered – loomed before them a shiver of apprehension rippled through Etta. It was the biggest ditch they had ever tackled – but this was no time to doubt herself or her horse.

'We can do this!' whispered Etta, her heart beating hard. She knew her trusty steed relied on her to give him confidence, to present him at the yawning ditch at the perfect place for take-off, at the perfect speed. She couldn't – she wouldn't – let him down!

Despite her resolve, for a fraction of a second Etta felt her confidence waiver – before she heard a shout of, 'You can do it Etta!' It was the voice of her loyal and famous show-biz comedian boyfriend who hated football, and who had always supported her choice of career, sticking with her through thick and thin.

With renewed confidence Etta closed her legs around her brave horse's sides. Hearing a shout of HUP from his rider, the beautiful grey launched himself into the air. A moment later the pair galloped away from the hideous ditch that had been the downfall of so many riders before them, all fear gone. Both of them looked forward not only to the next jump, but to a glorious round in record time, and to advancing their glittering career. They were on track to international equestrian glory...

'Are you sure you want to go, Etta?' says Becky. 'You don't have to, you know.'

I look up. Everyone is looking at me. AGAIN.

'I'm sorry, what did you say?' I ask Becky.

'It's your turn, Etta, but you don't have to jump if you don't want to,' says Becky kindly.

Gathering Silver's reins I nod my head. 'Of course I do!' I cry, and Becky looks puzzled. Haven't Silver and I just tackled Badminton? A telegraph pole is going to be a doddle!

And actually, it is. I hardly notice Silver bouncing over it. When we all move on into the woods and tackle the steps (upwards, which I'm sure must be more comfortable than downwards), Silver just pops over them like they're nothing (which to him, they probably are). Once everyone has jumped every jump (poor Amelia is looking like she might need resuscitation at this point, having exhausted herself on Poppy – and I feel a sorry for her because I know what Poppy is like, and I'm grateful not to be the one riding her), we line up at the start once more. Now we're to go one at a time to tackle the five jumps we've already jumped. It will be like riding a proper cross-country course!

I daren't start imagining things or Becky might refuse to let me go on, thinking I'm scared. As Pearl sets off on Pip, Olivia asks me whether I am all right, which is embarrassing but I'm not surprised because I think my face is doing that thing it does again. Something is niggling me. There is something about my imagined Badminton success in the back of my mind, refusing to be acknowledged, and I can't think about it right now because I'm too busy and I have to concentrate!

So when Becky says it's my turn I close my legs around Silver and he bounds forward just like a real event horse so I have to grab the neck strap to stop myself getting left behind. As we tackle the jumps it feels just right, like we're flying, and that we ARE at Badminton, and this is not just a brilliant day but THE PERFECT DAY. When everyone has jumped Becky says we've all been fantastic, and we ride around the field and have a long canter before walking the ponies back to the yard.

Afterwards, when I untack Silver (I can do that now, too) and give him a cuddle he nuzzles me, and I know he has enjoyed our time together as much as I have. I just wish he were mine so we could have lots of perfect days like today.

When I get home I show Mum and Dad my badge, and they are suitably impressed. I ring Nana Susan and send her a picture of it, and she is wildly enthusiastic.

'At this rate, Etta,' she tells me, 'we'll have to get you a pony of your own!'

If only. If only that pony could be Silver. It occurs to me that I am *almost* one of those people I saw on the Pony Club website who can DO (the not very scary) THINGS! Well, a bit closer to them, anyway.

When I show Shona my badge she looks down her nose at it and says it's not exactly an Olympic medal, is it.

There are times when I wish I were an only child.

CHAPTER NINETEEN

When I ask Hebe whether she is going to continue to go to Drama Club now *A Town Divided* is dead and buried, the reply I get is less than polite. It isn't like Hebe to use language like that, which clearly demonstrates the depth of feeling that for her, Drama Club is SO OVER! So I'm thinking I'll knock it on the head, too. I mean, now my dreams of being a famous actress seem to have turned to dust and I no longer have the difficult choice between a career in theatre or in film – or even television – there doesn't seem to be much point in putting myself through the emotional turmoil of being in close proximity to Nat.

And that's another thing: I am coming to realise Nat isn't the man of my dreams – no doubt because my dreams seem to have reached that conclusion for me, what with all the football references gate-crashing his dialogue whenever he's the Black Knight, or anyone else I make him up to be. I can't have that going on. I mean, my made-up life needs to be my own. If I'm not in charge of it, and if I can't get it to do whatever I want then I might just as well stick with real life – that takes no notice of what I want either. I mean, that's THE POINT of having a made-up life!

The other plus of not going to Drama Club is that my eyesight will no longer be assaulted by Ms Pertwee's dress (non)sense. It's beginning to give me headaches. So, like I said, I think I'll knock Drama Club on the head. Give it a miss. Wave it goodbye. Send it packing. Kick it up the backside and tell it good riddance. Get thee behind me, Drama Club!

'What's big, red and eats rocks?' shouts Max Rybart as he passes me in the corridor on the way to our social science class.

'A big, red rock eater,' I tell him, sighing.

'Oh,' he says, looking crestfallen.

'You told me that one yesterday,' I say.

'Oh,' he says again. 'Never mind, this one will slay you…'

I raise my hand, palm towards him. I am in no mood for Max Rybart's jokes. I am too depressed due to my dwindling career choices, my disappointment in Nat and my inability to control my own fantasies. That is enough to be getting on with – too much, if I'm honest. Max Rybart shrugs his head like it's my loss, sends a wink in my direction and attempts to slay someone else with his joke.

There is something in my head about Max Rybart that I try to remember. Something I should know or think about or something. But I just can't retrieve what it is. It stays annoyingly out of reach – just like Nat Black.

Hebe rushes up behind me, mobile in hand. 'Hey!' she says, in one of those voices that indicates that I WILL want to know what she has to say. Like if I don't listen, I'm going to seriously MISS OUT. So I put on my *you have my full attention* face and she pulls me into a space between two rows of filing cabinets, below a poster informing pupils that the sports day will go ahead come rain or shine, so basically get over it (in not so many words). The tone of this poster suggests bad weather is forecast, and everyone has been asking how that might influence proceedings in the hope that rain might be an acceptable get-out clause. The poster provides the answer: it isn't.

'You will *never* guess what I've just heard!' Hebe says, her voice a confidential hiss, her eyes wide as saucers, her red hair framing her face like a lion's mane.

'What? What?' I say, playing along. I mean, I may not be destined for cinematic or theatrical glory but that doesn't mean I can't still put in a performance when required. I've still GOT IT, so to speak. I just can't see myself performing in front of an audience much larger than my solitary friend.

Hebe takes a deep breath and then lets it all out in one go, without spaces, like all the words are strung together: 'AMELIAISGOINGOUTWITHNAT!!!'

I catch my breath. Hebe nods frantically like her neck has been replaced by a spring, her eyes still wide. She looks a bit crazy to be honest.

Amelia. And Nat. Nat. And Amelia. I think I must be psychic. If I am, there must surely be a career opportunity there somewhere, possibly involving a colourful tent, a paisley scarf, huge hoop earrings and a crystal ball…

'Come in my dear and cross my palm with silver,' said Madam Estrano in a rasping voice. Fortune-teller to the stars, celebrated psychic and general all-round mystic, she sat in her tent at a circular table, on which rested a heavy, tapestry cloth and a crystal ball.

'Do you want to know your future?' Madam Estrano asked, the silver coins on her headscarf glinting in the gloom. 'Give me your hand, my pretty, and let us see what life has in store for you…'

Well that's never going to work, is it? I have no idea about my own future, let alone anyone else's. On the other hand, haven't I already fantasised this very scenario? Haven't I already foretold the future? It's just like…

The castle was bathed in the silvery light from a full moon as Princess Amelia rode across the drawbridge to the waiting crowd. It was with a heavy heart that Estra watched Sir Nathan, the Black Knight, turn and catch his breath at the first glimpse of his bride. The ruby and silver coronet emitted a shimmering light, matched only by the sheen on Princess Amelia's flaxen hair. As one the congregation sighed at the sight of so beautiful a bride.

Gently helping Princess Amelia from her palomino's bejewelled side saddle, the Black Knight led his betrothed to the ancient altar where the wise old elder stood, staff in hand, his silver beard almost to his waist. With the sacred golden cord of Azbathria he bound the right wrists of the couple lightly together before turning to face the crowd.

'Does anyone here present know any reason why the joining of these two young people – the Princess Amelia and Sir Nathan, the Black Knight – should not take place? If so, make your utterances now or forever hold your tongue for this is a sacred union and must be pure.'

How Estra longed to speak, to confess her love for the Black Knight, of her desire to take the place of Princess Amelia. Catching sight of Maximus the Jester she thought she saw a strange look cross his face, so unlike his usual expression of mirth and merriment. Could Maximus be fighting his own demons? Could he, too, be struggling to come to terms with this marriage for reasons unknown to her? Or was there another, very different reason why the jester's gaze held her own?

The moment passed and Estra remained silent. For even she could see that destiny could not be denied, that she had no right to interject, no possible claim on Sir Nathan. She had thought he could be hers but now, seeing with her own eyes the love between the couple, the inevitability of their joining, Estra knew that her cause – as well as the Black Knight – was lost to her. And then, with a certainty she had never felt before, Estra knew that the Black Knight had never been hers, just as she had never really been his…

'Did you hear what I said?' asked Hebe.

Of COURSE Amelia is going out with Nat. I mean, isn't that just so predictable – Amelia with her perfect hair, and Nat with his dark and smouldering good looks? Weren't they always destined to get together, just like Julia and Ricky from-the-wrong-side-of-town? What's that thing people say? It is a case of *life imitating art*. That's what's happening. Come to think of it, I watched it happen when they were sitting below the stage as I was rehearsing Julia's part. The two of them weren't talking, they were FLIRTING!

'You all right?' asks Hebe, looking anxious…

Etta emitted a deep, heart-rendering sob and sank to her knees. The love of her life had abandoned her, left her for another. He had been bewitched by the beautiful and popular Amelia Armitage.

'Someone fetch a doctor,' cried Hebe, who could see the distress in her friend's eyes. Hebe knew Etta's love for Nat was more than just a crush, and she feared the shock would be too much for her to endure.

Etta clutched at her chest. She felt as though Amelia Armitage had plunged a knife into her breast, and she could feel her heart shattering into a thousand tiny fragments, broken beyond repair. She would never recover. She would never love again…

I wait to feel the searing pain in my chest, for my heart to signify it has been shattered into a thousand pieces – only I don't feel anything, really. I know by the look on Hebe's face that she is waiting for me to do something spectacular like scream and shout and throw myself on the floor and beat it with my fists in a broken-hearted, total loser sort of way but actually I just stand there, with my odd-ball thinking face on, giving this revelation considerable thought.

Because I have fancied Nat, like, forever. Or have I just fancied the Black Knight with whom, in my head, I've shared countless adventures? Because after hearing Hebe's news something weird seems to be happening – namely nothing. I DON'T CARE. Nat was a habit and it seems I'm cured – it's official.

'Oh, okay,' I say, realising my voice sounds a bit bored. Because I suppose I am bored – with Nat. Or rather, I'm bored with *fancying* Nat. I'm bored with always imagining scenarios where we're together. It suddenly seems so exhausting and pointless, especially now.

'Is that all you have to say?' asks Hebe. She looks a bit disappointed – maybe she was *hoping* I would throw myself on the floor and beat it with my fists. I mean it would liven up the day a bit and give everyone something to talk about but to be honest I wouldn't throw myself on this floor. I mean, you don't know half of what everyone's shoes have left on it.

'Yes,' I tell Hebe with a resigned sigh. 'Amelia can have him – and his football fixation. I'm over Nat Black.'

And I am. Totally. Strange how that has happened – just like that. *Finito!* (That's your actual Italian for *the end*. At least I think it is. It sounds like it, anyway.) It's like I've been waiting for a switch to go off in my brain (and I wouldn't put it past devil hamster to have done it), activated by the news that Nat Black never has been, and never will be, mine. It's not surprising. I mean a dream is just that. It's not real life.

'Oh!' says Hebe. And then she says, somewhat briskly and matter-of-factly, 'Well, that's good. No worries, then.'

'That's right,' I tell her, as we extract ourselves from between the filing cabinets and head off towards our social science class.

'Is it the football thing?' Hebe asks me with a sideways glance. I think she's really disappointed about me not throwing myself on the floor and having hysterics.

I nod, even though I know it isn't *totally* the football thing.

'Yeah,' she says, 'I understand, babe. I mean there's always a deal-breaker. If it wasn't football it would be something else.'

'Like what?' I ask.

'Um, dunno really – but there's always something,' she assures me.

I nod again. Quite honestly, I can tell Hebe it's the football thing but really, with my hair and everything else considered, there was no way me and Nat were ever going to hook up. Not in real life. Nat has Amelia stamped all over him. He would never look at me because Nat Black is *waaaaaay* out of my league. I have finally come to acknowledge that.

'Of course,' Hebe begins in a different, rather careful voice that tells me she is about to say something I might take offence to, 'you do go on a bit about Silver, which might have been *his* deal-breaker if you had got together.'

I don't know what to say about this. On the one hand I can't believe anyone would think Silver might be a deal-breaker. On the other hand, I can imagine that Nat

Black thinks the same about football. So I (reluctantly) acknowledge that it might cut both ways. In any case, it isn't something I need to worry about because we are never going to get together, so neither of us will have the opportunity to bore the other with talk of horses or football, but I can appreciate what Hebe is saying.

I'm still a bit miffed about it, though. I mean, Silver is *way* better than football.

I wonder whether Nat will still crop up in my made-up life now the reality of him has been erased from my real life. You couldn't say the Black Knight was out of Estra's league (Estra has great hair), not until Princess Amelia showed up, anyway – and I think she only made an appearance because, deep down, subconsciously (with devil hamster's input), I knew she and Nat were destined to be together – like Julia and Ricky from-the-wrong-side-of-town. The real trouble is that I am NOT Estra. I am Etta – Etta with the funny hair and the ever-shifting career plans. Worse luck.

In the meantime I have another problem, which that poster has reminded me: sports day – and how to get out of running the 400 metres at same.

'I have to get out of running the 400 metres,' I tell Hebe. 'Any ideas how?' But we've arrived at our social science class, and she hasn't time to answer.

Mr Cromer takes social science. Mr Cromer has this annoying habit of preceding every other sentence with a long, drawn-out, *urrrmmmmmm*. After our last lesson, Max Rybart told us that Mr Cromer had uttered no fewer than fifty-seven *urrrmmmmmms* throughout the first fifteen minutes of our lesson. He lost count after that. Well, you would, wouldn't you – I mean, for a start you'd need more than five pairs of hands.

Several hundred *urrrmmmmmms* later (possibly an exaggeration, but not by much), Hebe and I are on our way to lunch.

'The way I see it,' says Hebe, as we join the queue for the salad bar, 'you need to have sustained some sort of injury to get out of it.'

'Out of what?' I ask, my mind on the choice between rice or potato salad.

'The 400 metres,' says Hebe.

'Oh, yeah,' I say, remembering that I'd asked her. But I'd already thought that. It's pretty obvious – but not so easy to think of how.

'Watcha ladies!' cries Max Rybart, on his way to the fish-n-chip queue. 'What's brown and sticky?'

'I dread to think,' says Hebe, rolling her eyes.

'Okay,' I sigh, taking the bait, 'what *is* brown and sticky?'

'A stick!' cries Max Rybart with a wink, and he takes himself off, chuckling to himself.

'Or be off stick, I mean *sick*,' suggests Hebe.

'My mum will see right through that,' I tell her.

A gloom descends upon me. I might be okay with Nat going out with Amelia but I can't help thinking it will impinge on my made-up life. I liked my made-up life as it was, before Princess Amelia showed up without so much as a by-your-leave, with her perfect hair topped by her ruby and silver coronet, and fancy side-saddle-bedecked palomino. The whole point of Azbathria is that the hero (Nat – up until now) is there for ME. He's MY hero, not Amelia's. Actually, if Azbathria is going to be full of Amelia and Nat, not to mention the jester, Maximus, I'll be quite happy not to have any more fantasies about it – EVER! I mean, it's getting quite crowded in there and it's tricky keeping control over everyone – which may explain why everyone keeps getting away from me and doing their own thing.

'You all right?' asks Hebe.

'Oh, you know,' I say. 'Life's just a bit rubbish at the moment!'

'Tell me about it,' she says, rolling her eyes.

CHAPTER TWENTY

When I get back home from school, Mum and Shona are curled up on the sofa, watching TV.

'What's on?' I ask, flopping down onto a chair. Wolfie leaps up onto my lap and lets me know how much he has missed me – which is more than I get from my kith and kin, who can't even drag their eyes from the screen to say hi.

'Shhhh,' says Shona, between bites of a ginger nut. 'It's almost finished.'

'It's one of Shona's old films,' whispers Mum.

'What's it about?' I ask, simply because I know it will annoy Shona.

'Do shut up!' says Shona.

See? I told you.

'Shona!' scolds Mum. 'It's quite complicated – that woman there is a doppelgänger.'

'A what?'

'Someone who looks exactly like somebody else, stupid!' says Shona.

'Shona, please don't talk to your sister like that,' says Mum. We both know she will.

'Except she really *is* the person she looks like,' Mum adds.

'So she's not a doppel... what you said?' I ask.

'That's right,' says Mum.

'Shhhhh!' says Shona.

The doppelthingy – or not – woman and some bloke are walking up some stairs inside an old tower – actually, he's flipping out a bit and is dragging her up the steps. It's well odd and the music is going a bit bonkers.

'Oh dear!' cries Mum as the woman, who may or may not be a doppelthingy, falls out the window and plummets to her death.

The credits roll.

'Looks like a cheerful tale,' I observe.

'You can't judge, you only saw the last two minutes!' hisses Shona. 'It's a *very* famous, *much* rated film, *actually*.'

'Shall I feed the hens?' I ask, wanting to stay busy to keep my mind off the Nat and Amelia thing and the 400 metres, and hopefully stop myself drifting off into another disappointing Azbathria instalment.

'Oh, would you?' says Mum. 'That would be a great help, thanks love.'

Mrs Brown comes scurrying over when I go to the feed bin where the chicken meal is kept, with Miss Piggy right behind her. At least I think it's Miss Piggy, and I'm fairly certain that's Mrs Brown. The hens are all doppelthingys, they all look alike. Anyway, the others come over, too, in that way hens run that looks like they're holding up their skirts so they can go faster, and they gobble up all the meal I put out for them. Seeing them all together they look like one of those *spot the difference* puzzles. If they were I'd be hard-pressed to find a single difference, especially as they don't stay still long enough for me to really get stuck into the identity parade.

There are two eggs in the shed, so I pick them up and take them into the house – after thanking the hens (it's only polite) – and, in another ploy to keep my mind active, get out one of Mum's cookbooks and locate the chapter on cakes.

'All-in-one sponge cake method,' I read out, passing up the more complicated cakes and bakes on other pages. Looking through the recipe it seems quite simple – I just have to bung all the ingredients in a bowl and mix thoroughly. Which I do – after I've located the scales and the flour, the butter and vanilla flavouring – which is brown, and looks like cough syrup.

With the ingredients all mixed up I can't find a cake tin, so I go back into the sitting room and ask Mum.

'What do you want a cake tin for?' she asks.

'I'm making a cake,' I tell her. I would have thought she might have guessed this by my request, but it seems not.

Shona snorts. 'A cake? You?'

'What do you mean, you're making a cake?' asks Mum.

I wonder whether I'm talking in a foreign language, which would be cool as my French isn't that good…

'A caaaaake,' repeated Etta, slowly.

'No, sorry, I still don't get what you're saying,' said her mum, shaking her head. 'You're just jabbering away in gobbledegook. Can you understand it, Shona?'

'No,' said Shona. 'But I never can. Etta's always spouting rubbish, and all I can ever make out is blah, blah, blah. It's all nonsense.'

'I'm not even sure that really is Etta,' said her mum, frowning. 'I mean, she looks like Etta, but she doesn't sound like her.'

'Maybe she's a doppelgänger!' exclaimed Shona.

'A CAKE, for goodness' sake!' Etta shouted in exasperation. Why couldn't her family understand what she was saying? She was speaking in perfect English!

'It's no use shouting,' said her mum. 'That doesn't help. Now, from the top, take it slowly and speak distinctly, whoever you are. What exactly are you trying to say?'

'I thought I'd give cake-making a bit of a go,' I tell her.

'I hope you haven't used all the butter,' Mum says. This is not how I expected the news of me becoming a master baker to be received. I expected some words of encouragement, words of admiration, words of expectant deliciousness. Instead, I am getting an inquisition of epic proportions which I feel is undeserved.

I repeat my request for a cake tin and, following Mum's directions, discover one in the cupboard where all the cookbooks are kept, which I failed to notice earlier.

When the cake mixture is in the tin I realise I was supposed to do something called pre-heat the oven, so it can warm up. Honestly, this cake-making lark is a right carry on – with a great many parts to it to think about. I turn on the oven and bung in the cake tin. The cake will have to take its chance.

I have done it. I have made a cake – dah-*daaaah!* If this works out, my Plan C could be a winner.

There seems to be rather a lot of stuff that now needs washing up – a bowl, spoons, a knife, scales – not to mention the worktop which seems to have more flour on it than I put in the cake. I load most of it into the dishwasher and wipe down the worktop, thinking there is much more work involved in baking than the television programmes would have us believe.

I realise I have forgotten to notice what time I put the cake in the oven. It is supposed to cook for about thirty-five to forty minutes, but I have no idea how long it has already been in. Peering through the glass door, I deduce the oven needs a scrub as all I can see is a lot of brown, baked-on goo on the door, and very little of the cake within.

'How's it going?' asks Mum, coming into the kitchen.

'Er, good,' I tell her.

'How long has it got to go?'

'Um, well, probably about ten minutes,' I guess.

Mum peers into the oven. 'It looks done to me,' she says, opening the door.

The cake sits in the oven, all puffed up and cake-like, brown in the middle and ever-so slightly burnt around its perimeter. It looks, I hardly dare say, rather good. At least it looks like a cake.

'Turn it out, then,' says Mum, whipping out a wire cooling rack from nowhere like a magician. Except I can't. It won't come out. The cake is stuck inside the tin.

'What did you grease the tin with?' asks Mum.

'What did I what the what with?' I ask. Now Mum's the one who is speaking in a different language.

'Oh,' says Mum. Then she says, over-brightly, 'Well, we'll leave it in the tin for now and turn it out later.'

We do not turn it out later. We cannot. It refuses to budge. When I said the cake was stuck in the tin I wasn't joking. We get around this by digging bits of cake out with spoons and eating it. It tastes good, but it isn't really how a cake should be eaten – a fact not lost on Shona who sneers a lot, but not enough to prevent her from eating a considerable amount of it, I notice. When the dip in the middle where we've scooped out bits is quite big Mum tips in a pile of strawberries, tops the lot with a few squirts of cream out of a can, and names the cake *Etta's pudding*.

That, as Nana Susan would say, is how to turn a potential disaster into a success. I think I may have a career in cake making after all – providing I polish up my act regarding timings… and cake tin prep.

A bit too full of cake, strawberries and cream, I go to my room and lie on the bed. Wolfie shoves the door open with his nose and it hits the wall with a loud bang, so I get up and close it, and then cuddle up with Wolfie. I need some time to think. I started thinking while I was making the cake and a few ideas popped into my head that I wanted to pursue. So I do that now. They are thoughts about Nat

Black and the Black Knight and my made-up life. I pursue these thoughts for a while until my head hurts.

After about half-an-hour Mum calls up to say the TV programme I like is on, so I stop pursuing my thoughts and go downstairs with Wolfie to watch it.

I think I may just have sorted out those few things in my head.

CHAPTER TWENTY-ONE

I am on the school sports field, in my PE kit, which means I have NOT thought of a way to get out of running the 400 metres. It isn't raining but it is overcast, and the sky looks all angry like it hasn't let us off the hook yet and is probably waiting until I line up before tipping a load of rain down onto us. Lots of parents have turned up to watch – including mine. Oh, and Nat's. Although I am over him (no, really, I totally am), I'm having trouble NOT taking an interest in what he does as doing so appears to have become a habit. It is very annoying – particularly when I can see Amelia talking with Nat's parents and they, of course, look pretty made up with his new girlfriend. Well, they would, wouldn't they?

Hebe is competing in the long jump. She's good at it, so she has no worries like I have. She isn't going to be humiliated. She isn't totally happy about it, though. I spot this as she completes her second attempt.

'Eeuk,' she says, brushing sand from her backside, 'I totally hate getting sand in my underwear – and my trainers. It's worse than going to the beach. When I've had a shower there's always a sorry little heap of wet sand left at the bottom of the cubicle, like I've been panning for gold.'

'You're in the lead,' I tell her.

'Yeah, I know,' she says, like I've told her the sky is blue – or rather grey.

'I'm rubbish at sports,' I tell her.

Hebe looks at me like I'm a bit dim. 'You do know I go to after-school athletics practice twice a week, don't you?' she asks me.

I just look back at her. I think she is trying to make a point but I'm not sure what it is.

'Maybe that's why I'm good at it,' she says.

That was obviously the point she was trying to make. I stare into the distance and think about it.

After what seems like a hundred more jumps (but is probably only about ten) Hebe is relegated to second place by a tall, leggy girl with the totally glamorous name of Olympia O'Brien, who has very long, bright pink hair in a plait that swings about like a pony's tail when she runs. She's only been at our school for two weeks and she wins with her last jump.

Bit cheeky, I think.

Hebe just shrugs her shoulders. I wonder whether Estra ought to be re-named Olympia. I know for definite that Etta would benefit from being renamed Olympia. Who wouldn't?

'Thank goodness that's over, now I can go and get all this sand off me,' Hebe says, wandering off to do just that, destined to leave the shower like she's some old gold prospector with a bashed-up hat, a shovel and a donkey.

Max Rybart comes thundering up, skidding to a halt in order to tell me he has just come third in the 100-metre sprint.

'Congratulations,' I say, because that is what you are supposed to say to people when they come third in something.

'What are you doing?' he asks.

'Nothing,' I tell him.

'Why are you in your kit, then?' he asks.

'I'm entered for the 400 metres,' I say.

'But you just said you weren't doing anything,' Max Rybart says.

'I meant now,' I say. 'I'm not doing anything NOW.'

'I can see that,' he says.

This conversation is going nowhere.

'I was thinking...' says Max Rybart, staring at something in the far distance. 'I mean, I was wondering...'

'What?' I ask.

'Do you ice skate?'

'Not especially,' I tell him because I never have, but saying a blunt *no* makes me sound like a loser.

'Want to?'

'What? Ice skate?'

'Yeah. Some of us are going ice skating next week. Fancy coming?'

I think about it. Ice skating. Could I ice skate? Could I be an ice skater? Could I do those jumps and spins and wear a sparkly dress and white boots? Yes, I think I could totally be an ice skater. Why not?

'Who else is going?' I ask. I have learnt to ask this question before committing to anything because if you don't, and the people going are none of your friends, or people you don't get on with so well, you won't have a good time and you'll wish you had said, *no, but thank you very much for asking.*

'Oh, er, Nat and Amelia and, um, maybe a few other people,' Max says a bit too casually.

I have a strange feeling about going ice skating with Max Rybart. I suddenly have a strange recollection about something in my made-up life, too.

'Um… can I let you know?' I say, playing for time and not wanting to say, *no, but thank you very much for asking*, because it sounds quite abrupt. Maybe if I play for time Max Rybart might take the hint and forget about ice skating. At least with me.

'Oh yeah, of course,' says Max Rybart, airily. 'Good luck in the 400 metres,' he adds, and then dashes off to talk to someone else.

I don't want to go ice skating with Max Rybart. I particularly don't want to go ice skating with Nat and Amelia. NO WAY do I want to go ice skating with them. I mean, it would be like being back in Azbathria…

The feast to celebrate the wedding of Princess Amelia and Sir Nathan, the Black Knight, progressed long into the night with the citizens of Azbathria enjoying dancing and merriment, as well as entertainment in the form of jugglers, dancers and musicians and, of course, the magic of the jester Maximus.

It was with a heavy heart that Estra watched the couple mount their horses (the impatient and snorting ebony-black stallion, and the golden palomino with the snow-white mane and tail) and ride off into the sunset, leaving their subjects to continue their celebrations long into the night. Suddenly, Estra knew she had no place in this part of Azbathria – she had, instead, a longing for home. Running to the stables she saddled Silverado and called to Wolf, riding out of the safety of the castle grounds to head home to her tribe far away.

But darkness was already closing in, and both Silverado and Wolf grew restless, anxious about being so far from familiar lands and wary of the sounds of the night – for who knew what dangers lurked within the forest, what evil forces were at work now night had fallen?

Bravely the trio ventured forth, striding out for home, the strength of their anxiety matched only by their yearning to see familiar places and much-missed faces. Suddenly Estra heard a low growl from Wolf and saw him glance behind them, his tail down, his ears pricked for any sound.

'What is it, Wolf?' the girl whispered, sensing his unease, and feeling her faithful steed, Silverado, tremble beneath her.

A shadowy figure emerged from the trees. Cromos, brother of the sly Tarituss, feared throughout the land as the most evil Heratos of all. Even if she had been unable to see him in the darkness Estra would have known instantly who it was by the very first utterance from his wicked and twisted mouth.

'Urrrmmmmmm Lady Estra,' growled Cromos, his eyes the colour of dirty pond water, his teeth irregular and pointed. 'Urrrmmmmmm what a prize you will make, my pretty, when I take you back as my prisoner – a prize for my brother Tarituss – indeed for the whole tribe. You shall make a fine sacrifice. Urrrmmmmmm surrender now or it will be the worst for you!'

'Never!' cried Estra, bored by the length of time it took Cromos to get to the point, what with all the urrrmmmmmm-ing she'd been forced to listen to. Tossing back her jet-black, shining locks, she drew her sword from the scabbard on Silverado's saddle. Beside her Wolf crouched down, eager to pounce upon their evil foe. Estra's gaze never faltered as she faced the ugly Cromos, determined to fight, confident in her ability with the sword, and in the loyalty of her companions beneath and beside her.

'Wait!' cried a voice. 'You are mine to kill, Cromos, with your wicked ways, your dire thoughts and your boring urrrmmmmmms. Prepare to die, you foul creature!'

Estra turned, expecting to see Sir Nathan, the Black Knight, but in his place stood another knight wearing armour of the purest copper, astride a fiery chestnut with a wide white blaze, a flaxen mane and hypnotic tail. Brandishing his sword, the knight spurred his horse towards Cromos who – coward that he was, and with an anguished cry of 'Urrrmmmmmm-ahhhhh' – turned tail and fled into the darkness.

'Who are you, My Lord? Reveal yourself!' demanded Estra, her sword ready to swing from one enemy to another.

'I am but a humble knight, My Lady,' replied her saviour, removing his helmet to reveal a face Estra knew. To

her astonishment she found herself gazing upon the jester, Maximus.

'But, but...' she stammered, '... I don't understand!'

'Forgive the deception, My Lady, for I am really Sir Maximilian D'Bart, from the land of Comedious. We, too, are at war with the Heratos, for they are a foul race. Allow me to escort you to your far-away lands, and act as your protector and guide.'

Estra gazed upon the not unattractive face of Sir Maximilian D'Bart. Many things were becoming clear to her – maybe for the first time – and she drew breath to speak.

'Thank you kind Sir, for the honour you bestow upon me,' she began, 'but I need neither protector nor guide. My friends and protectors are those you see here – the faithful Silverado and loyal Wolf. I need no hero save the one I see in myself. I must fight the hateful Herotos alone – something I've been unable to do until now since every time one of them appears, a noble knight of some description turns up and muscles in on the action, relegating me to a bit part, an also-ran, a feeble being who needs to be rescued. In future I shall save myself for I am more than a match for the hateful Heratos. Was it not I who did slay the Giant Chicken of Azbathria? I thank you for the offer, I thank you for your gracious assistance, but I really must now ask you to butt-out and let me see how well I might cope on my own!'

'Well,' exclaimed Sir Maximilian D'Bart, a little taken aback. 'I must say you have put your case most forcibly and leave little room for argument. By your leave I shall now withdraw. I beg your pardon at my untimely and unwelcome intrusion, and bid you good evening, Lady Estra. May I

wish you good fortune in your quest, and safe journey to your homelands.'

'Phew,' said Estra to Silverado and Wolf. 'Maybe now we can get on with our lives without knights popping up all over the place and saving us!'

That's weird, I think. But Azbathria has sorted out the strange feeling I had about Max Rybart in my made-up life because I now realise that he possessed more than a passing resemblance to my show-biz boyfriend who supported me when I was riding Quicksilver across country.

I know – freaky!

I am certain I don't want to replace Nat Black with Max Rybart. I really don't. It's too exhausting having ANYONE as a habit. And after some more thought I realise I don't fancy Max Rybart. He's just filling a vacuum left by Nat Black, and I don't think that's a good idea.

And then I get another feeling, but this is a good one: I feel as though I've been set free somehow. Like being Estra in Azbathria has sorted me out – like my made-up life has got my real life back on track. I have a strange feeling that I may not even go back to Azbathria. No, that's not right. If and when I do go back to Azbathria I won't keep being rescued. I'll rescue myself, thank you very much – because I can do anything in a made-up life. That's the point.

As I line up for the 400 metres with all the other competitors all doing that thing with their legs they've seen Olympic athletes do, you know, stretching and pulling them up behind them one at a time (obviously, they couldn't pull both legs up at the same time, they'd fall over), I wonder whether I might have sold myself a bit short. I wonder whether, with my new persona in Azbathria – you know, saving myself and being my own heroine – that maybe in my real life I could actually run my socks off and pull off an amazing victory...

'... and Etta Marshall is coming up on the outside track now, passing the back markers. I don't believe it! She's passing all the other competitors in a blistering finish! My-oh-my, how does she go so fast? Her legs are all a-blur! She's storming ahead. And she's done it! Etta Marshall has crossed the line in first place, miles ahead of everyone else! It's a new school record! What a talent!

'The amazing Etta Marshall will no doubt be picked for the next Olympic Games and will probably be voted School Sports Personality of the Year, as well as being awarded an OBE. I shouldn't be surprised if she's invited to be the schoolgirl face of track-and-field, an inspiration to up-and-coming athletes world-wide! She's a super athlete!'

'Good Luck Etta!' cries a voice I know. It's Amelia Armitage, waving from the sidelines, having apparently been surgically removed from Nat Black's side.

Now I know she didn't do it on purpose, and I fully accept that it is my responsibility, but when the whistle goes for us all to start I am half-turned towards Amelia and giving her a wave back, so all the other runners are a good ten metres ahead of me by the time I get myself facing the right way and my legs in gear.

I won't bore you with the details. You'll have guessed by now that I didn't storm ahead of the other competitors, I didn't cross the line in first place. Sports day took place in my real life, not my made-up one so I doubt I shall ever trouble the selectors for the Olympic squad (not for running, anyway). *Last* is not a placing. Last by fifty metres is even less of a placing. If my name was Olympia and I had great hair I may have stood a chance, but Etta with the weird hair was doomed from the start. Maybe I still need my made-up life after all. Or, maybe – and I think this is the point Hebe was trying to get across – I should have put in a bit more preparation for the event instead of just hoping I'd be able to wriggle my way out of competing at all.

By the time I stagger across the finish line the 400 metres is old news, and everyone has lost interest and drifted off to watch the high jump. I'm not kidding myself that the result might have been different if I'd had a good start, but I might not have been so far behind. It takes so long for me to get my breath back I think I may be dying.

'I take it you broke no records,' says Hebe, appearing from the changing rooms in her school uniform and sucking on a cough candy twist, her self-worth intact and unquestioned by her second place in the long jump.

I nod. I am still puffing and cannot tell her that the only record I broke was the one for taking the longest time EVER to complete the 400 metres. If this is running I think I'll stick to riding Silver, let him do all the work. It's so much easier using my legs against his sides than pounding around a track on them, prep or no prep. As I bend over and suck in air I wonder whether I've got asthma. Between puffs I suggest this to Hebe, having decided not to return to the subject of my lack of training, even though the thought is still parked up in my mind.

'Doubt it, babe,' she says, between sucks on the cough candy. I can smell it even with my head down between my knees. Eventually she is proved right and my breathing returns to normal. So does my face – though it is a bit red, according to Hebe.

'It's even redder than when you catch sight of Nat Black,' she says, unhelpfully.

'I've told you I'm over him,' I say, as we collapse under a tree at the far side of the sports field.

'Oh yeah, I forgot,' says Hebe, seeing how far she can poke the cough candy out of her mouth with her tongue without losing control over it.

'I'll laugh if a fly lands on that just as you suck it back into your mouth again,' I tell her.

'Some friend you are... oh no!' cries Hebe, as she misjudges it and the cough candy is propelled out of her mouth like a torpedo to land on the grass. For a second I can tell she is considering picking it up and brushing it off, but you know how sticky a sucked cough candy can be, and she decides against it.

Despite our rather inspired hiding place my mum and dad manage to track us down, and I sit through five squirming minutes of them telling me how it's not the winning but the taking part that counts (really?), and how proud they are that I competed (pull the other one). I decide neither of these platitudes would ever crop up in Azbathria, when and if I return...

'Oh Sir Oliver, I know you were well and truly thrashed by Sir Nathan in the joust,' said Princess Amelia, snottily, 'but you must be very proud of yourself for having the courage to even bother to turn up. I mean, all the winning knights need a target, and we are always short of volunteers due to the rate vanquished knights are felled, not to mention the terrible injuries inflicted upon them. Someone has to lose – and today was your day to do just that.

'Now be a good chap and run along. Nobody wants to hang out with the Off-white Knight who's just been shown up as a total loser in front of everyone. You'll just be a laughing stock. Besides, you're making a terrible mess, what with that fatal wound of yours bleeding all over the grass...'

I knew that Princess Amelia harboured a nasty streak!

CHAPTER TWENTY-TWO

Something happened at Pony Club today and I'm not sure whether it was a good thing or a bad thing. It has the potential to be a BRILLIANT thing, but I have a feeling it may just turn out to be a rubbish thing.

We'd all had a lecture on how to care for ponies who live out in fields, and then a riding lesson (Pearl is on holiday so we didn't have to suffer her bossiness). I was glad I was down to ride Silver as I wanted to run a few ideas past him, and grooming him before the lesson gave me the ideal opportunity. I didn't expect him to come up with any answers – I'm not that stupid – but I just wanted to get my ideas off my chest and into some sort of order, and Silver is a good listener.

Because the thing is, as I told Silver as I brushed his mane, it's all very well having a made-up life where I'm different to how I see myself in my real life, but I've come to the conclusion that it's probably better to make my *real* life as good as my made-up one. No, not as good – BETTER! I mean, having dreams is all right but most of the time dreams just don't come true, no matter how hard you dream them, and no matter how much other people say you should follow them. Try transplanting my dreams in Azbathria to my real life!

And sometimes dreams come up with all the wrong ideas – I mean, I'm imagining I'm always being rescued when I ought to be rescuing myself. I need to address this (and I have already started, I mean, I told Sir Maximus to get lost). Judging by the way Silver looked at me I think he agreed. Take that time with the dragon: I totally had that in the bag, what with my improvised tree branch weapon and everything. But instead of dealing with the problem myself Sir Nathan popped up to steal my thunder. It should have had a very different outcome...

'Stop where you are, foul beast of the devil!' commanded a voice, and both damsel and dragon turned to see a handsome knight on his ebony steed, a steel-tipped lance in his hand.

'Sir Nathan, the Black Knight...' gasped Lady Estra, sweeping her tumbling locks from her face with one hand, the other resting on her hip as she tapped her toe impatiently at this turn of events, '...and his impressive, yet slightly anxious horse! What on earth are you doing here, sticking your oar in?'

'Er, well...I...um...' Sir Nathan frowned, his face showing confusion. Usually, his arrival was met with relief and gratitude, not impatience and a frosty glare.

'Can't you see I've got this?' snapped Lady Estra, tilting her chin skyward.

'What, with that piece of firewood in your hand?' asked Sir Nathan, raising his eyebrows and ignoring his horse's snorting and head shaking.

(Hmmm. Actually, that is a point...)

'Silverado, come quickly!' cried Lady Estra, hurling the branch away. As her faithful steed galloped to her side she grasped instead the quiver of arrows and bow hanging from his saddle. *'Now I'm fully armed and ready to tackle the foul beast!'* she cried.

'Do you actually know how to use those things?' asked the Black Knight, earning himself a withering look from the damsel. *'You don't want to do yourself a mischief.'*

'You need have no worries on that score!' cried Lady Estra, her eyes flashing with indignation.

'What's that tapping sound?' asked the Black Knight.

Turning around, they both observed the dragon leaning against a tree, drumming its talons against the trunk in the manner of one bored and kept waiting. 'When the two of you have finished your little tête-à-tête*,' it drawled sarcastically, 'and have decided which one of you is up for a bit of fire-fighting, maybe we can get on? It's way past my lunch time and I could, quite literally, murder a nice toasty snack.'

'That's me!' cried Lady Estra. 'Only to be clear I'm up for the fire-fighting thing, I'm not volunteering to be a snack.'

'We'll see about that!' snarled the dragon, licking its lips.

'Okay hot stuff, put 'em up!' cried Estra, fitting an arrow to her bow. 'Impressive use of French, by the way,' she added in appreciation, being quite cosmopolitan herself.

'Evening classes,' explained the dragon with a shrug. 'Just because I'm a dragon, it doesn't mean I shouldn't strive to improve myself.'

'Excuse me,' interrupted the Black Knight, 'but what exactly am I supposed to do while you two are doing your thing?'

'Can you speak French?' asked Estra. 'Pardon! I mean parlez-vous Français?'

'Is that relevant?' asked the Black Knight, more confused than ever, and wondering whether he'd made the right career choice. Damsels these days didn't seem to appreciate being rescued at all. They seemed more interested in his horse.

'Oh go and rescue someone else – Amelia for instance,' Estra shouted over her shoulder as she drew back her bow and took aim at the dragon. 'Can't you see I've got my hands full here?'

(*Tête-à-tête, in case you were wondering, is your actual French for having a bit of a chat. You're welcome – feel free to drop it into the odd conversation to prove how cosmopolitan *you* are.)

Yes, that revised dragon scenario is much more how it should have been. I shouldn't need anyone fighting my battles for me – I bet Silver doesn't. I need to save myself rather than wait around for some knight to do it. It doesn't really matter whether I *can* or not, the point is that I *try*. It's about making an effort. It's *my* made-up life so I can make it up how I like. And how I like in future is about me being in charge of me and my destiny, no-one else. I can't help thinking that waiting around for someone to rescue me smacks of having the very *wrong attitude*. That's no way to get on in life.

Look at Nana Susan. She doesn't let her gentlemen callers run her life for her. As soon as they get a bit above themselves and try to take over they're out on their ear. Old news. Gone. That seems totally the *right attitude* to me. I expect it might be different if they weren't so keen to boss her about, if they didn't want to run things. I wouldn't mind a knight who fought *with* me, a knight who wanted to form a partnership instead of swooping in and taking all the credit. That would be nice – but so far they don't seem able to help themselves, they just have to take over and run the whole show. That's not having the *right attitude*, that's just ill mannered.

And what about when I'm not in Azbathria? I mean it's all very well but what if there *isn't* a handy knight around every corner to rescue me? I haven't noticed a stack of them falling over themselves to help me in real life. No gallant hero swept in to rescue me from the 400 metres, or made sure Amelia didn't get to play the lead in *A Town Divided*, or even fixes things so I always ride Silver, never Poppy. Even if they had, or did, how will I learn to cope if someone else muscles in every time the going gets a bit tough? Granted, in Azbathria I might have been burnt to a crisp and eaten by a dragon, but how will I know whether I can deal with a crisis if I just stand aside and let somebody else take charge? It isn't on, it really isn't.

Just dreaming about things won't make them happen – it just wastes time, which is what I explained to Silver. I'm wasting time in my made-up life, I said, as I struggled to get his tail to behave itself, when I could be doing something to make my real life happen. I'm wasting my *real* life. Imagining how things could be isn't the same as putting in some effort. I mean, the reason Hebe's good at long jump is because she *practises*. For real.

I stopped then, and Silver chewed his hay thoughtfully and I could tell he was giving my words some consideration. I had a feeling he wanted to tell me that sometimes my made-up life needs not merely tweaking but rubbing out and starting again. Because dreams are dreams, and real life is real life.

Take my hair: it's never going to be like Estra's. My hair is like Silver's tail. It's my USP and I need to learn to live with it. Silver doesn't worry about the state of his tail; he's very chilled about it.

So with my thoughts rearranged I saddled Silver (perfectly, according to Becky, yay!) and we all had our lesson. And I felt quite good about having sorted a few things out that had been bothering me. I felt, for once, that I've actually started to have the *right attitude*, which helped me feel very positive. That might have been enough excitement for one day only when I'd put Silver away, Olivia pulled me over to show me a new notice on the board.

And that was when things started to go pear-shaped.

SUMMER HOLIDAY PONY SHARE read the headline. Underneath it explained how during the summer holidays clients (that's us riders) can put their names down to share one of the school ponies. For a modest sum, it said (I don't know what the riding school thinks is modest, but the sum they quoted would not be considered modest in the Marshall household – we're still waiting on that Saxon hoard), sharers can care for a school pony for two whole days in the week (grooming, mucking out and cleaning tack), with a lesson and a hack included on each day, PLUS a lesson at the weekend. If I could do that, it would be like Silver was a little bit mine. It would be like it is in Azbathria where I have Silverado all to myself.

'I'm going to ask my mum if I can share Cracker,' Olivia said, her eyes shining. 'Why don't you share Silver?'

I mumbled something that could have passed for, *what a great idea, I'll do that*, and we both left the yard to find our respective parents' cars and go home. Suddenly, my day had turned from positive to negative and far from feeling good, I now felt a bit flat. Well, actually, totally squashed. So much for having the *right attitude*. That had backfired, big time.

'You're quiet,' said Mum. 'Usually, after Pony Club you're bouncing off the walls.'

I hadn't noticed the car having walls, but that seemed to me to be a cue, if ever I'd heard one, to introduce the idea of Silver-sharing – and possibly more…

'Guess what?' asked Etta.

'I couldn't possibly,' her mum replied, crunching the gears as they approached a roundabout.

'For a modest sum I can part-share Silver during the summer holidays!'

'Oh how wonderful, darling,' said her mum, beaming at her as she swerved around another car. 'And you're right, the cost is terribly modest – virtually nothing at all!'

'I knew you'd say that,' said Etta.

'But it's true! Now run along and reserve Silver right away. You don't want to be disappointed! And who knows? If all goes well maybe we can look into buying Silver so he'll be totally, totally yours!'

A niggling little feeling in the pit of my stomach told me that the above scenario was as likely as me growing wings. It would be more like...

'Guess what?' asked Etta.

'You want to share Silver during the summer,' sighed her mum, braking hard as they approached a junction.

'That's right!' said Etta. 'Can I?'

'Of course not. The cost is way too high and you need a new school uniform. You've grown out of the old one. Now don't sulk, it's your own fault for growing all the time...'

Sadly, a much more likely outcome.

I couldn't help thinking that this part-share might be an opportunity to see whether I could cope with something in my real life. In Azbathria I could probably dig up some gold, or trade in a jewel from my tunic to raise some money. In my real life I was wracking my brains to think of something I might be able to sell so I could share Silver for the summer holidays. Or trade. What could I trade for the modest sum Chesterton was asking for a part-share in Silver? I mean, if I could part-share Silver it would be totally brilliant.

So I didn't tell Mum about the sharing thing because I was scared she'd sigh, and use her *try to understand how things are* voice that prepares me to brace myself for not getting what I ask for, like she used to do when I was younger and kept asking for a pony. Pony-share isn't cheap, and I didn't trust myself to speak in case I lost it when the inevitable answer of, *What? How much? I'm sorry, Etta…* was given. I'm not a baby, but imagining Silver being part-shared by Amelia, or Pearl, brought a lump to my throat, and I totally needed to get a grip…

'Who are you part-sharing?' asked Pearl, her nose in the air, her plait swinging from side-to-side in a particularly menacing, snake-like manner.

'I'm not part-sharing anyone,' said Etta, sadly.

'Oh my God, really? How can you bear it?' said Pearl. 'I've got Silver. He's going to have to work very hard this week because I want to gallop and jump everywhere.'

'But you can't!' cried Etta, running to Silver's stable and throwing herself in front of the door.

'Oh can't I? Just watch me!' said Pearl, brandishing her riding crop which, as Etta watched, grew longer and longer, and whippier and whippier, until it was as long as Pearl was tall.

'NO!' cried Etta, as Pearl pushed her aside and led Silver out of his stable. Mounting, she turned the beautiful grey pony towards the school.

'Come on you lazy creature,' shouted Pearl, and she brought the whip down hard on Silver's grey flank.

As Silver cried out in pain Etta grasped the whip, pulling it out of Pearl's hand.

'No matter!' cried Pearl. 'I'll just use my spurs instead.'

Etta could hardly believe her eyes when she saw the viciously long spurs strapped to Pearl's boots.

'Now clear off you pathetic loser,' sneered Pearl, jabbing the spurs into Silver's sides and galloping out of the yard...

I know Becky would never let Pearl do any of those things (and I'm sure Pearl wouldn't want to, to be honest. She's bossy and annoying, not cruel), but even seeing Pearl riding Silver would be just as painful.

So that's what happened – you're totally up to speed. And now I'm sitting in my room with Wolfie, thinking hard. My first thought is to ask Nana Susan for help – but she's already paid my Pony Club fees and asking her would be well cheeky. I know Mum wouldn't be impressed. I have to come up with something quickly. It's like I need to put my thoughts into actions. I need to put more effort into my real life, and get real things done as per my new plans and *attitude,* as discussed with Silver.

After about half-an-hour of thinking I have a list of ideas:

1. Ask Mum and Dad whether I can have money for my birthday and Christmas – only NOW!

2. Ask whether Nana Iris and Nana Susan can be included in this idea, too, to swell funds.
3. Make cakes and sell them (I don't rate this one because Mum will probably want me to pay for the ingredients, and I can't see potential customers being too impressed by cakes they have to dig out of the tins. Besides, if I have to include the tins because my cakes are stuck to them, it will seriously crush my profit margin).
4. Get Wolfie cracking on tracking down that Saxon hoard (could be a long job, and time is of the essence with this problem).
5. Offer to clean the car, like, forever (I'd rather not).
6. See whether Shirley wants her car cleaned (no – it's far too big and I can't reach the roof).
7. See whether the Robinsons want their car or van cleaned (I'd REALLY rather not).
8. Sell something (I haven't got anything).
9. Get a summer holiday job. (I got quite excited about this one until I realised that if I were working, I wouldn't be able to look after and ride Silver two days a week. Besides, jobs for schoolgirls aren't exactly plentiful.)

That's it.

I'm rubbish at this. So much for making my real life happen. No wonder I'm always being rescued in Azbathria!

After all that thinking, I go downstairs and sit on the sofa. Only I must slump a bit, which alerts Mum to my mood which is why she asks me again what the matter is.

'Nothing!' I reply, even though this is a blatant lie because I can't get the reality of how I CAN'T part-share Silver out of my mind. It's devil hamster again, resident in my brain, pounding away on his wheel, all glinty-eyed and preventing me from thinking of anything else. Far from hiding the pain quite well Mum has noticed I'm not myself. So even though I am a good actress, some things you just can't hide.

'Yes there is,' says Mum, like my head's transparent and she can see devil hamster inside it, jumping up and down and brandishing a placard on which is written, *there is something the matter, there totally is!*

'No, no, it's nothing,' I lie again, a bit breezier this time.

'Out with it!' Mum commands me.

I can see she isn't going to let it go, and I don't think I can pretend nothing is wrong any more so I shrug my shoulders and tell her about Silver and the part-share thing, and how modest the sum of money is (without using the word modest, so she doesn't think I'm being flippant), and I finish by saying I know it's too expensive and that I don't expect it to happen, and even though I've thought and thought I can't think of a way of financing it myself, although I'd like to more than anything.

Mum lifts her hand to stroke my hair, then remembers what happens when she tries so she changes her mind and diverts her hand to scratch her nose as though that had been her intention all the time.

'I know,' I say. 'I totally know that it's too expensive. It's all right.'

It isn't all right of course, but I'm getting used to lying about it.

'Okay,' says Mum. Only she can't stop herself from going on to say it sounds to her that the riding school is on to a good thing, getting their clients to pay money to look after their ponies in the holidays, which only proves how much she doesn't understand. But she does add, 'You're being very grown-up and brave about this, Etta, and I really appreciate it.'

I can't help thinking that being grown-up and brave doesn't seem to be getting me what I want. I still feel wretched. Having the *right attitude* stinks.

We watch *Move to the Country* together to take our minds off it. Only the people who are moving to Devon want to buy a house with stables and land for their horses, so instead of making me think of something else it just reinforces the fact that I WON'T be riding Silver all summer long.

Thanks *Move to the Country*. Thanks a lot!

CHAPTER TWENTY-THREE

When school breaks up for the summer holidays I am still having my lesson every Saturday morning. Plus, there are several Pony Club rallies due to take place not only some weekends but also in the week, so I suppose I still have lots to look forward to. After all, the Pony Club rallies cost a bit so maybe I'm being unreasonable about the share thing. I don't think the attitude I'm adopting is totally right, but I am trying. It's just proving a lot harder than I ever thought it would be, especially as I'm not looking forward to seeing who is going to be part-sharing Silver. It is bound to be up on the notice board, and as Olivia will be all fired up about sharing Cracker I can't promise that my attitude won't plummet. Or disappear entirely. What I mean is there are bound to be lapses. I'm not Amelia.

As I haven't got the hang of stopping time (at least in my real life), Saturday comes around like it always does and Mum takes me to Chesterton as usual and I go into the office to see who I'm riding. There is no Pony Club rally this week so I'm just having my usual lesson. Amelia is already there and so is Pearl, and they're staring at the notice board. From the loud squeals I can hear I take it they're each part-sharing a pony.

'Hello Etta!' says Amelia. 'We're just finding out who we're part-sharing in the holidays.'

Told you.

'I've got Dixie,' says Pearl, grinning so broadly, she looks as though someone's shoved a plate into her mouth. Her lips seem to be spread across her whole face in one big smile. Part of me sighs with relief – at least Pearl hasn't got Silver.

'I'm sharing Poppy,' says Amelia.

'Oh, bad luck,' I say. Poor Amelia, fancy getting Poppy – talk about the short straw (but at least it's not Silver).

'Oh no,' Amelia says, 'I *asked* for Poppy.'

'Why?' I ask her, astonished.

'She's so good for my riding,' Amelia explains. 'I figure if I can get a tune out of Poppy, my riding will really benefit. Don't you think?'

I do that. Think, I mean. Amelia takes my breath away sometimes. She looks at the big picture (being a better rider) rather than enjoying herself (riding an easier pony and having some fun), as Nana Susan might say.

Amelia clearly has her attitude all sewn up and understands how riding difficult ponies can improve her riding. I thought I was halfway to getting the hang of this attitude thing, but no.

'Why are you always riding Silver?' asked Amelia. 'He does everything right all the time.'

'Sounds like you've just answered your own question,' said Etta, puzzled.

'Do you remember when you were riding Poppy, and you were so determined to get her over the jump – because you couldn't face the thought of turning around and approaching it again – and you DID IT?' said Amelia.

Etta thought back…

'And then you rode Dixie for the first time,' said Amelia, 'and you were worried about it, and didn't know whether you could cope? But you concentrated and really THOUGHT ABOUT YOUR RIDING, and it worked because you rode Dixie really well?'

Etta's brain worked overtime… (not least because Amelia suddenly seems to know a lot about me and my thoughts all of a sudden!)

'Plus,' Amelia continued, 'you gained your Grooming a Pony badge at Pony Club, despite worrying you wouldn't. And you've learned enough now to look after Silver. It mattered to you, so you worked hard at it all. And now you can do those things.'

'And your point is?' asked Etta.

'The harder you work at something, the better you are at it!' cried Amelia, in frustration. 'It's like Hebe practising the long jump. Honestly, Etta, must I spell it out for you?'

'Er, well, yes please, if you don't mind,' mumbled Etta. 'If you do that I'll be able to look at it from time to time to remind myself of what I should be doing!'

Well that's an eye-opener, I think, taking it all in. Trust Amelia to understand that – and me. Or at least I imagine her to. So because I've imagined her to understand, it must mean that *I* understand. After all, I'm the one who put all the words in her mouth. And that might just mean that I've been cultivating the *right attitude* for a while now. I just didn't realise.

I can't help wondering whether Amelia will be so positive after six weeks of relentless and exhaustive kicking trying to get Poppy over jumps and through the woods. Her legs might fall off. Or she might just get totally fit. Or fit for nothing. Or a totally better rider because of all that effort she is going to be putting in. I'm looking forward to seeing whether she still has the *right attitude* at the end of the holidays, despite her turning up in my made-up life and letting me know that I have, after all, developed the *right attitude* when it comes to riding and looking after Silver.

But then I think (because I can't stop my thoughts, they're off and away up the road and over the hill, charging about in all directions like Wolfie does) that maybe Amelia asking to ride Poppy is like me deciding not to be rescued in Azbathria any more. Maybe we are both taking charge of our own destinies in our own way. If that's the case then I feel a bit better about it, almost like I've beaten her to it, like I thought of it first. I just didn't quite get it until now.

The office door opens and Olivia bursts in. 'Have I got Cracker?' she asks, pushing past Pearl and gazing intently at the list on the board. When she jumps up and down and punches the air I take it she has.

'Congratulations,' I say, swallowing down the lump that's in my throat, and trying not to be insanely jealous of everyone achieving their dream. I can't bring myself to look at the list. I can't bring myself to learn who is lucky enough to be looking after Silver in the holidays.

MY Silver.

'Hurrah! We're all going to have a great summer!' Olivia says – a bit tactlessly I think, seeing as I'm standing there all pony-share-less and trying to put on a brave face. Some of us are going to have a greater summer than others, and I decide to look at the OTHER list to see who I am riding on the lesson to take my mind off what I SHAN'T be doing all summer.

I'm down to ride Pip. Great. I've not even got Silver on my lesson today. Then I remember that from now on I'm going to take charge of my own destiny – to say nothing of embracing the challenge of riding other ponies, just like Amelia does – and give myself a bit of a shake. Honestly, how come I forget things so quickly? It's only been five minutes! I blame devil hamster.

Becky has said that Pony Club members are now allowed to tack up the ponies, so I go to Pip's stable and do just that. He snorts a bit and puts his head on a tilt as if he's worried that I might put his saddle on back-to-front or something. So I speak reassuringly to him as I put it on the right way round, hoping he'll realise I'm not totally useless. Unlike Silver, Pip doesn't volunteer to take the bit by opening his mouth but sticks his nose in the air, clamping his teeth shut as if he's daring me to make him. As Pip is quite a lot taller than Silver his head is now out of reach, so I slide my hand up his neck and over his nose and gently draw his face down to my level.

'Come on, Pip, open wide,' I tell him quietly, easing my thumb between his lips where he has no teeth. This is why I love Silver, I tell myself, because he's so obliging. But then I remember how nervous I was when I first put a bridle on a pony, and how I'm much more confident now, and how I'm not worried about Pip's little ways because I know how to overcome them.

Amelia in my made-up life is right – I've learned such a lot at Pony Club without really noticing and it's only now, when I think about it, that I appreciate just how much. I can tack up and groom and pick out hooves and muck out and clean tack and lead ponies in and out of their stables – all things I wanted to be able to do but couldn't before I joined the Pony Club. And now I can even get Pip to open his mouth and take the bit because I'm not worried about putting my thumb in his mouth, or afraid he might bite me. I'm not even stumped when he puts his head up out of reach because I know how to cope. I've been so busy learning all this stuff – stuff I wanted to learn – that I haven't taken the time to acknowledge just how far I've come. Until now.

I give Pip a pat when he does open his mouth, and make sure his mane and forelock are smooth and comfortable under the headpiece and browband. All the while I try not to think about how much more Olivia, Amelia and Pearl will learn pony-sharing all summer. I'm afraid they will leave me behind. I won't even be able to make an effort or cultivate the *right attitude* because I won't be there.

'All right in there?' asks Jade, popping her head over Pip's half-door.

'Yes thank you,' I reply, getting ready to lead Pip out of the stable.

'You must be delighted about Silver,' says Jade.

Uh-oh, I think. This is where Jade lets the cat out of the bag about who has Silver all summer. I know it isn't Amelia, Pearl or Olivia. Maybe it's Kayleigh or Emma. I wish I had closable ears so I can't hear her, but Jade just keeps on talking, and my ears stay open so I can't help but listen.

'I hoped you'd get him, you two are made for each other,' she says.

'Yeah, well...' I say, trailing off because I can't think of anything else to say.

'Your mum was very insistent,' Jade continues, oblivious to my pain. 'Becky tried to get her to agree to you having Amber but she wasn't having it. It was Silver or nothing!'

I open my mouth to say something, but nothing comes out. Jade seems to be talking nonsense.

I check carefully to make sure I'm in my real life, not my made-up one.

'Er, Jade, would you mind holding Pip for a minute while I get something from the office?' I ask, handing Pip's reins over to her.

'Okay, but be quick!' she says, tightening Pip's girth.

I want to run but it's not allowed so I walk really quickly, my heart thumping in my chest. By the time I get to the office and look up at the notice on the board, the notice I was too cowardly to look at earlier, I can hardly breathe. I'm so scared that I won't see what I so desperately want to see. What I think, despite everything, I MIGHT see.

But there it is. The list of part-sharers and the ponies they are sharing in the summer holidays. And half-way down the list is Silver's name. And next to Silver's name is mine. Not Estra's. Mine. *Henrietta Marshall.* Never have I been so happy to see my own name.

Silver is going to be part-mine for the whole summer holidays! It'll be like he's really mine – for two days a week anyway – and I decide I really will try to happily ride the other ponies the rest of the time, honest, promise, I'm not even joking. I'm going to be grooming Silver and keeping his bed tidy and feeding him and grooming him and cleaning his tack and grooming him – as well as RIDING HIM! And I promise, there and then, to nobody at all (because nobody is listening) that Silver is going to be the best looked-after, part-shared pony in the whole riding school for the ENTIRE SUMMER!

'Aren't you supposed to be on the lesson?' asks one of the students taking bookings.

I walk back to collect Pip, but it's like I'm floating above the yard. And even when I see Amelia riding Silver on the lesson I don't mind because she's only going to ride him for an hour. Soon, Silver is going to be mine for the whole summer (sort of).

And when Pip runs out at the jump the first time we approach it I don't mind because Silver is going to be mine (for two days a week), and my dreaming about it caused Pip to run-out because I wasn't paying attention, so I don't think it's too important in my real life but rather just a hiccup.

And even when Pearl tells me (with a pout and in a bossy voice) that I'm too close to her on Dixie I don't mind because Silver is going to be part-mine (all through the summer holidays).

When Mum collects me in the car I give her a huge hug and thank her and promise I'll clean out the hens all summer and help her with the housework (a bit reckless of me because I HATE HOUSEWORK!) and Mum says she's glad I'm happy, and that my mature attitude (*mature*, you notice, not *right*, but I decide the two are interchangeable) when I didn't think I could have what I wanted helped swing it for me.

'I know it's not cheap,' I say, gulping.

'No, it isn't,' says Mum. 'But don't worry, we can still keep Shona in ginger biscuits, and Wolfie won't have to go without his chew toys!'

'I'm so excited!' I say.

'You really love Silver, don't you,' says Mum.

I nod and tell her about him (again!) and about his tail being his USP, and how he listens to me and tries his best when we jump, and explain how he never tries to eat grass on hacks, or go too fast. And I think Mum actually gets how much I love him because she listens and doesn't interrupt or tell me I'm silly to love a pony – like I know Shona would.

'I was watching the last part of your lesson the other day,' says Mum, 'and I thought how good you looked in the saddle, and how confident – even when you were jumping.'

For the second time that day I'm astonished. 'I didn't think you ever watched the lesson,' I say. 'I didn't think you were interested.'

'Of course I'm interested, Etta,' says Mum. 'I'm interested in everything you do, and I sneak a look now and again. And I'm really proud of how much you've learned. Becky says you work hard and that you've come on in leaps and bounds because you make a real effort, rather than wanting other people to help you out and do things for you. She says you're one of her star pupils.'

And I don't know what to say, but I feel all warm inside because I really want to ride well. I feel made up that Becky not only thinks my riding has improved, but that her thoughts about me making an effort echo my new philosophy about my real life. Who knew Becky could see it when I couldn't?

'I love going to Pony Club,' I tell Mum.

'And you got that badge, too!' says Mum. 'Your dad and I are very impressed with how hard you've worked. We want you to enjoy the summer holidays and continue with your interest. We worry that you spend too much time daydreaming – Becky says you still have trouble concentrating sometimes. It's good to have a hobby.'

That's more news to me, I had no idea my parents were aware of my daydreaming…

'What's Etta doing?' asked her dad.

'Oh she's staring into space again,' said her mum. 'It's as though she's in her own little world! (That's spooky!) *Where do you suppose she goes?'*

'Somewhere wonderful, I expect,' said her dad, 'like scoring the winning goal for Chelsea, or tinkering with an old Porsche.'

'No,' said her mum with a smile, 'she's far more likely to be shopping for new clothes, arm-in-arm with her sister, or training hard for the school's sports day.'

'I expect you're right,' Etta's dad agreed, nodding thoughtfully...

Well, that's a relief! I'd rather they were delusional about my daydreams than know about Azbathria. I decide not to pursue that avenue of thought, but to concentrate more on the hobby aspect instead.

'Like you've got the hens for a hobby,' I tell Mum.

'Oh, well, yes I suppose so,' she agrees, pulling a face. I take it she doesn't count the hens as a viable hobby. 'We just think it's good for you to get out in the fresh air and take part in some sport,' says Mum. 'And since you've been to Pony Club I've noticed you've become more responsible, helping with the hens and things.'

I have? Oh, okay, maybe I have.

'And promise me one thing,' Mum adds, looking deep into my eyes.

Uh-oh, I think, here it comes: A CONDITION – be nice to your sister, put as much effort into your schoolwork as you do at Pony Club, that sort of thing.

'That you'll tell me all about your days at the riding school with Silver,' she says.

'Done deal!' I tell her and we high-five, even though we both know it's a bit naff.

And later I wonder whether I ought to make more effort at school. It won't be as much fun as all the things I do at Chesterton, that's for sure, but if it works in my made-up life and it works with Silver, who's to say it won't work at school?

Even running the 400 metres. I know I didn't make much (oh okay ANY) effort there. I could have PREPARED more (like preparing the cake tin before pouring the mixture in). Only I can't help thinking that if I had then I might not only have wasted the time it took to run the 400 metres at sports day, but a whole lot more time before in preparation that was never going anywhere. I mean, I doubt practising could have made me run any faster – you're either fast or you're not. And I'm not.

This whole attitude concept might need a bit more thought.

CHAPTER TWENTY-FOUR

These summer holidays are the best EVER! I love being responsible for Silver's welfare, it's as though he is really mine. I wish he was, but this is the next best thing. On my part-share days I catch Silver in from the field and give him his breakfast. Then I groom him, making sure he totally shines. It's hard work because he's grey but I don't mind because… well, because he's Silver.

Olivia and I ride Cracker and Silver on our morning lesson. We are lucky that our share days coincide – Amelia and the others are sharing on different days because the ponies can't all be shared on the same days as they need to be available for pupils on the regular lessons. During lunchtime Olivia and I clean tack together. We aren't allowed to go into the stables during lunch because the ponies are resting. I think that means they need a rest from US, because we'd be in with them all the time if we could.

Yesterday, when he saw me approaching him in the field, Silver made a little snuffling noise with his nostrils, like he was pleased to see me! (I'm sure the carrot he could see in my hand had nothing to do with it.) I feel we've totally bonded. Plus, Becky put an actual mini JUMPING COURSE up in the school and we went round it without any faults or losing our way. We're jumping higher now, and it feels like flying (even in my crushing body protector). It was so good I didn't drift off into my made-up life and imagine we were at Hickstead, or the Horse of the Year show. What I mean is that riding Silver is better than anything I can make up, so I don't need to.

As I am getting Silver tacked up to go on a two-hour ride Jade tells us we're going to gallop. I've never galloped before, but I know Silver will look after me and I'm really excited. Amelia is doing well with Poppy (we see each other at Pony Club rallies where we update each other on how we're getting on), and I can't wait to find out whether she will be able to get Poppy to gallop when she goes on her two-hour ride. If she does manage to, I reckon she'll deserve a medal! She may also need to be revived with oxygen *if*, of course, Poppy *does* actually gallop. It could be a first – assuming Poppy knows how.

My two days a week at Chesterton are so packed with things to do I've started a diary which I write in every night, describing what I've done and how I feel about things. I read out bits of it to Mum so she can share in what I've been doing as per our agreement. I don't mind because it means I get to re-live my day. I also think it might be a good thing to write down what I learn on my lessons so I can look back every few months and remind myself how much I've progressed. It will be a record of my achievements (I might not record any disappointments). Oh, and we're taking some more tests – I mean *badges* – at the end of the holidays, so I'm revising for those, too.

I'm enjoying writing my diary – much more than I ever thought I would. I'm wondering whether I might be a writer when I leave school. I might have a go at writing a book this winter when I'm not riding so much. I didn't know what I could write about but then I thought I could write about Azbathria and the Black Knight, and Princess Amelia and the evil Heratos – and Silverado and Wolf, of course.

I haven't had much time to visit Azbathria lately as I've been too busy with Silver and the Pony Club and looking after the hens for Mum to thank her for paying for my part-share of Silver. It's been full-on. So maybe I really am making my real life happen like I planned, and have no need to make things up any more. Oh, and Max Rybart never did ask me again to go ice skating, so that's a relief! I think he only asked me because I laugh at his jokes. I don't laugh because they're funny, I just think someone needs to.

I meet up with Hebe a couple of times a week on my non part-share days. She's taken up cross-country running. Well, she is sporty whereas I'm not. I don't really count riding because it isn't something you can do at school, or *for* the school, even though it is a sport.

As for Nat Black… I think he's still seeing Amelia, and I still don't care. Silver is the love of my life right now and that suits me fine. Shona keeps sneering at me, telling me I ought to marry Silver if I love him so much, but she doesn't understand, and it's not like she's got a boyfriend so she can't talk. At least Silver is real and alive. I might tell Shona she ought to elope with some wallpaper, or a lamp.

On our two-hour ride Olivia and I ride next to each other like we're on our own ponies, and we're both excited about galloping. We ride farther than we ever have along the bridleways until we get to a big field where we're going to gallop.

'Now keep behind me, and ease gently into canter,' instructs Becky. 'The ponies will simply stretch out and go faster, and you won't feel much difference. Just remember to lean forward and take the weight off the saddle and onto your knees – but only a little bit, not as much as you do in your jumping position.'

She's on a big bay mare called Blossom who has a white blaze running down her face and over her nostrils, and I think she might be a good horse to include in Azbathria if I can make up a suitable rider for her. Maybe Becky could be a queen of some far-distant lands. I'll give that some thought.

I glance at Olivia and she grins at me, and we start off cantering nice and steady (although Cracker is going sideways, of course). I can feel Silver's legs going faster and faster under me so I lean forward as tears stream down my cheeks, torn from my eyes by the speed. Becky is totally wrong about not feeling a difference; galloping is really fast!

I know I ought to slow Silver down a little but I don't want to, even when he takes me upside of Becky and Blossom before overtaking them so we are in front of everybody. It feels as though Silver is going as fast as a racehorse…

Crouching low over Silver Charm's sleek, well-bred neck, apprentice jockey Etta Marshall kept her mount at a steady pace, tucked in at the back of the field and away from trouble. The colourful ripple of jockeys and racehorses made their way up the hill, then along the smooth turf of the racetrack towards the downward stretch, moving like relentless, rippling waves on a stormy sea. Etta could hear nothing but the whistle of the wind in her ears as she and Silver Charm galloped after the others. Then they were hurtling down the hill, approaching the famous Tattenham Corner, sweeping around towards the crowd. Cries rose above the pounding of hooves and shouts from the other jockeys – all desperate to win the biggest race of all: the Derby!

Silver Charm, sensitive to his rider's urging, easily passed several horses in front of them, their jockeys open-mouthed in surprise as the outsider thundered by. Only three horses to go – and Etta could see the winning post ahead, hear the roar of the crowd and smell the sweat on the horses as they gave their all.

'Not too soon,' Etta whispered to her mount, her hands steady on the reins.

Only three furlongs to go… now two… now one…

'Go!' she cried, urging on the eager Silver Charm with hands and heels while the other riders reached for their whips.

They passed the white-faced chestnut with the flaxen mane, Comedy Star, with no laughs forthcoming from his jockey, the equally flaxen-haired Max Rybart. Golden Prince, with talented Amelia Armitage in the saddle, was next to be overtaken as Silver Charm galloped his heart out for his jockey. Ahead, Etta could see the tail of Dark Ebony, and hear the horse's laboured breathing as champion jockey Nathan Black desperately urged the big horse to greater effort.

Nathan Black's expression as the dappled grey swept past Dark Ebony to win by a short head was one of incredulous surprise, the roar of the crowd drowning out any words he might have uttered.

They had done it! They had won the Derby! Silver Charm was assured of his place in the history books and his jockey, Etta Marshall, was the new darling of the crowd...

'Got a bit carried away there, didn't you Etta?' I hear Becky say as Silver drops down to a canter then a trot, before finally coming to a halt at the edge of the field.

'Oh, sorry,' I say, wiping the tears from my face and giving Silver lots of pats on his silky neck. 'It wasn't Silver's fault.'

'Never mind,' Becky laughs. 'I can see that Silver was enjoying it as much as you. You two are made for each other!'

It seems my made-up life hasn't gone away completely – and I don't want it to. But now my real life, in its different way, is just as good.

This book is printed on paper from sustainable sources managed under the Forest Stewardship Council (FSC) scheme.

It has been printed in the UK to reduce transportation miles and their impact upon the environment.

For every new title that Matador publishes, we plant a tree to offset CO_2, partnering with the More Trees scheme.

For more about how Matador offsets its environmental impact, see www.troubador.co.uk/about/